Praise for Beth Kendrick's Novels

Cure for the Common Breakup

"Beth Kendrick has reminded me once again exactly why I love her books so much. *Cure for the Common Breakup* is packed with humor, wit, and a lot of heart. A charming and exceptionally entertaining story! I can't recommend this book highly enough."

—Jane Porter, national bestselling author of *The Good Wife*

"Beth Kendrick has written a sharp, sassy, surprisingly emotional story that will make readers laugh out loud from page one and sigh from the heart at the end. Light and lovely perfection!"

—Roxanne St. Claire, *New York Times* bestselling author of the Barefoot Bay series

"Utterly delightful! Summer Benson will charm and disarm her way into the hearts of readers as easily as she does the residents of Black Dog Bay."

—Meg Donohue, *USA Today* bestselling author of *All the Summer Girls*

The Week Before the Wedding

"Kendrick proves she is the leader of the pack when it comes to fashioning cheekily clever love stories, and her latest will delight readers with its delectably acerbic wit and charmingly complex characters."

—*Booklist* (starred review)

"In an engaging story about matters of the heart, Kendrick perfectly captures the struggle between who we really are and who we want to be. With its endearing characters and page-turning plot, this novel balances humor and emotion in a way that begs it to be read in one sitting."

—*RT Book Reviews* (4½ stars)

"A delightful romp with depth."

—Heroes and Heartbreakers

The Lucky Dog Matchmaking Service

"Graced with a stellar cast of captivating characters (including an adorable pack of scene-stealing canines) and written with both sharp wit and genuine wisdom, Kendrick's latest effervescent novel is a hopelessly, hopefully romantic treat."

—*Booklist* (starred review)

continued . . .

"Wonderful! Kendrick manages to cook up a tender, touching, and very funny story about the complicated relationship of two sisters torn apart by their own stubbornness and brought back together by love and pastry. With a fresh plot and richly layered characters, *The Bake-Off* is a winner."

—Ellen Meister, author of *The Other Life*

Second Time Around

"Kendrick deftly blends exceptionally clever writing, subtly nuanced characters, and a generous dash of romance into a flawlessly written story about the importance of female friendships and second chances." —*Chicago Tribune*

"A touching and humorous look at love, loss, and literature." —*Booklist*

"Extremely engaging. . . . [Kendrick's] characters were easy to fall in love with." —Night Owl Reviews

"Kendrick is an undeniably practiced hand at depicting female bonds." —*Publishers Weekly*

"A funny, charming story about the power of female friendship, and a must read for all English majors, past and present."

—Kim Gruenenfelder, author of *Wedding Fever*

The Pre-nup

"In the exceptionally entertaining and wonderfully original *The Pre-nup*, Kendrick writes with a wicked sense of humor and great wisdom about the power of friendship, the importance of true love, and the very real satisfaction of romantic revenge done right." —*Chicago Tribune*

"The three female leads all captivate." —*Romantic Times*

"[A] highly entertaining story." —Fresh Fiction

"Clever, wise, and wonderful, *The Pre-nup* is Beth Kendrick at her best."

—Jane Porter

"Witty, juicy, and lots of fun! Say 'I do' to *The Pre-nup*."
—Susan Mallery, *New York Times* bestselling author of *Only His*

"A smart, funny spin on happily-ever-after!"

—Beth Harbison, *New York Times*
bestselling author of *Always Something There to Remind Me*

Also by Beth Kendrick

cure
for the
common
breakup

Beth Kendrick

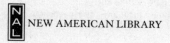
NEW AMERICAN LIBRARY

New American Library
Published by the Penguin Group
Penguin Group (USA) LLC, 375 Hudson Street,
New York, New York 10014

USA | Canada | UK | Ireland | Australia | New Zealand | India | South Africa | China
penguin.com
A Penguin Random House Company

First published by New American Library,
a division of Penguin Group (USA) LLC

First Printing, May 2014

 REGISTERED TRADEMARK—MARCA REGISTRADA

LIBRARY OF CONGRESS CATALOGING-IN-PUBLICATION DATA:

Kendrick, Beth.
Cure for the common breakup/Beth Kendrick.
    p.   cm.
  ISBN 978-0-451-46585-6 (pbk.)
  1. Single women—Fiction.   2. Man-woman relationships—Fiction.
I. Title.
  PS3611.E535C86 2014
  813'.6—dc23   2013049130

Printed in the United States of America
10 9 8 7 6 5 4 3 2 1

Set in Granjon
Designed by Alissa Rose Theodor

for Chandra Years,
a true friend

acknowledgments

Thank you to . . .

Danielle Perez, the best editor in all the land.

Amy Moore-Benson, the best agent in all the land.

Kimberly Camarillo, who patiently answered my endless questions about life as a flight attendant. (I'm sure I got some of it wrong. Blame me, not her!)

Kresley Cole, my own personal Coach Taylor.

Kresley Cole's fabulous mom, who knows how to make an entrance.

Marty Etchart, a good sport and a great writer.

Jane Porter and Barbara Ankrum, for so many acts of grace and guidance that I cannot even begin to list them.

Shannon Kinney, Heidi Padley, and the "Montessori Mom Mafia": Michelle Elquest, Kami Mooth, Anna O'Brien, Cori Zdebel, Kim Nudi, Sarah Behof, and Betsy Etchart.

As always, I owe boundless love and gratitude to my awesome family, especially Joe and Tai, who introduced me to the Delaware shore.

cure for the common breakup

**Specialty drink at the
Whinery in Black Dog Bay, Delaware**

Ingredients:
Sweet vermouth, freshly squeezed orange juice,
champagne, twist

Instructions:
Fill a highball glass with ice (a tall glass, 12–14 ounces).

Fill halfway with chilled, freshly opened sweet vermouth. (If vermouth is room temperature, chill 3 ounces of it with a few stirs of ice and strain over the fresh-ice-filled highball. Vermouth, like wine, is best when freshly opened and kept refrigerated.)

Add a splash of freshly squeezed orange juice.

Fill with champagne/sparkling wine.

Finish with a twist and a straw.

The cocktail will naturally layer and is delicious enjoyed either layered or gently stirred together.

Recipe created by mixologist Adam Seger, CCP
Creator of Hum Liqueur and Balsam Spirit

cure

for the

common

breakup

chapter 1

"Good evening, ladies and gentlemen. This is your captain speaking."

"He's so hot." Summer Benson nudged her fellow flight attendant Kim. "Even his voice is hot."

"Welcome to our flight from New York to Paris." Aaron's voice sounded deep and rich, despite the plane's staticky loudspeaker. "Flying time tonight should be about seven hours and twenty-six minutes. We're anticipating an on-time departure, so we're going to ask you to move out of the aisles and take your seats as quickly as possible."

Summer leaned back against the drink cart in the tiny first-class galley. "Ooh, I love it when he tells me what to do."

Kim, a petite Texan with a sleek blond bob, rolled her eyes and started checking the meals that had arrived from catering. "Get a room."

"As soon as we get to Paris, we will," Summer assured her. "And then we're going to walk by the Seine and go to the Eiffel Tower and eat croissants. If it's cheesy and touristy, we're doing it. I actually packed a beret."

"I was wondering why you had two gigantic carry-ons," Kim said. "That's a lot of luggage for a three-day layover."

"One bag's half full of scandalous lingerie," Summer replied. "I left the other half empty so I can buy more scandalous lingerie." She frowned at a snag in her silky black nylons. "These eight-hour flights are hell on my stockings. This pair was my favorite, too. They're all lacy at the top. Hand-embroidered."

Kim's jaw dropped. "You're wearing thigh-highs? All the way to Paris? Do you hate yourself? Do you hate your veins?"

"When I'm on a flight to Paris with my boyfriend, I don't wear support hose. Not now, not ever."

"And do you hate your feet?" Kim glanced down at Summer's patent leather stilettos. "I don't have a ruler with me, but I'm guessing those heels are higher than two and a half inches." She shook her index finger. "Airline regulations."

"Airline regulations also state that we have to wear black shoes and black tights with a navy uniform," Summer said. "That doesn't make it right. Besides, France has laws against ugly shoes. You can look it up."

"You're going to be begging for flats by the time you're through with the salad service," Kim predicted.

Summer had to admit that her coworker had a point—international first-class service didn't offer a lot of downtime. Between distributing hot towels, drinks, place settings and linens, appetizers, salads, entrées, fruit and cheese, dessert, coffee, cordials, warm cookies, and finally breakfast, a sensible flight attendant would wear comfortable footwear.

Summer had never been accused of being sensible.

"The only thing more high-maintenance than the meal service is me," she said. "I refuse to be hobbled by a few plates of lettuce."

Kim ducked out of the galley with a pair of plastic water

bottles. "Hang on. I'm going to go check if the pilots want anything before takeoff. Want me to say hi to your boyfriend?"

"Sure, and ask if he has any M&M's. I forgot to bring a fresh supply, and he knows I'm an addict."

Two minutes later, Kim returned from the flight deck, walking as fast as her polyester pencil skirt permitted. "I just saw Aaron!"

"Score." Summer held out her palm as Kim handed over a bag of candy. "He truly is the best boyfriend ever. I'll have to keep him around for a while."

"For a while? How about forever?" Kim clutched Summer's forearm and gave her a little shake. "He has a diamond ring for you!"

Summer pulled away and braced both hands on the narrow, metal-edged countertop.

"It's gorgeous!" Kim squealed. "He was showing it to the first officer when I opened the door."

Where was an oxygen mask when you needed one? Summer inhaled deeply, smelling stale coffee grounds and the plummy red wine Kim had just uncorked for a passenger.

"I . . ." She waited for her emotions to kick in. She should laugh. Cry. Faint dead away. *Something.*

"He's going to propose in Paris! How romantic." Kim looked as though *she* might faint dead away. "A guy like him, with a ring like that . . . God, you're so lucky."

All at once the emotions kicked in. Complete, overwhelming terror, served up with a side of denial. "Slow down—slow down." Summer sagged back against the counter. "This is crazy. I mean, Aaron and I have a great time together, but we've certainly never talked about marriage."

"Well, why else would he buy a diamond ring?"

"Maybe it's for his mom. Or his sister." Summer scrambled for any plausible explanation. "Maybe he's carrying it for a friend, like a drug mule for Cartier. He's not proposing—he's just smuggling!"

"No way. You should have seen his face." Kimberly clasped her hands beside her cheek. "He looked so nervous. It was adorable." Her rapturous expression flickered for just a moment. "He made me promise not to tell you. Oops."

"Oh my God," Summer rasped.

"*I know!*"

"Oh my God." She grabbed the nearest bottle of wine and took a swig. "Don't serve that."

"You know where you should go?" Kim's eyes sparkled. "There's a great little boutique hotel right off rue du Faubourg Saint-Honoré. Hotel de la something. I'll Google it. Super-swanky, super-secluded." She shook her head. "I guess wearing thigh-highs and four-inch heels was a good call, after all."

Summer took another bracing sip of wine and wiped her lips on the back of her hand. "I can't believe this."

"Me, neither!" Kim planted her hands on her hips. "We've all been drooling over Aaron Marchand for years, and you get to spend the rest of your life with him? Not fair. You've landed the unlandable bachelor."

"Well . . ." Summer realized, as she forced herself to release her death grip on the wine bottle, that her hands were shaking. "I haven't landed him yet. I mean, this ring is still speculation and hearsay at this point."

"*Pfft.* I know an engagement ring when I see one." Kim pursed her lips in a little pout. "One less tall, dark, and handsome man for the rest of us." She sighed, then frowned at Summer. "Wait. Why are you freaking out?"

"I'm not freaking out." Summer straightened up and cleared her throat. "But, you know, let's not get ahead of ourselves. He hasn't actually asked. I haven't said yes."

Kim laughed. "Come on. You wouldn't say no to Aaron Marchand." Her eyes widened. "Would you?"

Summer ducked her head and let her hair fall over her eyes. "Well . . ."

Kim wrapped her fingers around Summer's arm again and demanded, "How old are you?"

"Um. Thirty-two."

"Thirty-two," Kim repeated. "And you've done your share of partying, yes?"

Summer nodded. "I'm sure you've heard the rumors. They're all true."

"Okay, so you've had your fun. But, let's face it, you're not twenty-five anymore."

"Twenty-five is a state of mind." Summer tried and failed to free herself from Kim's grasp.

"You're never going to do better than Aaron Marchand. You know that, right?"

Summer stared down at her shiny patent shoes.

"What are you waiting for? Why on earth would you say no?" Kim threw up both hands in exasperation.

Summer darted around her fellow flight attendant and escaped into the first-class cabin. "Hold that thought. I have to go do the dog and pony show." She took her place beneath the TV monitor while the safety demonstration video played. While she pointed out the emergency exits, she scanned the sea of faces, looking for any sign of potential troublemakers.

But tonight the passengers looked docile and weary, most of them ignoring her as the video droned on about inflatable slides and oxygen masks. An elderly couple was already sleeping in the third row, the wife resting her head on her husband's shoulder.

Summer found a thin navy blanket and draped it across the couple's armrests. Then, she dashed to the bulkhead and dialed her best friend, Emily's, number.

When Emily's voice mail picked up, Summer started raving into the receiver: "Hey, I know you're in Vancouver and you probably have thirty thousand things going on right now, but I need a consult. I'm about to take off for Paris with Aaron. The pilot, remember? The one who's all perfect and dreamy and nice? Well, he's about to ask me to marry him. *Marry him.* Out of nowhere! Like an ambush! What should I say? What should I do? Call me back, Em. I'm scared."

She hung up, rested her forehead against the cool, curved plastic walls of the cabin, and forced herself to arrange a smile on her lips before she turned back to the passengers. As she walked through the cabin to do her final safety compliance check ("Fasten your seat belt, please. . . . Here, let me help you with that tray table"), she was waylaid by a passenger with an English accent and a red soccer jersey. He exuded entitlement and the smell of stale beer, and she guessed he was either a professional athlete or a professional musician.

"Could you take this, doll?" He handed her a magazine that had been left in his seat pocket.

"Of course." When Summer took the magazine from him, he brushed his fingers against hers.

"You're gorgeous. Has anyone ever written a song about you?" He met her gaze, then gave her a thorough once-over. Charming, cocky, and incorrigible. A year ago, she would have been all over him.

But she had finally outgrown bad boys. She had finally moved on to a good man. The kind of man she should marry.

"Twice, actually." Summer laughed at the passenger's expression. "What, you think you're the only musician to ever fly commercial?"

"Anyone written a song about you that people have actually heard?" He grinned gamely. "Won Grammys? Gone platinum?"

"Sounds like someone could use a big glass of ice water."

He leaned into the aisle until the side of his head grazed her hip. "What's your name?"

She gave his perfectly coiffed hair a pat. "I'll be right back."

"What's that?" Kim asked when Summer squeezed into the galley to dispose of the magazine.

"Oh, 4C found it in his seat pocket." Summer glanced at the photo on the cover: a quaint seaside village featuring golden sand dunes and gray cedar-shingled houses. The headline read: *The Best Place in America to Bounce Back from Your Breakup.*

"Black Dog Bay, Delaware." Kim peered over her shoulder. "Never heard of it."

"Me, neither. I don't think they even have an airport in Delaware."

"Black Dog Bay. Where all the stores sell Ben & Jerry's and Kleenex."

Summer laughed. "And multiple cats are mandatory."

"And the official uniform is sweatpants and a ratty old bathrobe."

"And *Steel Magnolias* is on TV twenty-four/seven."

Kim tossed the periodical in the trash. "What you need is a magazine all about awesome honeymoon destinations. Because when Aaron Marchand says, 'Will you marry me?,' you say, 'Yes.'"

"We're number two for takeoff," Aaron's voice intoned. "Flight attendants, please be seated."

Summer buckled herself into the jump seat by the bulkhead, facing the passengers in coach. As the plane began to taxi, she automatically "bowed to the cockpit," tilting her head in the direction of the flight deck as a precaution against whiplash.

As always, she devoted the last moments before takeoff to conducting a mental inventory of the emergency medical equipment and glancing around the cabin for ABAs—able-bodied assistants— who could potentially help out in a crisis.

Then they were lifting off and she was thinking about Aaron. Visualizing a diamond ring and fighting back the sour taste of bile in her throat.

It wasn't that she didn't love him. She did love him, more than she'd meant to.

But could she keep his heart without wearing his ring?

Thump.

She heard a loud bang and felt the plane shudder.

"What was that?" A woman gasped. Passengers started murmuring in both English and French.

Summer put on her best flight attendant face, striving to convey both competence and nonchalance as the passengers looked to her for guidance. Her job was to keep everyone calm and safe. And to figure out what the hell was going on.

The plane continued to gain altitude, but something about the alignment was off. Her stomach lurched as the cabin tilted suddenly.

"Oh my God!" someone screamed. "Fire!"

Summer saw the bright streak of flames out the window and knew, with sickening certainty, that an engine was on fire.

We're going to die.

Every muscle in her body locked up, and for a long moment, she was frozen. Her mind went blank.

And then years of training overrode her panic. She grabbed the gray plastic interphone next to her seat and dialed the code for the flight deck.

She pressed the receiver to her ear and waited to hear Aaron's voice, telling her that everything would be fine.

The pilots didn't pick up.

As soon as she hung up, Kim rang from the galley: "Did you feel that? What's going on?"

"I'm not sure." Summer was acutely aware of the panicked

gazes of the passengers. "It's possible one of the engines is damaged." She lowered her voice. "Fire."

Kim sucked in her breath. "What did the pilots say?"

"Nothing yet. I tried to reach them, and they're not picking up."

Kim didn't respond to that; she didn't have to. They both knew what it meant.

Summer put down the phone and concentrated on calming the passengers in coach. "Yes, I felt that, too. Yes, I see the flames. But don't worry, the pilots have this under control. We're all trained for this sort of thing and, you know, the plane can fly perfectly well with only one engine."

We're going to die.

She kept her hand clamped on the interphone, waiting to hear from the flight deck. But there was nothing.

The plane stopped climbing.

Halfway through her breezy explanation of aerospace engineering, the plane tilted sharply and plummeted downward. People started screaming again.

After what seemed like an eternity but was probably only a second or two, the plane leveled off again, and Summer started breathing.

Still no word from the flight deck.

The cabin lights blinked off and the screams faded into tense silence. Her memory summoned snapshots of her past, the proverbial life flashing before her eyes.

She'd seen the northern lights in Sweden and fed baby elephants in Thailand. She'd danced at Carnival in Brazil and gone snorkeling on the Great Barrier Reef. She'd traveled all over the world having once-in-a-lifetime experiences.

But she'd never had a garden.

She'd never learned to play the piano.

She'd never let herself fall completely in love.

This is the worst bucket list ever.

If she weren't so petrified, she'd laugh. Pianos were for singing along to and draping oneself across while wearing a sequined gown. And a garden? Really? That was crazy talk. She'd never even *wanted* a garden.

As for love, well, she could try, right? She could open up and let herself be vulnerable. She could accept Aaron's marriage proposal and settle down and live happily ever after.

I can't.

She white-knuckled the vinyl seat cushion and tried to keep a smile on her face. Tried to slow her heartbeat and catch her breath and say something comforting and authoritative.

The plane pitched sideways again and plummeted down through the darkness. The thick shoulder straps of her seat belt bit into her flesh despite the sensation of weightlessness. She heard the rush of her pulse in her ears. She felt a flood of adrenaline coursing through her limbs.

She forced herself to keep her eyes open as she braced her body for the impact she knew was coming.

chapter 2

Two days later

*B*efore she even opened her eyes, Summer could smell roses. The floral perfume was stale and cloying, almost nauseating in the warm, dry hospital air.

She lay motionless while she regained her bearings, mentally reviewing the few facts she'd been able to retain over the past forty-eight hours:

My head is concussed.

My back is burned.

My ribs and spleen are tore up from the floor up.

Walk it off.

She was safe. No matter how many times she repeated that to herself, she still couldn't quite believe it. Even though she could feel the tissue-thin cotton of the hospital gown on her shoulders and the starched bedsheets against her calves, even though the confusion of the last few days was punctuated with flashbulb memories of doctors and nurses changing her bandages and asking her questions ("Can you tell me your name?" "Can you tell me what year it is?"), she couldn't recall anything about how she'd gotten from the plane to the hospital.

She remembered prepping for takeoff to Paris. She remembered the bag of M&M's and Kim teasing her about her shoes and the British passenger who smelled like a distillery. She remembered the plane's sudden lurch and the screams in the darkness and the acrid smell of smoke. But then there was a gap, a thick and impenetrable mist clouding her memory. All she knew for sure was that she'd been in a New Jersey medical center for two days now, and a dozen red roses had arrived with Aaron's signature on the card.

So she understood, on a detached, intellectual level, that she was safe. Her body would mend.

Aaron was safe, too. He'd been busy with debriefings and corporate damage control, but he'd be here as soon as he could. In the meantime, he'd sent flowers she could smell even in her sleep.

So now she had to open her eyes, start patching reality back together, and figure out what to do next.

Or at least try to get her hands on some good drugs.

She took a deep breath, wincing as sharp pain shot through her rib cage, and surveyed the tiny private room. Her lips were chapped, her throat parched. There was a plastic tan water pitcher just out of arm's reach—*so close, yet so far*—on a low metal table. Various electronic monitors hummed and beeped, and a flimsy shade covered the steel-framed window.

She startled as she heard a soft rustling from across the room. Her neck ached as she turned her head to glimpse a shadowed figure seated in the vinyl recliner next to the door.

"You're awake," Aaron's voice said.

She could hear him, but she couldn't see him. Just like the moments before takeoff. Overwhelmed by emotions she couldn't even name, she had to try three times before her dry throat would swallow.

"You're here." Her voice came out thin and hoarse.

"I've been here all afternoon." He got to his feet, cutting a striking silhouette in the late afternoon shadows. The handsome hero, straight out of central casting.

She had dated handsome men before. Fascinating, witty men who were long on charisma and short on integrity. They wined and dined her. They enthralled her. They left her at the first sign of trouble.

Until Aaron.

He was so much more than handsome; he was honest and hardworking and respectful and loyal. The kind of man that every woman hoped for.

Summer had never seen herself as the marrying type, and in fact had strict rules in place: *Never stay in one place too long. Never stay with one man too long.* She knew what would happen if she broke these rules. If she needed a man more than he needed her. She had experienced the fallout firsthand.

Kim was right. Summer should be able to do this—to grow up and settle down and form lasting attachments. Her friends were all getting married, having babies, buying houses. Being adults. Being normal. They made it look so effortless, this transition from reckless youth into stable families. As if the whole thing couldn't unravel at any second.

She loved Aaron; he loved her. He had literally saved her life. She should marry him.

I can't.

"Why didn't you wake me up?" She struggled to sit up straighter, wincing and reaching for the water pitcher.

"You need your rest." He intercepted the pitcher and poured lukewarm water into a clear plastic cup. "Ice?"

She shook her head again, heedless of the pain, and gulped the water. Despite the steady drip from the saline IV, her body craved fluid. She felt empty inside, almost hollow.

He adjusted the window shade, and as golden sunlight streamed in, she saw worry and fatigue etched in the lines of his face. The sparkle in his blue eyes had gone flat, and his devil-may-care grin had given way to an expression of grim resolve. He still wore a crisp navy pilot's blazer, but he'd unfastened the buttons of his white shirt, and she could see a patch of gauze taped to his collarbone.

And, in that moment, both of them half-hidden and half-revealed in the shadows and sunlight, she sensed something different about him, a subtle shift in the way he looked and spoke to her.

"Come here." She put down the cup and stretched out her hand to him. "Are you okay? What happened to your shoulder?"

He took a single step in her direction. "Nothing, just a scratch."

"That's a pretty impressive bandage for 'just a scratch.'"

"It's nothing," he repeated. "You got banged up pretty good, though. I've been calling two or three times a day for updates." He came closer and smiled down at her. "You look great."

She tried to laugh, but it came out as a cough. "You lie."

"It's the truth." He brushed a strand of hair back from her cheek. "Not a scratch on that perfect face."

"Tell that to my spleen." As she gazed up at him, she felt the same hot rush of attraction she'd experienced the first time she'd met him.

His right hand patted his blazer pocket, then fell away. Reached again and fell away. And then she remembered: the ring.

She picked up her cup as her throat went dry again.

"I'm sorry I couldn't be here with you the whole time," Aaron said. "But legal had to interrogate me. And then the public relations team had their turn."

"Public relations?"

"Oh, yeah. They want to make sure they spin this as a victory against all odds rather than an equipment failure that justifies a lawsuit. I had to go on one of those morning shows yesterday, and tonight I'm booked for some cable news interviews. Hence, the uniform."

"I bet you did great. You're very photogenic, and—" She broke off as his hand drifted back to his pocket.

He rocked back on his heels. "That's what the public relations team said. They had the first officer go on air with me. Kim, too. Said her Southern accent was good for the company image. They wanted you, too, but . . ."

Summer let her head settle back against the pillow. "I'm an unreliable witness whacked out on pain pills and prone to passing out."

"They didn't use those exact words." He finally came close enough to kiss her, pressing his lips against the top of her head. "Does that hurt?"

"No." She tilted her face up so he could kiss her on the mouth. "Thank you for the flowers." She nodded at the bouquet. The rose petals had gone dark and crisp around the edges.

His hand went all the way into the pocket this time, and he started to extract something before he changed his mind and put it back. "Summer. You know I love you." He sat down next to her on the bed.

"I love you, too," she forced out.

"How much do you remember about the landing?" he asked. She finally drew a breath. "What?"

"The doctors won't tell me much since I'm just your boyfriend and not your husband."

She stilled. "Uh-huh."

"And your family isn't . . . They're not returning my calls." He shifted his weight. "I looked up your dad's office number on the university Web site. His department secretary said he's out of town. And your mother . . ."

He gazed at her, a glimmer of pity in his eyes.

Summer lifted her chin and stared at the roses.

He waited for her to respond for another long minute, then gave up. "Anyway, from what I've managed to get out of the nurses, you don't remember much."

"Yeah." She laced her fingers together and squeezed, wondering where he was going with this. "Everything after takeoff's a little hazy. They told me one of the engines blew out?"

He nodded. "I had to make an emergency landing. We didn't have time to circle and dump the fuel, so things got pretty exciting for a minute, but we made it."

"Is that why I have burns on my back?"

"Like I said, things got a little exciting."

"But you saved us," she said. "You're a hero."

"*You're* the hero," he corrected. "Once we got back on the ground, people were trying to get out the emergency doors, and a little boy fell in the aisle. You managed to push back the crowd and pull him up."

Summer suddenly wanted an extra dose of morphine. "I let go of the door handle?"

Aaron nodded. "That's how you got hurt. You fell onto the tarmac."

"Which is why we're not supposed to let go of the door handle." Summer shook her head. "That's like, flight attendant 101." She closed her eyes and concentrated, sifting through her consciousness for any recollection. "I really . . . I can't remember any of that."

"The whole thing was over in less than five minutes," Aaron

said. "But those five minutes changed everything." He reached into his pocket.

She held her breath and waited for him to produce the ring. And waited. And waited.

He continued to look at her with that wistful expression. "I do love you, Summer."

"I love you, too." She smiled. "We're even."

He stood up and turned his back to her. "There's so many things I want to say to you, and I don't know where to begin."

She couldn't stand this any longer. "I know about the ring, Aaron."

He froze, then turned to face her. "You do?"

"Kim told me everything." She waited for him to look up.

"Okay, then." His hand moved back to his pocket. "Kim was right. There was a ring."

"'Was'? Past tense?"

He caught her gaze and held it. "When I said I love you, I meant it. I've loved every minute we've spent together. You're fun. You're spontaneous. You make me laugh."

"Okay," she said faintly. "But . . . ?"

"I love you. But I don't love you enough."

She went perfectly still.

He watched her face. "Say something."

She took a moment, cleared her throat. "You're breaking up with me?"

He lifted his shoulders and blew out a breath. "I've been carrying that ring around for months."

Her stomach clenched. "Months?"

"I wanted to ask you to marry me. I really did. But it never seemed to be the right time. And after a while . . ."

"You were going to propose in Paris," she insisted. "It would have been perfect."

"It would've been," he agreed. "But we didn't make it to Paris. And maybe that's a sign." He turned his face away. "Please don't take this personally. My whole life has changed in the last few days. I've realized that all the clichés are true. Life is short. We can't do things halfway. And you and I, we had fun, but we're not marriage material. There's something missing. I wish I could explain it better, but I can't."

She took her time sipping the lukewarm water.

"You'll be fine." He couldn't even look at her. "You're the strongest woman I know."

Walk it off.

At this, Summer finally regained her voice.

"Go." Her voice came out flat and low. "Just go."

"I'm sorry." He reached for her, but she flinched away.

"Don't apologize," she said. "I don't want apologies. I don't want explanations. I just want you to go."

Still, he hesitated.

Her voice got louder, sharper. "Please."

As the door closed behind him, she felt the prickle of tears in her eyes, but she managed to compose herself. Aaron was right about her strength—she had always been resourceful and resilient. When life got hard, she didn't stop—she put one foot in front of the other, moving faster and farther until she pushed through the pain.

She would survive this, she knew. She always did.

And in the end, Aaron wasn't the one who got away. He was the one who reminded her of everything she'd been trying to get away from.

The room seemed to close in on her. She couldn't bear to stay here, confined, inhaling the scent of dying roses with every breath. So she did the only thing she could under the circumstances: She hit the call button, and when the nurse arrived, she announced,

"Bring the consent forms or whatever I need to sign. I'm discharging myself, effective immediately."

Before the nurse could start arguing, the door swung wide again and a firm, feminine voice rang through the room: "Simmer down, crazycakes. No one's going anywhere."

This time, Summer couldn't hold back her tears. "Emily?"

chapter 3

"I'm kind of insulted that you're surprised to see me." Emily shooed the nurse away, handed Summer a box of tissues, and pulled up a chair to the bedside. "You crash and burn—literally—and just expect me to go about my business? I don't think so." Even after a long flight and zero sleep, Summer's former stepsister maintained her deceptively ladylike poise. "Besides, I had a feeling you'd try a jailbreak."

Summer clawed at the back of her hospital gown. "You're not supposed to be here. You're supposed to be on some fancy film set, telling everyone what to do."

"Well, aren't you lucky that I decided to take the red-eye and direct all my bossiness at you?"

"Where's Ryan?" Emily's husband could always be counted on to support a jailbreak.

"Back in Vancouver, telling everyone what to do in my absence." Emily grabbed Summer's hands and pried them off the fabric. "Stop thrashing around. You're going to rip the rest of your spleen in half, and then you'll never get out of here."

"Oh, please. When have a few gushing head wounds ever

stopped us from having a good time?" Summer squeezed a wad of blankets in her fists. "Speaking of which, we've never been to New York together. Let's freshen up, grab the train to Manhattan, and find someplace fabulous to catch up over a cocktail."

Emily stared at her. "What's going on with you?"

"Nothing."

"Something."

"Nothing! I'm just tired of wasting away in bed like an invalid. Let's go do something fun!" Summer couldn't hold still.

"You've been through a lot." Emily adopted the soothing, condescending tone the medical staff had been using. "Let's check in with your doctors and see if we can get something to help with the agitation." She reached for the call button.

"I'm not agitated!" Summer grabbed the plastic water pitcher and hurled it at the vase full of roses, which toppled off the table and shattered on the tile floor in a spray of water and glass shards.

There ensued a long silence. The only sound was the muted clicking of the IV monitor.

Emily rose, strode over to the bathroom, and came back with a stack of industrial paper towels. "Clearly, you're not agitated in the least."

"Get me out of here." Summer closed her eyes while Emily mopped up wet rose petals. "Please. I'm begging you, Em."

Emily tweezed a hunk of glass between her thumb and index fingers and dropped it into the wastebasket. "I will consider it. But you need to stop throwing stuff. If I wanted drugged-up divas hurling vases at me, I would have stayed in Hollywood."

"Fair enough." Summer paused. "But technically, I didn't even throw it in your direction."

"Keep it up." Emily pushed the rose petals into a pile. "I've got a 5150 with your name all over it." She glanced up. "Where is everyone? Where's your dad?"

"Poetry conference in Ireland."

Emily opened her mouth, then obviously thought better of what she'd been about to say.

"He's giving the keynote speech, Em. You know the rules. Keynote speech trumps daughter." As did NPR interviews, Pulitzer Prizes, nights at the bar with his writer buddies, and fawning literary groupies.

Not that she was keeping track.

"He brought some new girlfriend with him," Summer continued. "Sweet. Young. Thinks my dad's bullshit is 'an artistic temperament.' The usual."

Emily laughed, and for the first time since the plane crash, Summer felt normal. "Bless her heart."

"I've never even met her, but she's already sending me journals and telling me I should write poetry like my father."

"Just like all your English professors," Emily said. "The Benson name didn't hurt your GPA."

Summer nodded. "That and a made-up dead grandmother will get you a C in comp lit."

Emily shook her head. "Shameless."

"You're the one who whipped up the fake death certificate on Photoshop."

Emily grinned at the memory. "Masterful work, if I do say so myself." She cleaned up the last of the puddle and settled back into her chair with an expectant look. "Well, where's Captain Hunky?"

Summer hesitated.

"I saw him on *Good Morning America*. Well, I didn't see him, but my mother did." Emily rolled her eyes. "She sent me the video clip, and she wants me to give you the following message: 'He gives my ladybits turbulence.'"

Summer burst out laughing. "I love your mom."

"And she loves you." Even though Georgia, Emily's mother,

had divorced Summer's father years ago, they still considered themselves family. "So, where is he? I assumed he'd be here, dabbing your fevered brow."

"I believe you have Captain Hunky confused with a Brontë book hero," Summer said.

"Don't play coy with me." Emily braced her elbows on the armrests and leaned forward. "Did he propose yet? I need all the juicy details."

"Well . . ."

"The TV anchors asked him if he had a girlfriend, but he was very discreet."

"I bet he was." It took Summer a few seconds to work up the nerve to say the words. "He didn't propose. He . . . left."

Emily frowned. "Like to go make more media appearances?"

"Like to go find someone else. Someone he actually loves. Someone who's, quote-unquote, 'marriage material.'"

She summarized the breakup to Emily, whose expression cycled from scandalized disbelief to murderous rage and back again.

"Just so we're clear." Emily rummaged through her handbag. "He actually said the words, 'I love you but I don't love you enough'?"

Summer flinched. "Sounds worse every time I hear it."

"When did all this happen?"

"Approximately two minutes before you got here."

"I will kill him." Emily redoubled her search efforts in her bag. "*Kill him*. Damn it, TSA took away my nail file." She reached over and squeezed Summer's hand, her eyes brimming with sympathy. "Oh, honey, I—"

"Do not." Summer snatched her hand away. "Do not look at me; do not touch me; do not speak to me in that tone of voice."

"But you—"

"I'm fine. I'm the strongest woman he knows. I'm easy to walk away from because I'm all scrappy and shit."

Emily's jaw dropped. "Is that what he said?"

"I'm paraphrasing. But it's okay because, you know, he's right. I'm not marriage material. I have strict rules against it, in fact." Summer straightened the sheets. "This was bound to happen sooner or later. The poor man realized I was out of his league and decided to go back to playing JV. It's fine."

"It's *not* fine." Emily was practically frothing at the mouth. "He can't break up with you while you're in the hospital recovering from all kinds of internal injuries! This will not stand. I am going to hunt him down—"

"No one's hunting anyone down. Like I said, it's fine." Summer willed herself to believe this. "I refuse to be the woman some guy settled for."

Emily sprang to her feet. "He can't—"

"He can, he did, and you know what?" Summer waited until Emily stopped fuming. "I had it coming."

Emily's eyebrows shot up. "What does that mean?"

"You know exactly what it means." Summer stared out the window. "He didn't love me enough because I made myself impossible to love. Next topic?"

Emily sat back down. "Have you considered talking to a counselor?"

"I don't need a counselor! What I need is a bottle of vodka and a full night's sleep without someone barging in to check my vitals every twenty minutes." Summer pulled the IV needle out of her arm, gasping at the pain. "And then I need to hole up somewhere quiet. Somewhere I don't have to worry about seeing Aaron's face all over the television."

Emily gave up her role as the designated voice of reason. "You're right—we need to break you out of here and go find some vodka."

"This is what I'm saying."

"But then I want you to come back to Vancouver with me."

Summer shook her head. "Don't worry your pretty little head about me. Go back to bossing the rest of the world around. I'll be fine."

Emily was already dialing her cell phone. "I'm booking you a room at the hotel where the crew is staying."

Summer confiscated the phone and turned it off. "That's sweet of you, but really, I just want to be by myself for a while."

Emily's look of concern deepened. "For how long?"

"I don't know." *Until every single molecule of my being isn't in pain.*

"Don't let him do this, Summer." Emily's brown eyes flashed. "Don't let him make you doubt yourself."

"Please. No man can make me do anything." Summer flopped back against the pillows. "I'm just tired. I'm *exhausted*. I need to pick a time zone and stick with it for a while."

"Where will you go? Home?"

"Home" was a tiny apartment shared with two other flight attendants, and nothing had ever sounded less appealing. "I can go wherever I want. I have like a million frequent-flier miles at my disposal." Even as she said the words, she knew she wouldn't be flying anywhere. Not while her burns and bruises still ached. Not while the mental image of the airport made her heart race and her stomach churn.

"I will help you however I can," Emily vowed. "Whatever you need to heal."

"Really?"

"Really."

"Can you go get Scarlett from the long-term parking lot and drive her down here?"

Emily smiled. "You still have Scarlett?"

"But of course. That car has outlasted every relationship I've ever had."

"And where will you be driving off to?"

For a moment, Summer's mind went completely blank. Then she remembered the cover of the travel magazine. The magazine she'd laughed at minutes before her entire life went down in flames. The mecca for people who hadn't been loved enough. "Black Dog Bay."

"Where's that?"

"Delaware."

"Delaware?"

Summer nodded.

"What's in Black Dog Bay, Delaware?"

"Ben & Jerry's and *Steel Magnolias*."

chapter 4

TURTLES CROSSING—NEXT 5 MILES

Summer had seen a lot of road signs in a lot of cities all over the world, but this was a new one. The yellow diamond featured the black silhouettes of one big turtle followed by two smaller turtles.

She snapped out of the daze she'd fallen into, took a sip of warm, watery diet soda, and tried to get her bearings.

Last night, she'd waited until Emily had fallen asleep in the vinyl recliner, then watched a clip of Aaron's TV interview a dozen times. The man gave good sound bite. He managed to appear serious but approachable, responsible but easygoing.

A few days of public relations training had rendered him almost unrecognizable—how was this the same guy with whom she'd planned to share a naughty corsets-and-croissants weekend? With whom she'd considered, even in the most abstract terms, spending the rest of her life?

She knew she should be grateful that he'd been honest and left before they'd made a huge mistake. She'd seen what happened when people stayed in a relationship because they *had* to; the deceit of "mature adults" bound by obligation.

Countless married men propositioning her on flights.

Hungover honeymooners who wouldn't even speak to each other on the way home from Tahiti.

Her own parents.

Yes, she should have felt relieved. But she didn't.

So she'd stuffed a trash bag full of personal belongings into the trunk of her 1982 red Mercedes convertible and pulled out of the hospital parking lot at dawn, despite the protests and warnings of a dozen medical experts.

If you're going to be self-destructive, might as well go all the way.

She'd crossed the state line into Delaware two hours ago, and spent the morning navigating stop-and-go beach traffic on a highway lined by marshes and lush green trees. Every few minutes, she had to give herself a little shake to stay focused, but she should be approaching the turnoff for Black Dog Bay any minute now. The muted rattle of ice from her soda cup reminded her that she hadn't eaten since . . . um . . . a long time. She didn't want to eat, or talk, or think. She just wanted to drive until she could see the ocean.

She turned on the car radio and scanned through the static until she found a local station, which was playing an old Pet Shop Boys song she remembered from middle school. She turned up the music and forced herself to sing along.

The car rounded a curve and she saw a weathered white wooden sign embellished with the outline of a black Labrador: WELCOME TO BLACK DOG BAY. Summer followed the arrows and turned off the highway onto a narrow asphalt road.

She rolled down the windows of the car to let in the damp, tangy ocean breeze. She couldn't see the water yet, but she could literally taste sea salt in the air.

Now what?

She hadn't actually planned out this trip past the drive to the shore. After years of last-minute schedule changes and twelve-hour layovers, she didn't worry about researching tourist attractions or making hotel reservations in advance. She just charged ahead, armed with bravado and a few spare pairs of underpants, and so far, it'd always worked out. This morning, she'd been so desperate to get on the road, to physically distance herself from all her injuries. To escape.

And now she'd arrived at her destination, and her entire being still hurt. Her head still ached. Her ribs protested with every breath.

At least her heart had stopped breaking. Now she felt numb, which was a decided improvement.

The foliage thinned as the bay came into view. The ocean looked dark and cold, in stark contrast to the pristine, pale sand dunes. One side of the road was lined with quaint little brick shops, the other with stately, gray shingled houses. Across the white-capped waves, she could see the yellow triangle of a sailboat and a tiny seaplane towing a banner.

Traffic was light, but the sidewalks were crowded with vacationers who had clearly come straight from the beach. Lots of flip-flops, khaki shorts, and straw hats.

Her grip on the steering wheel loosened and the muscles in her shoulders relaxed as she rolled past a shop window painted with a black dog eating an ice-cream cone. She hadn't realized how much tension she'd been holding on to until she let some of it go.

This was why she'd come. To recharge. To heal. To figure out what the hell she was supposed to do next.

She reminded herself of the cardinal rule of travel: When in need of a mood adjustment, try snacking, showering, and sleeping.

Hoping to find an inn, she turned left at the next stoplight and continued on a newly paved road that narrowed as the houses on either side grew ever bigger and grander. This was not hotel territory. This was million-dollar summer home territory. She sped up a bit as she drove around the bend, looking for a driveway she could use to turn around.

That's when the Taylor Swift song came on.

The mournful lyrics and dulcet vocals hit her like a sack of oranges to the stomach. The clouds dissipated, and as the afternoon sun blazed down, all the tears she hadn't been able to shed in the hospital gushed out, blurring her vision and shocking her with their force.

She raised her arm to wipe her eyes on the sleeve of her short-sleeve shirt. Then Taylor launched into the chorus, and Summer started sobbing, gasping for breath. Her whole face was soaked. Her entire body shook.

And when she glanced back at the road, a tiny green turtle had meandered in front of her car.

She slammed on the brakes and spun the steering wheel, missing the turtle by inches.

She did not, however, miss the white trellis bordering the lawn of one of the beach houses. Even though she was driving slowly, the Mercedes was built like a tank, and the wood gave way with a splintering crunch as the convertible plowed through the rose-bushes and onto a white gravel driveway.

"Shit." She stomped on the gas and backed up, launching chunks of dirt and a spray of gravel across the road. Once the car's tires were back on the asphalt, she cut the engine and jumped out to assess the damage.

A screen door slammed and a male voice called: "Are you all right?"

Summer shaded her eyes and peered up at the porch of the house. Although situated on prime beachfront property, this home was relatively modest compared with the multistory architectural behemoths on either side. Two stories of weathered brown cedar siding and white-trimmed windows, surrounded by a low-slung porch. The yard left room for a larger garage or a guest cottage, but instead, the owner had devoted the space to rows and rows of what appeared to be rosebushes.

Rosebushes upon which she had perpetrated vehicular manslaughter. "I'm fine. I just . . . Sorry! I'm sorry."

She heard the thud of footfalls on wooden steps as the homeowner approached her. Despite the humidity, he wore faded jeans, mud-spattered work boots, and a long-sleeved navy T-shirt that set off gray eyes and a chiseled jawline. The combination of rugged and sensual features was startling—Captain America at a Milan photo shoot. He was tall and lean, with a hint of windburn on his cheeks and thick brown hair sun streaked with bronze.

Rustic outdoorsmen weren't Summer's type, but something about him . . . He looked like he could ravish you so right and then stride off to chop a cord of wood.

"You ran over my roses." His tone was both accusatory and incredulous.

"It was an accident. There was a turtle." She swiped at her eyes and struggled to regain her composure. "Came out of nowhere."

He stared at her for a moment, his eyes narrowing.

"I've never been to Delaware before." Summer drew in a ragged breath. "I didn't realize. About the turtles."

He crossed his arms, his gaze intensifying. "Are you drunk?"

"No!"

He stepped closer. "Yes, you are."

"I am not. I'm completely sober." To prove her point, she got right in his face and blew out a huge lungful of air. "See? Diet Coke. No rum!"

He didn't back down. "I don't see a turtle."

"It's right here!" She jabbed her index finger at the patch of asphalt where she'd seen the tiny green desperado, but realized the road was empty. "It was moving surprisingly fast."

"Uh-huh." The guy pulled a cell phone out of his back pocket. She noticed half-moons of fresh dirt under his fingernails. "I'm calling the cops."

She put her hand on the sleeve of his cotton shirt. "I swear to you, I'm stone-cold sober."

He looked down at her fingers, then back up to her face. "Your eyes are red and bloodshot and you're babbling about a turtle that doesn't exist."

"It exists! I'm just a bad driver, okay? Why is that so hard to believe?"

He paused mid-dial. She took her hand off his forearm.

"You're just a bad driver?" he repeated. "Running over fences and ripping out rosebushes is your standard operating procedure?"

"No. There were extenuating circumstances."

"I'm waiting."

She clenched her fists and stared down at the muddy tire tracks. "I was lost and I was crying at a Taylor Swift song on the radio, okay? Are you happy now?"

"No." His voice was so flat that she couldn't gauge any emotion, so she glanced back at his face. His expression remained impassive, but she thought she caught a little flicker of amusement in those gray eyes.

"Did you, uh, did you plant all these roses yourself?" she asked.

"Yes."

"Sorry again. Look, this place is breakup central, right?" The wind picked up, blowing her hair across her face, and she pushed it back with one hand. "You must have Taylor Swift–induced car wrecks all the time. Am I right?"

He shifted his weight. "You're sure you're not drunk?"

"Believe me, I'd *love* to be able to blame this on alcohol. But no. Anyway, I'll fix your lawn. And your roses. And this . . . fence thing . . . whatever you call it. I'll fix that, too."

"Don't worry about it. I'll handle it."

"Give me twenty-four hours," Summer said. "It'll be like this whole thing never happened. Trust me; I'm very efficient."

He shook his head. "All I ask is that you turn off the radio. The roads will be safer for turtles and trellises everywhere." He dusted off his hands, clearly dismissing her. "Drive carefully."

Over his shoulder, beyond the porch railings, she could glimpse the blue of the ocean. "The view from the front of your house must be amazing."

"It is."

She waited for him to elaborate, and when he didn't, she tried, "Do you live here year-round?"

She wasn't sure why she was trying to keep this conversation going. The guy was covered in dirt and Irish Spring–scented sweat, he was annoyed about his yard, and he no doubt wanted to perform triage on the half-dead roses and grieve in his manly, wood-chopping way for the all-dead ones. He was telling her, not so subtly, to get gone.

And yet she held her ground, surrounded by plant carnage and listening to the ocean and watching his gray eyes darken in the sunlight.

He watched her watching him. "What exactly are you looking for?"

She blinked. "Excuse me?"

"You said you were lost. What are you trying to find?"

She had to force herself to break eye contact. "Somewhere to stay. A decent hotel."

"Go to the Better Off Bed-and-Breakfast." He pointed in the

direction she'd come from. "Back to that main road, turn left at the intersection, then take your second right."

Summer laughed. "Shut up. It's not really called the Better Off Bed-and-Breakfast."

His eyebrows rose just a fraction of an inch. "Business name is registered with the town."

"Really? That's awesome. Do you think they'll have any rooms available?"

"They'll work something out." He started back toward the house.

"I promise you, I'm coming back to fix your landscaping situation."

"Please don't."

"I'm trying to be nice." She called after him as he started up the porch steps. "I'm Summer, by the way. And you are . . . ?"

He lifted his hand in a wave and didn't look back.

chapter 5

$\mathcal{S}$ummer arrived in downtown Black Dog Bay approximately
three minutes later. As she drove through the main drag (two lanes
of traffic, one dotted yellow line, speed limit twenty-five), she had
to smile at the business names: the Retail Therapy boutique, the
Jilted Café, the Rebound Salon. This must be the section of the
community that catered to the breakup crowd. She noticed a
woman strolling down the cobblestone sidewalk wearing baggy
green yoga pants and carrying a handbag Summer had eyed cov-
etously in the window of the Chanel boutique in Paris. This town
was half kitschy tourist trap, half gentrified old money.

The street dead-ended in a quaint little town square consisting
of white park benches, a wooden gazebo, and a large bronze statue
of what appeared to be a big, shaggy dog. Beyond the town square,
the beach and boardwalk beckoned. The bay created a semicircular
inlet, and Summer could see rows of sleek, modern beach houses
featuring walls of plate glass windows . . . plus one huge mansion
painted violet. The house, sprawled across at least an acre of prime
beachfront property, was the color of a fresh bruise.

Summer started speculating about what kind of homeowner

had enough wealth to buy such an estate and the chutzpah to paint it purple. Then she spotted a sign hanging from an iron lamppost, BETTER OFF BED-AND-BREAKFAST, and followed the arrows to a large, saltbox-style house with white clapboard sides and green shutters. An orange striped cat sat on the front step, twitching its tail and basking in the sun.

The parking lot was packed with a diverse assortment of cars: soccer mom SUVs, sporty coupes, vintage hippie vans, and even a shiny mint green Vespa scooter. Summer managed to maneuver Scarlett into a space (well, okay, it wasn't technically a space, but it *would* have been if everyone else had parked properly) between a silver BMW sedan and a rusty pickup truck with a visible gun rack.

After she turned off the car, she settled back into the driver's seat and tried to muster the energy to collect her bags and go inside. She knew there were basic tasks she had to attend to—eating and showering came to mind—but the mere idea of those activities overwhelmed her. So she made a deal with herself: If she could force herself to go inside and navigate the check-in process, she could stay in bed for the rest of the day. For the rest of the week.

Moving at a glacial pace, she stepped out of the car and started up the flagstone path to the entryway. While the bed-and-breakfast's exterior harkened back to a bygone era, the interior had obviously been recently remodeled. The lobby was airy and full of sunlight, with ice blue walls and windows facing the ocean. The back door stood open, beckoning visitors to a deck lined with wicker sofas and Adirondack chairs.

A stout, pink-cheeked redhead bustled in to greet Summer. "Welcome to the Better Off Bed-and-Breakfast. You must be Summer?"

"I am." Summer glanced around. "And you must be psychic."

"No, no, I'm Marla." When the redhead smiled, she looked so

warm and maternal she might as well be wearing an apron and rolling out pie dough. "But I've been expecting a tall, beautiful blonde. Dutch called and gave me a heads-up."

"Dutch," Summer repeated. "Is that the guy whose fence I ran over?"

"That's right. Dutch Jansen." Marla regarded her with a hint of reproach. "He works so hard on those roses. It's a crying shame."

"It was an accident, and it wasn't even my fault! I blame the turtles and Taylor Swift."

"Of course, honey." Marla nodded as if this made perfect sense. "How long do you think you'll be staying with us?"

But Summer wasn't finished with their first talking point. "Hang on. So this Dutch guy. He said I was a tall, beautiful blonde?"

Marla's eyes widened as she picked up a coffee cup from a side table. "He said . . . Well, I guess I inferred . . . Do me a favor and don't tell him I said that, okay?"

"Absolutely. I'm just surprised, because he was not having any of my tall, beautiful blondeness at the scene of the crime. He couldn't get away from me fast enough."

"Well, as I said, he puts blood, sweat, and tears into those rose-bushes."

"Dutch Jansen." Summer filed this name away for future investigation. "So he grows roses and he knows the owner of the local B and B."

"Oh, Dutch knows everybody. He's the mayor."

Summer froze. "He is?"

"Mm-hmm. Didn't really have much of a choice; it's Jansen family tradition. His grandfather was the mayor, and then his father—until he died. Dutch took over as soon as he was old enough to run for office."

Summer patted her windblown, unwashed hair. "I ran over the mayor's landscaping."

"Sure did!" Marla hummed a happy tune as she rearranged the wildflowers in a blue milk vase. "Now, let me get you settled in before the dinner rush starts. How long do you think you'll be our guest?"

"I'm not sure, exactly. I know it's the height of tourist season. What's your availability like?"

"Well, we don't technically have any vacancy, but I'll squeeze you in somewhere. Though I'm afraid all our ocean-view rooms are taken."

"That's fine," Summer said. "I just need someplace quiet to crash." She winced as the word left her mouth, her mind flashing back to the near disaster in the plane.

"Here." Marla patted a sofa piled with embroidered throw pillows. "Have a seat while I ask my husband if we can put you up in the attic room."

"Wait. You run this place with your husband?"

"Mm-hmm. Theo—that's him out there." Marla pointed out the window at a burly, bearded man sanding a bit of peeled paint from the porch railing. "Isn't he a cutie?"

"I guess, but what about the whole better-off-breakup theme? Shouldn't you be single?"

Marla chuckled. "Oh, why, bless your heart, honey, that's the *guests*. Not the locals. There are three types of people in Black Dog Bay: year-round residents who have jobs and families and bills to pay, the rich summer people from Baltimore and D.C., and the heartbreak tourists."

"Heartbreak tourists," Summer repeated.

"That's what we call them. Mostly women, although we do get the occasional man. Two years ago, I rented a room to a groom who was left at the altar. He stayed in our best suite for a week, smoking cigars and heaven knows what else. The place smelled like a humidor by the time he checked out. We had to rip out the carpets and replace the drapes." Marla shook her head at the memory.

"Don't the rich summer people object to the heartbreak tourists?"

"Not really. Most of them figure we're better off with weepy women than rowdy college kids. Besides, this town was founded by a filthy-rich socialite. Lavinia Leighton. Her name's on the plaque by the dog statue down at the town square. Her husband left her, ran off with some floozy actress. She lost her lifestyle in New York, all her fancy friends, and she came down here to start fresh." Marla plucked a book from the shelf beneath the window seat and showed Summer the title: *The History of Black Dog Bay.* "You can read all about it if—" She broke off midsentence as a lanky woman wearing a woven black sun hat and oversize sunglasses strode in. "Would you excuse me for just a moment?"

"Take your time." Summer collapsed onto the sofa.

Marla rolled up the sleeves of her pale pink shirtdress and hurried over to intercept the newcomer, who was tugging at a locked drawer in the front hall table.

"Celeste, honey, no." Marla wedged herself between the woman and the table. "Step away from the cell phones."

"Where's the key?" The woman ripped off her hat and ran her fingers through long, tangled hair. "Forget everything I said yesterday. Just give me my phone."

"Absolutely not." Marla adopted the demeanor of a stern finishing school headmistress. "This is for your own good."

"One text." Celeste grabbed Marla's hand. "That's all I'm asking for. One last little text. For closure."

"Consider your dignity."

"Fuck my dignity!"

Marla didn't bat an eye. "Now, now. You don't mean that."

"I do, too!"

"Texting him's not going to make you feel better." Marla adopted the tone of voice you'd use to soothe a spooked horse. "This is just your brain chemistry resetting itself back to normal. That's what Hollis says. You're not in your right mind—you're a junkie in withdrawal."

The willowy brunette glanced down at her trembling hands, her expression mutinous. "I know exactly what I want, and it's to text that miserable, selfish SOB and tell him that . . . that . . ."

"What?" Marla planted her hands on her ample hips. "That you still need him? That you can't live without him? That you know you two still love each other deep down?"

At this, Celeste burst into tears. "You don't know him! You don't know me!"

Marla engulfed the distraught guest in a motherly hug and handed over a box of tissues—but no phone. "There, there. Let it all out. The first three days of detox are the hardest. I promise it gets easier."

Summer marveled at the innkeeper's maternal warmth and "tough love." Marla hugged you when you needed a hug and confiscated your cell phone when you were jonesing for the rat bastard who broke your heart. How did some women step so effortlessly into the Mom role? And what would it have been like to have been born to one of them?

What would it have been like to have a mother who stayed instead of left?

"When?" Celeste sobbed into Marla's collar. The dry-cleaning bills around here must be astronomical. "When will it get easier?"

"Tomorrow," Marla promised. "And the day after that and the day after that. You're bottoming out and it's miserable. I know. But you're going to get through this. If you text him right now, you're restarting the clock and undoing all our hard work."

"But I—"

"Here." Marla wriggled out of Celeste's bear hug, reached into her dress pocket, and pulled out a hammer. "You'll feel better."

"But you—"

"Run along." Marla made little shooing motions with her hands. She didn't even glance at the smears of lipstick and mascara on her dress. "Give it all you've got for fifteen minutes and if you still want your phone after that, we'll talk."

Celeste accepted the hammer, still scowling. "Don't lie. You're not giving me my phone back in fifteen minutes."

Marla waved her fingers. "Toodle-oo."

Celeste stomped off, hammer in hand, and left her sun hat abandoned on the rug.

Summer stared after her. "What was that all about?"

Marla picked up the hat, dusted it off, and placed it on a hook next to the front door. "What was what, dear?"

"Where's she going with that hammer? Why are you holding her cell phone hostage?"

Marla shrugged. "Hotel policy. I make all the guests surrender their phone when they check in. It prevents backsliding."

"Backsliding," Summer echoed.

"Begging, pleading, threatening." Marla ticked these off on her fingers. "Regrettable calls and texts at three a.m." She smiled up at Summer and held out her palm. "Speaking of which, dear, if you'd be so kind . . ."

Summer clutched her purse strap protectively. "You want my cell phone?"

"Just for a few days."

"You can't have it. I'm very important. And busy. I'm getting calls from my employer, the media—people need to be able to reach me."

Marla didn't argue. She just stood there, smiling, with her palm outstretched.

"Look, I get that you don't know me, but I don't backslide. When I'm done with a man, I'm *done* with him." She swallowed hard. "And I definitely don't beg."

Marla's smile softened. "What's his name, dear?"

Summer swallowed again. "He, uh . . . You've probably seen him on TV over the last few days. He's the . . ." She couldn't force the word "pilot" out, let alone "Aaron." "Can I have some water, please?"

Marla bustled off to the kitchen and returned with a glass of pink lemonade. "I'll take that cell phone now."

Summer sighed and surrendered the lifeline that kept her tethered to the hope that, any minute now, Aaron would come to his senses and reach out to her. Apologize. Repent. Beg her to take him back.

Decide that she was worth loving.

"Take good care of her," Summer said as Marla locked the phone in the drawer.

"I'll love it like it was my own," Marla promised. "And if you need to make calls, you're welcome to do so. In the common areas. Under supervision."

Summer took one tiny sip of the cold, delicious lemonade and almost gagged. Her body wanted nothing to do with food or drink right now. "So this is like breakup boot camp?"

"Mm-hmm. With homemade blueberry muffins for breakfast."

Summer suppressed another gag. "And what's with the hammer?"

"We have a storage room in the basement. A few years ago, I asked Theo to put some hammers and nails down there for the guests. There's something about swinging a hammer that really helps you start to heal from a bad breakup. Local contractors drop off old bricks and tile. The smashing can be very therapeutic."

"I bet." She would have to give it a try, right after she took a four-day nap.

"Would you like to take a whack at it, so to speak?"

"No, I'm okay." Summer hadn't realized how exhausted she was, but now that she'd settled into the sofa cushions, she couldn't seem to get up.

"Maybe you'd like to try the yoga and meditation class later," Marla suggested. "Or kickboxing. We've got something for everyone."

"Mmm." Summer's eyelids drooped.

"Maybe after a little rest."

Summer let her cheek rest against the embroidered fabric of a pillow. "Mmm-kay."

"Tell you what." Marla's voice sounded very far away. "I'll just have Theo take your suitcase up to your room and you can set a spell right here. Where are your bags, pumpkin?"

"Car." Summer used her last remaining stores of energy to fish her keys out of her pocket. "Red convertible. New York plates."

"All righty." Marla eased Summer's ankles up onto a footstool. "We'll get you properly checked in later. You just stay right here and take care of yourself."

"Always have, always will."

Summer knew that life must have continued on around her—guests coming and going, attempting cell phone coups and borrowing hammers—but she remained oblivious to it all. For hours, she napped in a patch of light like a cat. At sundown, she mustered just enough energy to walk from the lobby to the back porch, where she collapsed into an Adirondack chair.

Marla appeared with a glass of water and an invitation to a game of Trivial Pursuit starting in the lobby.

"No, thank you," Summer replied. She touched a drop of condensation on the glass, then drew her fingers away as if burned. "I'm good right here."

This was a lie. She was not good. She was, in fact, the opposite of good. As the shock of the last few days wore off and her physical injuries started to heal, she was wrecked, ravaged, bleeding out from wounds no one could see.

Walk it off.

But she'd finally reached her breaking point, here at the water's edge. She couldn't take one more step.

"I'll leave your room key right here." Marla regarded Summer, her gaze warm and perceptive. "We call it room number fourteen, but it's really the attic. Can I get you anything else, honey?"

"No, thank you," Summer said. "Nothing."

She stretched out her legs and watched the sunset fade into dusk. She didn't move. She didn't speak. She barely breathed.

She just sat, listening to the waves and feeling the weight of her body. After years of racing through airport terminals and cramming carry-ons into overhead bins and traipsing through crowded bars and cafés and hotels, she craved stillness and solitude. She wanted to feel the support offered by the sturdy wooden chair. She wanted to watch the world passing her by.

chapter 6

I feel like I'm getting a CAT scan.

The next morning, Summer woke up to the sound of the tide coming in. She stared at the ceiling, which was only about three feet above the top of the bedposts. Because of the steep slope of the roof, the bed had been positioned in the center of the narrow attic, and the walls, floor, and beams had all been painted pale blue. The space didn't allow for a dresser or table, so her trash bag (or her "luggage," as Marla insisted on calling it) rested on a spindly wooden chair wedged between the footboard and the wall. Bright morning sunlight filtered in through the white wooden shutters, bouncing off the blue walls and giving the impression that the whole room was submerged in seawater.

"Sorry about the close quarters," Marla had said last night as she led Summer up to the inn's fourth floor. "I hope you're not claustrophobic."

After years of squeezing herself into tiny airplane galleys and lavatories and economy-class middle seats, Summer was not claustrophobic. She hadn't realized how many people were until she'd undergone multiple tests and scans in the hospital after the accident. "You okay?" the medical techs kept asking. "No issues with anxiety?"

She could fit herself into the tiniest pocket of space, as long as she knew the situation was temporary. As long as she was en route to another destination.

She turned over on her side, adjusted the white cotton sheets, and realized she was still wearing the same clothes she'd worn yesterday: a casual black shift dress and lightweight cardigan she'd borrowed from Emily.

This couldn't go on any longer. She *had* to shower—a real shower with shampoo and conditioner, not just a cursory rinse in a tiled hospital stall with no water pressure. She had to comb her hair and do something about her nails. The polish had chipped to the point that she looked like she'd drawn red amoebas on the end of each finger.

Okay, so a shower and a manicure. She felt overwhelmed just thinking about it.

She glanced at the lopsided black trash bag, which contained her burned and bloodstained polyester uniform, the ridiculous lingerie she'd planned to bring to Paris, and the flimsy blue gown she'd swiped from the hospital. Obtaining new clothes would mean going back into town, finding a boutique, talking to people, trying things on. . . .

So much easier to just lie here all day than deal with these impossible logistics. She yawned and snuggled into the pillows. Just a few more minutes of sleep, and then she'd face reality.

"Wakey wakey," Marla practically sang. "Breakfast is served. Warm blueberry muffins are on the table."

Summer closed her eyes and ignored the innkeeper.

A succession of knocks. "Summer. Let's go."

Summer scowled and yelled in the general direction of the door. "I'm sleeping. Come back later."

Marla sighed audibly. "You leave me no choice. But just re-member, honey. You made me do this."

Summer yanked the covers over her head. "Do what?"

"Haul your carcass out of bed." Even on speakerphone, even from three thousand miles away, Emily Lassiter meant business. "Pronto."

Summer turned to Marla, who held up Summer's cell phone like an avenging angel. "How did you . . . ?"

"I dialed the 'In case of emergency' on your contact list."

Summer finally sat up. "This isn't an emergency."

"It is an emergency," Emily countered. "You're not eating; you're not hydrating; you're jailbreaking out of hospitals against medical advice."

"I'm sleeping!" Summer leaped up on the mattress, banged her head against the low ceiling, and clutched the back of her skull. "And let's not forget who helped me jailbreak!"

"She's up," Marla reported to Emily. She smiled sweetly and handed the phone to Summer. "I'll leave you two girls to chat. Oh, and your muffin is right outside on the hall table."

"You just lost a paying customer!" Summer yelled as Marla closed the door. To Emily, she said, "And you! Traitor. You should be happy I'm resting. The doctors told me to rest, remember?"

"They didn't tell you to go to bed and never get up again."

"Well, I'm *tired*."

Emily didn't say anything.

"What?"

"Nothing." Emily went from bossy to worried. "But I've known you since we were what? Twelve?"

"Something like that."

"And I don't think I've ever once heard you say you're tired.

You're always dragging me to some party or after-party or after-after-party."

"Well, there you go. I've got fifteen years of sleep to catch up on." Summer sat back down on the bed. "And I have nothing to wear besides my charred uniform, scandalous lingerie, and the hospital gown. So, you know. Facing the world's kind of a hassle right now."

"This problem has a solution." She could hear Emily clicking away on a keyboard. "It's called shopping online."

"Aren't you supposed to be busy making a movie?" Summer asked.

"Camera crew's setting up a shot." More clicking from the keyboard. "I'll overnight everything. You'll have it by tomorrow afternoon. Shall I order your usual? Leather pants? Stilettos that could double as murder weapons? Sequined everything?"

Summer yawned. "Maybe just a few shorts and tank tops."

"Excuse me?"

"Oh, and flip-flops. Nothing fancy."

"Would you put Summer on the phone, please?"

"The Delaware shore isn't really the place for sequins and stilettos."

"Well, at the very least, I'm sending you a bikini. Do you want halter top or bandeau top?"

"Emily . . ."

"Halter top or bandeau top?" The bossiness had returned in full force. "And if you say no bikini, I'm sending in the National Guard." There was a series of muffled thumps on Emily's end of the line. "Hang on. Ryan's wrestling me for the phone."

"Summer?" Ryan said. Summer had to smile at how manly and authoritative he sounded. Quite a change from the hyperactive college kid Emily had married on a reckless whim all those years ago.

"Yes?" Summer said.

"That jackass is a jackass."

Summer slid down to the oval rug next to the bed. "Uh-huh."

"Repeat after me," Ryan commanded. "I want to hear you say the words."

Summer picked at a strand of blue yarn and mumbled, "That jackass is a jackass."

"Again," Ryan ordered. "Say it like you mean it."

She closed her eyes. "Save the drama coaching for your actors."

"I'm a producer, not a director."

"Whatever."

"Tell her I'm flying to Delaware," Emily said in the background.

"No airport in Delaware," Summer informed them.

"I will fix this," Ryan said. "What do you need to feel better? Name it—it's yours."

Summer didn't realize she had spaced out of the conversation until Ryan prompted her with, "Hello? Benson? Name your price."

"That's sweet of you, but I swear I'm fine. I don't need anything."

Summer could hear Emily's muffled voice; then Ryan returned with, "Do you want to go out with Ryan Gosling? I can't promise anything, but I can make a few calls."

"I don't want to go out with anyone."

"It's worse than we thought," Ryan reported to Emily, who reclaimed the phone.

"Listen, missy. I'm going to check my text messages in one hour, and I better see a picture of you on the beach. With a margarita and a trashy celebrity gossip rag. Or else."

Summer stared at her feet and noticed that the tips of her toes were bruised. Kim had been right about those shoes. "Or else what?"

"Or else we're sending Ryan Gosling over to personally break down your door and read *Us Weekly* to you in bed."

"I guess I should wash my hair, then." Summer ran her fingers through the lank, tangled mess. "I don't know what the hell my deal is. I'm kind of freaked out, to tell you the truth."

"So am I," Emily said.

"I'm not some delicate flower who goes into mourning. Guys dump me. I dump them. So what? You know my rules. There's no reason for me to be boarding myself up in an attic and hibernating like this."

"Maybe you have post-traumatic stress disorder," Emily suggested. "Or maybe the whole thing with Aaron . . ."

"Oh no." Summer cringed. "I know that voice. That's your therapist voice."

"Is it possible that all this is dredging up—"

"No," Summer snapped. "I am in Black Dog Bay, Delaware. Know what this town is for? Getting over your breakup. Know what's it's *not* for? Overanalyzing a hot mess of a family history. Don't read too much into it. Don't feel sorry for me. Just mind your business and send over Ryan Gosling."

"Will do. In the meantime, promise me you'll eat something—anything—and walk around the block. I checked the weather online and it's supposed to be sunny and breezy there."

Summer could see slices of clear sky between the shutter slats. "It's gorgeous."

"Once around the block," Emily repeated. "Bonus points if you can bring yourself to buy a T-shirt."

"But I—"

"Great, so that's settled. Now, what's the phone number for the hotel? I need to talk to Marla for one more minute."

Under any other circumstances, the homemade muffin would've been delicious. Moist and crumbly, with plump fresh berries, it smelled delectable. Yet it tasted like cardboard. Everything tasted like cardboard right now, which was why Summer hadn't been eating. She managed to choke down half, followed by a glass of water and the multivitamin Marla had placed on the plate, then ventured out the B and B's lobby into the fresh air.

"Put on some sunscreen," Marla singsonged as she watered a plant. "You'll get burned."

"I want to get burned," Summer singsonged back.

She waited on the porch until her eyes adjusted to the blinding sunlight—*Note to self: Buy sunglasses*—then descended to the parking lot, crunched across a patch of gravel, and kept going down the street and around the corner, toward the town square. Her spirits lifted as her hair ruffled against her cheeks in the warm salty breeze.

A few blocks later, she spied the Retail Therapy boutique. The shop was across the street, but Summer could hear high-pitched wailing from fifty paces away. A rosy-cheeked little girl with a smocked blue dress, glossy brown ringlets, and the lungs of an opera star shrieked up at the sky while a woman in a yellow polo shirt knelt next to her. At first glance, Summer assumed that the woman was the little girl's mother or nanny, but then she noticed the logo embroidered on the woman's shirt—REBOUND SALON—and realized that this was a hapless civilian caught in the cross fire.

After years of handing out snacks and plastic pilot wings to sleep-deprived toddlers, Summer could tell the difference between a sweetie pie crumbling under stress and a hellion who'd been spoiled by overly permissive parents.

And this kid? Was a hellion.

Summer made eye contact with the frazzled brunette. "What's her deal?"

"I have no idea." The woman clutched at her shirt collar. "She just keeps . . ." She recoiled as the caterwauling continued.

"Hang on. I'll go find her owner." Summer's eardrums had withstood countless takeoffs and landings, but if they were ever going to rupture, now would be the time.

"Her mother's inside getting a manicure. She should be done soon."

"I'm on it." Summer took a quick inventory of the contents of her purse and was delighted to find a pack of gum, a deck of cards, and a miniature bag of M&M's. "Want to play Go Fish?" She offered the cards at arm's length.

"No!" The little girl snatched the deck and flung the cards into the air. Then she turned to the salon employee with a wicked little smirk. "Pick them up."

"Don't you dare pick them up." Summer opened the salon door with a new spring in her step. "Who belongs to that spirited cherub out there?"

"Are you referring to my niece?" A lithe, tanned blonde looked up from a table in the corner.

"Blue dress? Brown hair? Likes exercising her lungs and fifty-two-card pickup?"

"That's her. She's in time-out." The woman splayed her fingers and took her time examining her nails. "You know, this pink dried much darker than I was expecting." She frowned at the manicurist.

The salon employee went pale. "I'm sorry, Mrs. Sinclair."

Summer looked at the nail tech. "Did you pick the color?"

"No, but . . ."

The blonde crossed her legs and held up her ring finger. "And this one is chipped already. Look."

"Sorry."

"It's fine." Mrs. Sinclair heaved a weary, put-upon sigh. "I'll wait while you fix it."

The wailing outside started up again.

"Sounds like your niece needs you," Summer said.

"Yes, well, *I* need a decent manicure for the benefit ball this weekend."

Summer crossed her arms and stared down the blonde while the nail tech rushed through the polish repair, then recapped the bottle of topcoat with evident relief. "All set."

Mrs. Sinclair ignored Summer, scrutinized every millimeter of nail surface, and finally nodded. "That will suffice. Same time next week?"

"We have you in the schedule."

"Fine. Put everything on my tab." The blonde picked up a beige leather handbag adorned with designer-logoed hardware. She headed for the door with a grating little laugh. "Oops, I forgot to get my tip money out of my wallet and now I have wet nails."

"That's okay," the nail tech assured her.

"I'll get it for you," Summer volunteered. She plucked the wallet out of the handbag before anyone could protest.

Mrs. Sinclair made a little noise that was half gasp, half squeak. "What do you think you're doing?"

"Saving your nails." Summer opened the wallet and pulled out a crisp ten-dollar bill. "You're welcome."

"Ten dollars seems . . ."

"Like not enough since they had to provide child care services, too? Well, if you insist." Summer exchanged the ten for a twenty. "That's damn decent of you."

Mrs. Sinclair narrowed her eyes, but whatever she wanted to say was lost in a bout of her niece's screeches.

"Stop it this instant, Aviva," Mrs. Sinclair ordered.

"No!" The little girl gulped in a huge breath, gathering steam for the next round.

"Yoo-hoo!" Mrs. Sinclair's tone shifted from dragon lady to social butterfly as she lifted her hand in a friendly wave. "Ingrid!"

On the other side of the street, a slouchy teenager froze as if an FBI agent had just pulled a gun on her. "Mrs. Sinclair?"

"Fancy meeting you here!" The blonde strode through the scattered pile of playing cards and beckoned the girl over. "I'm so glad I ran into you. Natalie's birthday is next week, and we're having a little get-together on Saturday evening. She asked me to invite you."

The teenager approached slowly, her expression vacillating between shock and suspicion. "She did?"

"Absolutely." Mrs. Sinclair didn't laugh—she giggled. "Why do you look so surprised? Natalie simply adores you."

The teenager's slouch got even slouchier. She was tall and gangly, struggling through the awkward stages of adolescence on her way to statuesque. Despite her striking gray eyes, porcelain complexion, and thick russet hair, she radiated self-doubt. Her baggy, earth-toned outfit seemed chosen to help her blend into the background. "Uh-huh."

"Saturday evening, around six. And you know Nat—she's invited lots of cute boys. Bring your swimsuit." Mrs. Sinclair paused and then added, in a tone that was probably supposed to sound nonchalant, "Oh, and the adults are going to chitchat while you kids are having fun, so bring your brother, too."

Ingrid's eyes widened. "I don't know—"

"Then it's settled! We'll see you both on Saturday." Mrs. Sinclair pressed her palms together, then turned back to Summer. "I suppose I'll be going now, if you're finished rifling through my wallet." She oozed disdain as she glanced at Summer's nails. "And if I may make a suggestion, you really ought to consider getting a manicure, yourself."

"How sweet of you to care," Summer oozed right back. "Shall I have them put that on your tab, too?"

Mrs. Sinclair grabbed Aviva's wrist and stalked away, the queen of spades stuck to the bottom of her pristine white shoes.

One of the salon employees started to laugh. Then the others joined in, and finally the teenager. Summer realized that at least ten consecutive minutes had passed, and she hadn't once thought about plane crashes, Aaron Marchand, mistakes from her past, or fears of her future.

Things were looking up.

chapter 7

"*How* did you do that?" Ingrid gazed up at Summer with awe.

Summer threw back her shoulders and stepped into the little salon. "Do what?"

"You *handled* her."

"You did handle her," the manicurist agreed. "And *no one* handles Mimi Sinclair. She's the second-biggest bully in Black Dog Bay."

"Which is why someone had to handle her." Summer grinned and scanned the bottles of nail polish.

Ingrid trailed behind her. "But you . . . you took her wallet and her money and you lived to tell the tale."

"If looks could kill . . ." The nail tech shivered.

"Let her look." Summer picked out a shade of turquoise, then put it back. "I get glared at worse than that every time I tell people to turn off their cell phones before takeoff." She shrugged. "I'm a flight attendant. I absorb rage and wrath on a daily basis; it's my job." She glanced back at Ingrid. "And by the way, you don't have to go to that party."

The girl's cheeks reddened. "How do I get out of it? She didn't ask me to go; she *told* me."

"Yeah, well, I'm guessing she doesn't sign your paychecks. Your brother's, either. Blow it off."

Ingrid nibbled her lower lip. "I don't even know what I'd wear to something like that."

"Madras shorts and a stick up your ass. But it doesn't matter, because you're not going."

"Here, try this." One of the salon employees selected a coppery polish and handed it to Summer. "By the way, I'm Cori and you're my hero."

"Mine, too." The second employee offered a handshake. "I'm Alyssa. Your mani-pedi's on the house."

"Plus a deep-conditioning treatment." Cori regarded Summer's hair with evident dismay. "I insist."

Ingrid mumbled something that might have been "good-bye" under her breath and slipped out the door.

Summer introduced herself while Cori and Alyssa led her over to the shampoo basins by the back wall.

"You're going to be famous by nightfall." Cori handed Summer a yellow nylon smock. "The woman who stood up to Mimi Sinclair and lived to tell the tale."

"Most of our summer residents are great, but not her." Alyssa grabbed a stack of towels. "She's a nightmare. We call her the terrorist in tweed."

"Does she own that giant purple mansion on the other side of the bay?" Summer asked.

"No, that belongs to Miss Huntington," Cori said. "The first-biggest bully in Black Dog Bay."

Summer settled into the padded chair and positioned her head in the large black sink. "Really? No one who paints their house purple can be all bad."

Cori scoffed. "That's what you say now. Wait till you meet her." She examined Summer's hair and scalp, then gathered an array of shampoos, conditioners, oil treatments, and spray bottles. "She painted her house purple for spite."

"Ooh, sounds juicy," Summer said. "Who was she trying to spite?"

Alyssa shook her head. "Who can keep track of all her vendettas? There's so many of them."

Two hours later, Summer emerged from the salon with immaculate nails and freshly highlighted hair.

"You look stunning," Alyssa declared.

"I called Beryl at the boutique next door," Cori said. "She's expecting you."

"She'll take good care of you." Alyssa gave Summer a quick little hug. "We told her the whole thing about Mimi Sinclair."

"You did?"

"We did. You're a legend!" Alyssa picked up her cell phone. "Wait till I tell Jenna and Hollis and Marla and Theo."

"News travels fast around here." Cori grinned at Summer's stunned expression. "*Everyone* is going to want to meet you. How long are you staying, anyway?"

Summer paused. "I'm not sure. A week, maybe? Two weeks?"

"You have to stay until you see the dog."

"What dog?" Summer asked. "Do you mean the bronze statue by the boardwalk? I've already seen that."

Cori shook her head. "The black dog."

Summer stared at them. "Like a Labrador? A poodle? A cocker spaniel? Give me a hint."

"The black dog is what makes this town special." Alyssa exchanged a look with Cori. "You'll know it when you see it."

"You must be Summer, slayer of Mimi Sinclair." A buxom redhead with a ponytail and a forties pinup-style black dress greeted Summer at the door of the Retail Therapy boutique. "I'm Beryl. Delighted to meet you." She gave Summer's wrinkled outfit a once-over. "So what can I help you find?"

Summer shivered as her body adjusted to the arctic air-conditioning. "Something shapeless, soft, and ice-cream-stain resistant. A shroud made of Egyptian cotton and Teflon would be perfect."

Beryl turned on the heel of her cherry red sandals. "Oh, we don't carry shrouds."

"Okay, then a muumuu. Whatever. I'm not picky."

Beryl's smile never faltered as she led Summer toward the other side of the room. "Let's start over here. I've organized the racks according to the stages of breakup recovery."

Summer raised an eyebrow. "What, like denial and anger and bargaining?"

"Mm-hmm." Beryl's ponytail bounced when she nodded. "You're still in the grieving stage, so we'll start here."

Summer tilted her head. "How do you know I'm in the grieving stage?"

"Honey. You just asked for a stain-resistant shroud." Beryl clicked her tongue. "When you're ready, we have the 'rage and revenge' section over there, and then the 'single and self-confident' section over there." Beryl flipped through the hangers, pulling out flowy, simple skirts and dresses. "Here, try this on. And this and this and this." She loaded up Summer's arms with garments in muted blues and greens. "But don't buy too much—something tells me you'll be moving out of the grieving stage and into the party girl stage with a quickness."

"The party girl stage is my natural habitat," Summer conceded. "But I'm through with that. Really, who has the energy?"

"Uh-huh."

"Seriously, men are repulsive to me right now." Summer

pursed her lips. "I've learned my lesson—I'm going to simplify my life and stay single."

"Uh-huh." Beryl rolled her eyes and steered her toward the dressing room. "I give you two weeks before you're back in here, begging for shorter skirts and tighter tops."

Summer rerouted and headed for the cash register. "I don't have the stamina to try any of this on. Just give me some pajama pants and a magical hoodie with a never-ending supply of wine and cigarettes in the pocket."

"Here you go." Beryl handed her a featherweight navy sweater. "Wine and cigarettes not included."

"I'll take it." Summer slapped her credit card down on the counter. "Whatever you want to sell me. I can't afford to be buying a new wardrobe right now, but it turns out that I really don't care. How convenient."

Beryl picked out a gauzy gray sundress and a slate blue T-shirt with a striped skirt. "Sometimes you have to treat yourself." She bundled the clothes into a bright pink bag stuffed with pastel tissue paper. "Don't forget to eat and drink plenty of water."

"Is that the official town motto?"

"It's a fact. Heartache and dehydration are a dangerous mix." Beryl gave her a little pat on the arm. "Come back whenever you're ready for those halter tops and miniskirts."

"Never," Summer vowed.

"That's what they all say. See you soon!"

On her way out of the boutique, Summer had to pause and brace one hand against the doorjamb as she reeled under a sudden dizzy spell. *Definitely time to eat.*

She glanced around the nearby businesses in search of a café. The afternoon sunlight reflected off the bronze dog statue overlooking the boardwalk.

"There she is!" an angry voice cried. A posh, entitled voice that sounded familiar.

Sure enough, the terrorist in tweed stood across the street, waving a playing card and pointing out Summer to a broad-shouldered man in a gray suit.

"That's her!" Mimi Sinclair cried. "She littered! She tipped without my permission!"

The man turned around, and Summer realized he was the same guy whose roses she'd run over.

Except he wasn't the same, exactly. The Dutch Jansen she'd met in the garden had been windburned and rugged, with dirt in the creases of his knuckles. Now he was clearly Mayor Jansen, all silk tie and cuff links and immaculate grooming.

She hoisted her bag in greeting, then threw in a flirty little hair flip because, hey, old habits die hard and new highlights look good.

Mimi's scowl darkened. But Dutch's impassive expression finally cracked. He shaded his eyes from the sun, gazed across the town square at her, and smiled as if he couldn't help it.

And she had to turn around and hurry away, because she couldn't help smiling back.

chapter 8

"All right, ladies, it's campfire night." Marla, ever the nurturing den mother, rounded up the bed-and-breakfast guests at nightfall. "Grab your breakup debris and follow me. Theo usually gets the fire going, but he left for poker night, so we'll have to do it ourselves." She led the group out of the lobby and down to the starlit beach, where a circle of charred rocks surrounded a pile of twigs and logs. "Any volunteers?"

"I'll give it a try. All those years of Girl Scout camp are finally going to pay off." A stunning woman with dark skin, cropped black hair, and cheekbones to die for stepped forward holding a wedding gown. "Silk chiffon is good kindling, don't you think?"

"Silk chiffon is perfect." Marla handed out sweaters and blankets while the woman tossed the white dress into the fire pit. "We've had problems with certain fabrics over the years—acetate, anything polyester—but silk burns beautifully." She produced a can of starter fluid and sprinkled a few drops on the gown. Then she handed a pack of matches to the gown's owner. "Whenever you're ready."

The guests gathered together, whooping and clapping as the

woman lit a match and tossed it into the fire pit. The crumpled dress ignited with a whooshing sound. Someone produced a flask and started passing it around.

Summer stayed on the sidelines.

"Who's next?" Marla helped herself to a sip from the flask. "Don't be shy!"

The flames leaped higher as the guests piled on their unwanted mementos. Some of these were obvious reminders of failed relationships: engagement photos, love letters, anniversary cards. But some objects held meaning known only to their owners: a takeout menu, a carved wooden elephant, an old-school cassette tape that melted amid billows of acrid black smoke.

"Dagnabbit," Marla said as she moved upwind. "I forgot the marshmallows."

"I'll get them," Summer said, thinking about the Hefty bag up in her room. "Be back in a second." She ran to the inn and scooped up the scandalous lingerie she'd packed in her carry-on.

In her haste to incinerate all that satin and lace, she forgot to stop at the kitchen for marshmallows.

"That's okay, honey." Marla gave her a little sideways hug when she returned. "We do this three times a week. We'll roast marshmallows next time."

The lingerie burned quickly, as flimsy and frail as newsprint, and Summer found her mood sinking even lower while she watched the delicate material go up in smoke. As if it never existed.

"Let me guess," said the guest who'd torched her wedding gown. "Those belonged to the other woman."

"Are those actual garter belts?" Another woman made a noise of disapproval. "Lord have mercy—don't they just scream 'affair'? Well, it's easy to run around in sexy lingerie when you're not working full-time and raising two kids."

"No, they're mine." Summer sighed. "I wear that stuff every

day." She glanced down at her drab sundress, which she'd paired with a boring beige bra. "At least, I used to."

The first woman gasped in outrage. "And he cheated on you anyway? Just goes to show—"

"He didn't cheat on me," Summer said softly. "He just . . . left."

"Are you sure?" The rest of the inn guests crowded around to put their two cents in. "Just because he won't admit to it doesn't mean he's not cheating."

"You've got to check his phone records, his texts, his laptop. . . ."

"I'm sure." Summer rubbed the heel of her hand against her forehead. "He was planning to propose, but then he changed his mind."

"But why?"

"He didn't love me enough. And he knew it. So he left." And there it was: the unvarnished, unbearable truth. No righteous indignation, no sordid affair. She had been loved, and she had been found lacking.

"Don't look so sad," the other guests murmured. "You'll find someone else."

"Someone better."

"Someone who will appreciate a woman who wears thigh-highs every day."

"In fact, let's find him right now. There's a wine bar down by the boardwalk. We're all going over there after we finish up here."

"Come with us! It'll be fun!"

"Thanks, but I think I'm done for the night." Summer hunched into her oversize sundress.

"It's Friday night! Come on—a girl who has stockings like that knows how to have a good time on a Friday night."

"Maybe tomorrow," Summer said, feeling more lethargic by the minute.

"Are you sure? Lots of men come to town on the weekends. Hot men. Single men."

"One glass of wine," the wedding-dress pyromaniac cajoled her.

"You only have to drink half." The women swept her up in their camaraderie, alternately laughing and wiping away tears that they blamed on the smoke.

A few days ago, Summer wouldn't have been able to imagine herself in this state. She hadn't stayed home on a Friday night since she was grounded in high school—and even then, she'd found a way to sneak out of the house.

She was a good-time girl. That was why people liked her. That was how she compensated for everything she lacked.

"Fine." Cheers broke out as she relented. "I'll have half a glass. But you guys are buying."

If Barbie hired Hello Kitty to decorate her dream house, the result would be the Whinery.

The bar's interior was done up in various shades of pink, accented with black iron tables and chairs. The glossy black bar top was dotted with little silver bowls filled with candy. Dartboards (the cork dyed a lovely magenta) lined the back wall, and patrons had adorned these with photos of various exes. Soft, warm light emanated from frosted-glass sconces along the walls, and a crystal-bedecked chandelier hung just inside the entrance.

The place was packed with heartbreak tourists, and the ambience bounced between sorority sleepover and speed dating. A few intrepid men wandered among the throngs of newly single women, trying out pickup lines that were met with either indulgent laughter or blistering scorn. A dozen local residents kicked back in one corner, sipping wine and watching the drama unfold.

Summer's group split up as soon as they stepped in the door. Some of the women veered toward the dance floor, some headed back to play darts, and some made a beeline for a very, *very* handsome man holding court on the other side of the bar.

Summer wove her way through the throng until she reached the bar, where she was greeted by an athletic, snub-nosed bartender, who slung the pink-striped dish towel over her shoulder and offered a handshake. "You must be Summer. I'm Jenna."

"Hi." Bewildered, Summer shook hands. "How did you . . . ?"

"Rumor mill is always churning in Black Dog Bay. I heard you took on Mimi Sinclair."

Summer peered at the wine varietals listed on the chalkboard above the bar. "It really wasn't that big a deal."

"It's not a big deal—it's a huge deal. Taking on Mimi Sinclair means your first drink is on the house. It also means you get to call the tune." Jenna gestured to the stereo speakers blaring in the corners. "Is there anything specific you'd like to hear?"

Summer shrugged. "What're my options?"

"We have every breakup anthem you could want. Except 'I Will Survive.'" Jenna clenched her jaw. "My last nerve is going to snap if I hear that song one more time." She pulled up an iPod and scrolled through the selections. "What are you in the mood for? We've got pop: 'Villa in Portugal' by Pursuit of Happiness, 'Irreplaceable' by Beyoncé, Alanis Morissette's entire *Jagged Little Pill* album. Then there's country: 'You Lie' by the Band Perry, 'My Give a Damn's Busted' by Jo Dee Messina. And of course there's always the classics: 'You're So Vain,' 'These Boots Were Made for Walking,' and my personal favorite, 'Fist City.' What's your poison?"

Summer sank back on the tall iron stool. "I've never heard 'Fist City,' but I think I need to."

"Excellent choice. It's Loretta Lynn at her finest." Jenna

punched a few buttons, and the crowd cheered as twangy guitar notes opened the song.

"I guess I'll have a glass of Shiraz," Summer said.

"Nope. You need the Cure for the Common Breakup." Jenna grinned and explained, "It's our specialty drink. Pairs perfectly with chocolate and mood swings."

At the mention of chocolate, Summer started digging through the nearest silver candy bowl. "Ooh, do you have any M&M's?"

"I might." Jenna rummaged under the counter and came up with a snack-size bag. "Your wish is granted."

Summer ripped open the wrapping and poured the chocolate candies directly into her mouth. "I'm never leaving this bar."

"We get that a lot." Jenna sang along with Loretta as she lined up a bottle of champagne, a bottle of vermouth, and an orange. "The secret to this drink is, everything needs to be fresh."

"Even the ice?"

"Everything." Jenna got to work with an old-timey glass citrus juicer. "This drink is all about fresh starts. No tainting the future with the past." She filled the glass with ice, then uncorked the vermouth. She layered in the squeezed orange juice, then the champagne, and topped it all off with a straw and a festive twist of orange peel.

"Here's to new beginnings."

But Summer had to sit back and admire the drink first. "It's so pretty!"

"Yeah, plus it's symbolic. Looks like a sunrise, right? It's a new dawn. New day. All that."

"Wow." Summer laughed. "That's, like, so deep."

"Totally. I'm Tolstoy with a tip jar."

As Loretta Lynn wrapped up and the playlist queued up Travis Tritt's "Here's a Quarter," Jenna leaned over and murmured, "Don't look now, but your evening just got a whole lot better."

"What?"

Jenna nodded toward the very, *very* handsome man who had gotten to his feet and was now striding toward Summer.

"Here comes the other cure for the common breakup. Aka Jake Sorensen."

chapter 9

$\mathcal{J}$ake Sorensen embodied everything Summer loved in a man: confidence, charm, classic good looks, and complete emotional detachment. She'd had a hundred dalliances with a hundred guys just like him all around the world. It was as if the universe had compiled a list of her known weaknesses and built a sex-god prototype to her exact specifications.

Yet all she felt as he approached her was annoyance.

The crowds in front of him parted. The women he left in his wake all but swooned.

When he reached her side, he planted his hand next to hers on the bar top and opened with, "I've been watching you since you walked in. I can't take my eyes off you."

Summer glanced at the bevy of halter-topped hopefuls he'd abandoned on the other side of the bar. "What a disappointment for your fan club."

The corners of his eyes crinkled when he smiled. "I'm Jake."

She tilted her head and took in the broad shoulders, the thick, tousled hair, the smoldering sensuality in those dark eyes. "Let me guess: You're the designated rebound guy around here."

His smile got even more rakish.

"You sit there in your corner, all brooding and inscrutable, and wait for the ladies to swarm. You show them a good time, they keep you entertained for the weekend, and then you send them back home with a story to tell. Everyone's happy—no muss, no fuss, no messy entanglements." Summer raised one eyebrow. "Right?"

He paused, regarding her with renewed interest. "You disapprove?"

"Not at all." Summer popped another piece of chocolate into her mouth. "Everyone needs a hot rebound after a bad breakup, and I'm sure you're a delightful palate cleanser."

The smile returned, but this time, it was genuine. "I've cleansed a few palates in my day."

"Well, good for you. You're providing a valuable community service." She offered him a miniature 3 Musketeers bar. "But I'd assume that in a bar like this in a town like this, getting the girl has got to be ridiculously easy."

"Fish in a barrel." Jake took her hand in his. "Dance with me."

"If you insist." Summer slammed back the rest of her drink and let him lead her out to the floor. As he settled his hands on her hips and she looped her arms around his neck, she realized that their bodies fit together perfectly. He looked good. He smelled good. He felt good. The sex would no doubt be phenomenal.

And still . . . nothing.

"Something wrong?" His brow creased as she blinked up at him.

"Yeah, something's wrong. You're all hot and swarthy and lickable."

His hands drifted lower on her hips. "You think I'm hot and lickable?"

"Please." She rolled her eyes. "You know it. I know it. Everyone in this bar knows it."

He moved even closer and whispered into her ear, "Thanks."

She pulled back a few inches. "And yet, I have no urge to lick you."

"Ouch."

She slid her hands down from his neck to his elbows. "Well, do *you* want to lick *me*?"

A spark of humor replaced all the raw smolder in his eyes. "Eh."

"See? We're even."

His frown deepened. "I do want to lick you, in the abstract. But somehow . . ."

She threw up her hands. "I know. We're perfect for each other. We should be ripping each other's clothes off right now!"

"Yeah." He rubbed his jaw. "In the abstract."

She raced back to the bar and signaled to Jenna for a refill. "Oh my God. What's wrong with me?"

Jake stayed right by her side. "Nothing's wrong with you."

"Something's definitely wrong with me." She dabbed at her forehead with a pink cocktail napkin. "When the going gets tough, I have ill-advised flings with lickable men who don't call me the next day. Men like you. That's what I do! That's who I am!"

"Maybe you've evolved," he suggested.

"I *highly* doubt that." Summer shook her head and took a sip of her drink.

Jake gave her another once-over. "I'm guessing you get hit on a lot."

"Well, not to brag, but . . . yeah, pretty much. I'm a flight attendant. Goes with the territory."

"But you're here in the breakup capital of the world?"

"Yeah." She stiffened. "We don't need to get into all the details."

"Listen. A drunken hookup with some man-whore is not going to do anything for you right now."

"Excuse me? Did you just refer to yourself as a man-whore?"

He leaned back against the bar and scanned the crowd. "Trust me. I've spent enough time with enough women at this bar to know what's what. You don't need a guy like me. You need a guy like . . ." He inclined his head, indicating a man who had just walked in the door. "Him."

The man looked up, and Summer recognized Dutch Jansen. He looked even more rugged and masculine against all the frilly pink.

"*Him?* No. I ran down his roses in cold blood," Summer said. "That guy hates me."

"But you're looking at him."

"Oh, really? And how, exactly, am I looking at him?"

Jake flashed a diabolical grin. "You know. I know. Everyone in this bar knows."

Summer jerked her thumb toward the other side of the bar. "Shouldn't you be heading back to your fan club?"

"Go talk to him," Jake said. "Dance with him the way you just danced with me."

Summer laughed. "He can't *handle* the way I danced with you."

"Go on. Trial by fire."

"So you want me to, what? Just go over there and, like, ensnare him in my web of seduction? Like I'm the designated rebound girl?"

"I dare you."

Summer stared at the back of Dutch's head, debating. She did want to talk to him again. . . .

Jake paid for her drink and told her, "Look. Being with me is like falling down into a ditch. But being with him is like climbing Everest."

She scrunched her nose. "Climbing Everest isn't as big a deal these days. It's swarming with tourists, like Walmart on Black Friday."

"Okay, then, it's like climbing the K2. That tough enough for you?"

She took a deep breath, then shook her head. "I am not going to go dazzle some defenseless man with my feminine wiles—which are considerable, by the way—"

"I have no doubt."

"—just to make me feel better about myself. That is selfish. That is wrong. That is—"

Jake lowered his voice. "He's looking at you, too."

Summer's hand flew to her chest. "He is? Shut up. He is not."

"Go get him. K2, baby. Belay on."

chapter 10

"What's the most manly wine you have by the glass?" Summer asked Jenna over the bluesy opening riffs of Suzanne Rhatigan's "To Hell with Love."

"Probably one of the Cabernets or a Meritage." Jenna beckoned a striking, pale woman who looked oddly familiar. "Summer, this is Hollis. She owns the bookstore by the boardwalk."

"Two blocks over from where you gave that insufferable Mimi Sinclair a taste of her own medicine." Hollis slid into the seat next to Summer's.

Summer stared at Hollis, trying to place the fine-boned face and the melancholy green eyes. "Have we met before?"

Hollis glanced at Jenna, who explained, "Hollis used to be kind of famous."

"But enough about me," Hollis said. She pointed her straw at the Jake Sorensen fan club, which had reclaimed its president. "We saw you dancing."

"And we want to know why you're still here instead of steaming up the windows of his fancy beach house," Jenna said. "Explain yourself."

Summer turned up one palm. "He's not my type."

Hollis's jaw dropped. "Jake Sorensen is every woman's type. He's so charming."

"And mind-blowing in bed." Jenna fanned her cheeks. "I, uh, hear."

"You should see his back muscles," the woman on the other side of Summer chimed in. "Hi. I'm Chandra, and I have a thing for lats."

Hollis rested her chin in her palm as they all stared over at the designated rebound guy. "He's handsome, he's rich, and he's very mysterious, since he spends every summer here but no one has any idea what he does for the rest of the year."

Summer considered all this, then shrugged. "Yeah, no."

"If you say you're not ready, so help me, I will kill you." Jenna slapped her hand down on the bar. "It's Jake Sorensen! *Get* ready."

"Leave her alone," Hollis said. "If she's not ready, she's not ready."

"I'm ready," Summer lied. "But he's not the one I'm after."

Hollis and Jenna both leaned in.

Summer fixed her gaze on Dutch and said, "I want you to pour two glasses of Cab, please. And send them both over to him."

Jenna's eyes got huge. "To Dutch Jansen?"

"The mayor?" Chandra did a double take. "What is he even doing here on a Friday night?"

"Oh, his assistant forgot to drop off the renewed liquor license, so he offered to bring it by on his way home," Jenna said.

"I'm asking him out," Summer declared.

Hollis waved her off with both hands. "No, sweetie, you don't want to do that."

"Why not?"

Jenna and Hollis exchanged a flurry of furtive glances.

"Here's the deal: Dutch is the most eligible bachelor in Black

Dog Bay." Jenna mixed up a trio of fizzy pink drinks while she talked. "His family goes all the way back to the Dutch settlers who first landed on the Delaware coast."

"Hence, the name Dutch," Hollis threw in.

"Right. I forget what his real first name is. 'Mies' or something like that." Jenna paused to rattle a metal cocktail shaker full of ice. "And I'm not going to lie—every single woman in town wants to date him."

"So far, I'm not seeing the problem here," Summer said.

"The problem is, he doesn't date."

"At all?" Summer frowned. "Ever?"

"Not in Black Dog Bay." Jenna poured and served the drinks. "Not that I've ever heard of."

"It's very annoying," Hollis said.

"Very," Jenna agreed. "The man has no life. He goes to committee meetings; he grows his roses; he takes care of his sister. The end."

"No way." Summer narrowed her eyes and reassessed Dutch's starched white shirt and silk tie. "No one's that responsible. He probably has some secret, twisted double life. And I want in on it."

"Save yourself the frustration and find another rebound guy," Hollis advised. "Dutch is unlandable."

Something about that word triggered a surge of anxiety in Summer, and she realized Kim had used the same term when describing Aaron. "Oh, I'm not looking to 'land' anyone. I just want to have a little fun."

"I don't think Dutch Jansen is capable of fun." Jenna waved this away. "Trust me—it's a nonstarter. Women ask him out all the time, and he always says no."

"Well, he's never been asked out by me." Summer fluffed her hair and dredged through her purse until she came up with a tube of shiny red lip gloss. Although she hadn't packed any makeup for this trip, she tossed trial-size products in various handbags every time she went shopping and had amassed enough samples to stock a cosmetics counter. "I'm going to the ladies' room to get glamorous. And Jenna, while I'm in there, send Mr. Mayor two glasses of Cab."

Summer cursed her practical beige bra as she emerged from the restroom. The old arrange-your-neckline-to-expose-your-lacy-bra-strap gambit lost most of its potency when the bra strap wasn't lacy. Maybe incinerating every piece of European lingerie she owned had been a wee bit hasty?

But no matter. She still had red lips and her feminine wiles. She had done a lot more with a lot less.

Jenna was handing two wineglasses to Dutch, who wore a charcoal gray suit and a confused expression. He caught her gaze and held it, and in that moment, she saw him as everyone else in Black Dog Bay did: strong and stern and quietly authoritative. Someone who took his responsibilities seriously. Someone who was not to be trifled with.

And it only increased her desire to trifle with him.

As good as he had looked in jeans and work boots, he looked even better in a tailored jacket. She wanted to start peeling off the layers of civility, starting with his cuff links, until she uncovered the rough-hewn guy with windburn on his cheeks and calluses on his palms.

She stole a quick glance at his fingernails, and though the sweat and grime had been washed away, she could still see the strength and capability in those hands. She could imagine how those hands would feel on her skin.

After a week of feeling numb and hopeless, she was suddenly looking forward to something.

"Perfect timing," she practically purred as she sidled in next to him. "These are for us. It's the least I could do after that unfortunate incident with the turtle and Taylor Swift."

Jenna mouthed, "Good luck," and hustled back to the bar. Five seconds later, the music switched to the Pistol Annies' "I Feel a Sin Comin' On."

Dutch stared down at Summer with those piercing gray eyes. "How long have you been in town?"

"Two days."

"You've made quite an impression."

"That's kind of my thing." She tried to imagine she was wearing a sheer black bra as she worked her way through her repertoire of hair flips and coy smiles.

Dutch didn't smile back, but he didn't look away.

Summer grabbed her wineglass and took a sip. "Seriously, I feel awful about your roses. I don't know much about gardening—okay, I don't know *anything* about gardening—but if you ever need someone to come over and, you know, *mulch* . . ."

His lips twitched. "Mulch."

"Yeah, mulch. I understand that's some sort of gardening term?"

He doubled down on the staring, and she stared right back, until what had started as a come-hither gaze turned into a staring contest.

Clearly, he was a stubborn one.

But so was she.

She made a big production out of wetting her lips and taking another sip of wine that could nearly be classified as pornographic.

He blinked.

She swept her hair to the side, exposing her neck, and leaned in until she could smell the faint trace of Irish Spring on his skin. "Have a drink."

He pushed away his wineglass. "I don't make a habit of drinking with my constituents."

"I'm not a constituent. Hell, I've moved so many times I'm not even registered to vote anymore." She eased even closer as his lips twitched again. "I'm a bad, bad girl."

"Is there a point to this, Miss Benson?" He finally broke into a full smile. "Yes, I know who you are. I keep up on current events. Your employee photo has been in *Time* and *People*."

She wanted to call a time-out and ask him what the magazine articles had said. But any discussion of the emergency landing would lead to a discussion of Aaron. So she turned up the sultry a few more notches and murmured, "The point is, I'm just another tourist passing through. I'll be here for a week, maybe two, and then we'll never see each other again."

There was another long, loaded pause as they made eye contact.

But just when she thought she'd convinced him, he turned toward the door. "I better get going. Curfew."

She straightened up. "What time's your curfew?"

"Eleven. And it's not my curfew; it's my sister's."

She grabbed his wrist and examined his gold watch. "You have seventeen minutes. We better cut to the chase."

He stilled, allowing her to keep her hand on his sleeve. "What is it you want from me?"

From the way he said this, Summer realized that he must deal with people wanting things from him all day. Favors. Exceptions. Validation.

"I'm kind of hoping you'll go out with me." Heat flooded into her cheeks. Dear God, was she *blushing*?

He reclaimed his wrist and took a single sip of Cabernet. The wineglass looked even more delicate in his large, masculine hands. "You want to go out with me."

"I'm all up in your personal space with my hair and my red lipstick, am I not?"

He put down the glass. "I don't date."

She held up her hands and fanned out her fingers. "Listen, we don't have to label anything."

"I don't get involved with anyone in Black Dog Bay." He scanned the crowd and shook his head. "And I *definitely* don't pick up women at the Whinery."

"You're not picking me up; I'm picking you up. You can tell because I bought your drink."

"You're not picking me up." He started for the door.

"One week," she called after him. "One week you'll never forget, and then you'll never hear from me again."

He faltered midstride, checked his watch, then muttered something under his breath. "Enjoy your stay in Black Dog Bay. If I can help you with anything non-date-related—"

"You can't!"

He took another step toward the exit. "Drive carefully. Watch out for turtles."

She stopped batting her eyelashes and throwing her hair around and gave him a sweet, genuine smile. "It'll be fun," she promised. "Really fun."

He strode back to her side just long enough to tuck her bra strap under the neckline of her dress. The back of his thumb brushed against her collarbone, and he let his hand linger at the base of her neck for a moment. Then he ducked his head and murmured, so low that only she could hear:

"That's what I'm afraid of."

chapter 11

*O*ver the next few days, Summer explored the rest of the little town. She discovered the world's best M&M's brownies at the Eat Your Heart Out bakery. She sat on the beach and watched sandpipers race along the waterline. She fell asleep and woke up to the sound of the waves in the blue attic bedroom.

Physically, she was improving. Her back and head and ribs stopped aching. And last night, Marla had given back her cell phone.

"I think you're ready for this now," the innkeeper had announced with the air of a dean handing over a diploma. The handful of guests in the sitting room had applauded. "Summer Benson, you are now free to communicate with the outside world. But remember, please text responsibly."

Now that Summer could communicate with the outside world, she found she didn't want to. She couldn't very well hole up in Delaware forever, but she didn't have anywhere else she'd rather be.

On Sunday afternoon (was it Sunday? Who kept track?), she spotted the sign for Black Dog Books and headed in to say hi to Hollis.

"This is the best bookstore ever," she said as she entered the cozy little shop, which smelled of freshly ground coffee.

"Thanks." Hollis stood behind the counter with a latte and a surly-faced cat. "I try to keep it stocked with everything you might want during a breakup: self-help, romances, and of course murder mystery and suspense. There's nothing like a good serial killer story to soothe your shattered nerves."

The cat took one look at Summer, bared his teeth, and hissed.

Hollis scratched the cat's ears and rolled her eyes. "Ignore little Snidely Whiplash. He pretends to hate everyone."

"'Pretends'? He's very convincing."

"He's been with me since my Method acting days." Hollis paused for a sip of her latte. "I lived in Los Angeles in my previous life. Been here for five years now, which I guess makes me an honorary local."

"What did you do in L.A.?" Summer asked.

"I was your garden-variety model-actress-waitress." Even in the harsh morning sunlight, Hollis looked like she belonged in a facial moisturizer commercial. "I grew up in a little town in Nevada, and I was always the prettiest girl in school. Sang solos in the choir. I was sure I'd be a star if I moved to Hollywood. So I did, and guess what?"

"Well, if you'd lived happily ever after, I'm guessing you wouldn't have moved here."

Hollis nodded. "Turns out, Hollywood is full of waitresses who used to be the prettiest girl in their high schools. But I got lucky. After months of auditions, I actually landed a part in a movie."

"I thought you looked familiar. What movie?" Summer pulled out her smartphone. "I'm going to look up your IMDb right now."

"Oh, I used a stage name. And before you even ask, no, I wasn't doing porn or anything like that. Lots of actors change their names for various reasons."

Summer's finger hovered above the phone screen. "Okay, well, what was your stage name?"

Hollis kept going as if Summer had never spoken. "Anyway, while I was filming, I fell in love with my costar. Total cliché. And pretty soon, there was more drama off set than on set."

"Who was the guy?" Summer was dying for details. "What was the movie? Spill your guts, woman!"

"After everything blew up in my face, I had to leave L.A. I had nowhere else to go, so I came here." Hollis gazed out the window, the faintest hint of crow's-feet now visible at the corners of her eyes. "He still e-mails me sometimes. Texts me, too." She shook herself back to reality. "I have no idea how he got my cell number."

"Do you ever want to write him back?" Summer asked. "Sorry—what was his name, again?"

"I used to be tempted, back when he e-mailed. Now that he texts, not so much." Hollis smiled. "I can forgive a lot of things, but text-speak isn't one of them."

"So breaking your heart is bad, but spelling it 'u' instead of 'y-o-u' is worse?"

"Infinitely worse." Hollis shuddered.

Summer nodded. "Remind me never to text you."

"We have grammar and syntax for a reason." Hollis shook her fist. The cat dived for cover. "Whatever happened to punctuation? Whatever happened to nuance and subtlety? *Whatever happened to the shift key?*"

"Calm down," Summer urged. "Deep breaths."

Hollis took a moment to collect herself. "Anyway, I gave up on being the next Julia Roberts and came out here and now I get to spend every day with my books and Snidely Whiplash. Couldn't be happier."

Summer looked around at the floor-to-ceiling bookshelves, the earthenware cookie jar by the cash register, the fluffy white cat curled up in the window. "I bet there are lots of literary-minded men around here who would be delighted to use their shift key on you."

Hollis laughed. "I'm not ruling anything out, but right now, I'm happy with the status quo."

"But isn't that the whole point of Black Dog Bay? Getting over an old relationship and finding a new one?"

"Not at all. We got a lot of media coverage last year, and the extra tourist business is great, but the journalists got it wrong. Black Dog Bay has never been about finding love. It's not about getting revenge or making your ex sorry or hooking up with some good-looking guy who knows his way around a shift key."

"Damn," Summer muttered.

"It's about healing. It's about letting go of the past and reenvisioning the rest of your life. You can read all about it in *The History of Black Dog Bay.*" Hollis pointed out a stack of books by the cash register. "But while we're on the subject of good-looking guys, what's going on with you and Dutch?"

"Nothing yet," Summer replied. "But don't worry. I'll wear him down."

"I hope you do. That man is in dire need of a love affair. He's spent the last decade working and raising his little sister and being entirely too responsible. He needs a woman like you. I can see it now: the two of you strolling on the sand, making out while the waves crash . . . all very *From Here to Eternity.*"

Summer laughed. "Weren't there a lot of beatings and deaths at the end of that movie?"

"Details, details. Here's a little something to get you in the right frame of mind." Hollis selected a trio of steamy romance novels. "Come back when you're ready for more. And if you're interested, book club meets every Tuesday evening. We love new members."

"Oh, I probably won't be here long enough to go to book club."

"No? How much longer do you think you'll stay?"

"Well." Summer's savings were dwindling and she couldn't afford to stay at the Better Off Bed-and-Breakfast indefinitely. But it wasn't like she could go back to flying the turbulent and terrifying skies. "I don't know."

"You're not ready to leave yet." Hollis ran Summer's credit card and put the books into a paper bag. "You haven't seen the black dog. Plus, you really should have a scandalous summer fling with Dutch. He—" Hollis *shh*ed both of them as a teenager entered the bookstore. Summer recognized her as the girl she'd met on the morning of Mimi Sinclair and fifty-two pickup.

"Hi, Ingrid." Hollis stepped out from behind the counter. "How are you? Did you like *Mrs. Dalloway*?"

Ingrid considered this, her gray eyes solemn. Along with her coltish frame, she had the wardrobe of a ten-year-old tomboy and the demeanor of a senior citizen. "Yeah, but it was kind of bleak."

"Have you read any Thackeray? Try *Vanity Fair*." Hollis started back toward the literature section.

Summer blocked the aisle. "Virginia Woolf? Thackeray? What kind of summer reading is that?"

"The awesome kind," Hollis replied. "Thackeray has a very sly wit."

"Save that for AP English." Summer plucked a few paperbacks from the romance shelves and handed them to Ingrid. "You know what you need? Jackie Collins, Danielle Steel, and Kresley Cole. You're welcome in advance."

"This is Ingrid *Jansen*." Hollis shot Summer a pointed look. "Dutch's sister?"

"Yes, we met during my little brawl with Mimi Sinclair." Summer offered a handshake. "Summer Benson."

"Is that your red convertible parked outside?" Ingrid asked.

Summer nodded.

"I like it." The teenager laced her fingers together. "Is it old? Sorry, I mean vintage?"

"You were right the first time—it's old." Summer laughed. "Her name's Scarlett."

"Like Scarlett O'Hara?"

"Exactly. My stepsister, Emily, named her. I wanted to call her Belinda Carlisle, because, you know, 'Car-lisle,' but I was out-voted."

Ingrid furrowed her brow. "Who's Belinda Carlisle?"

"Okay, now *I'm* old." Summer winced and changed the subject. "So? Did you end up going to Mimi's daughter's party on Saturday night?"

Ingrid stared down at the cover of the Jackie Collins novel. "Yeah."

"Uh-oh. What happened?"

The teenager shrugged and slouched at the same time. "I didn't look right."

"What do you mean?"

"I dressed up, but my clothes were all wrong." She hunched deeper into her baggy T-shirt. "And I don't know how to do makeup and stuff."

"That's because you're brilliant." Hollis sniffed. "You have better things to do than obsess over boys and bronzer."

Ingrid didn't respond at first. Finally, she muttered, "That's easy for you guys to say. You were probably born knowing how to deal with boys and bronzer."

"Well, I'm sure Summer here will be happy to help you," Hollis said.

Ingrid's huge eyes got even huger. "Really?"

Summer jerked her head up. "What, now?"

"Why don't you two head down to the drugstore and pick out

some blush and some lipstick?" Hollis pulled two oatmeal cookies out of the jar on the counter and prepared to send them on their way.

"Could you give us one second?" Summer asked Ingrid. She pulled Hollis over toward the window, where Snidely Whiplash took a halfhearted swipe with one paw.

"What are you doing?" She returned the cat's surly stare.

"Come on, help her out," Hollis whispered. "In the words of Cher from *Clueless*, the poor girl is screaming for a makeover."

"Then you do it," Summer whispered back. "She doesn't even know me."

"Yes, but she's obviously very impressed with your car and your moxie."

"Well." Summer paused to preen for a moment. "I do have a lot of moxie."

"Besides, Dutch is ridiculously overprotective of her. He's like Captain von Trapp in *The Sound of Music*." Hollis appealed to Summer with an Oscar-worthy display of pathos. "She doesn't have a mother, poor thing."

At this, Summer felt her resolve crumble. "What happened to her mother?"

"Her parents died in a boating accident. The whole thing was tragic." Hollis touched her fingers to her lips. "No one ever taught her all the stuff a girl needs to know in high school. She needs a mentor."

Summer threw up her hand. "Let's get one thing straight: I am nobody's mentor."

They both peered back at Ingrid, who was scuffing the toe of her ancient sneaker into the carpet and tugging on the ends of her unruly russet hair.

And in those soulful eyes and restless fidgeting, Summer recognized a girl like herself—a girl who had been torn away from the people who mattered most. A girl who believed she was easy to leave and hard to love.

She heaved a mighty sigh and gave in. "Fine."

"Yay!" Hollis gave a little golf clap.

"But this isn't gonna end well."

"What do you care? You're leaving soon anyway, right?"

"Good point." Summer slid on her sunglasses and beckoned Ingrid to follow her. "All right, let's go. And if your brother asks, we spent the whole afternoon reading Thackeray and drinking tea with our pinkie fingers crooked."

Ingrid took the lead as they exited the bookstore to the sound of Snidely Whiplash's discontented yowls. "The drugstore's just around the corner and two blocks to the left. But I was hoping—"

"Hold that thought." Summer grabbed Ingrid's hand and inspected the chapped skin and peeling cuticles. "What happened here?"

"I spent yesterday working in the garden and teaching swimming lessons at the country club. They put a ton of chlorine and chemicals in that pool." Ingrid tucked her hands into her pockets. "Forgot moisturizer, I guess."

"The makeup can wait—you need a manicure, stat."

"Oh, I don't get manicures," Ingrid said.

Summer stopped walking and lowered her sunglasses. "Never?"

"Never."

"Why on earth not?"

"I don't know." Ingrid hunched down again. "It just seems kind of frivolous."

"That's the whole point."

"You spend all that money and then the polish chips off."

"Yeah." Summer took Ingrid's elbow and steered her toward the Rebound Salon. "And then you get another manicure."

"An endless, futile cycle. I'd rather spend the money on books and the time reading."

"Did you just use the word 'futile' in reference to a manicure?" Summer held open the door and waved to Cori. "You are way overdue for a day with someone like me."

"Why do you look like you're having a nervous breakdown?" Summer watched Ingrid peruse the rows of nail polish.

"There's too many colors." Ingrid looked vaguely panicked. "I don't know which one to pick."

"Is there a shade called 'futile fuchsia'?" Summer asked Cori. She turned back to Ingrid. "Look, I know you're new to this, so here's a tip: Mani-pedis are supposed to be fun. If you're angsting over color choices, you're doing it wrong."

"Well, what are you getting?" Ingrid asked.

"Maroon. But I'm kind of a brazen hussy like that."

"I'll get the same color," Ingrid said.

"You sure you're ready for red? Maybe you should start out with something a little more low-key. Peach? Pink? Bronze?"

"Maroon." Ingrid set her jaw.

"Maroon it is." Summer settled into a cushy massage chair and kicked off her flip-flops. "After this, we'll hit the drugstore and do a quick cosmetic application tutorial."

"Can we take the convertible when we go to the drugstore?"

"Sure."

Ingrid's face lit up for a moment, but then she said, "Well, it's only a few blocks, so it's kind of a waste of gas."

"Not only will we take the convertible, we'll put the top down. You can drive, if you want."

"Oh, I can't drive." Ingrid perched in a massage chair, her posture prim and perfect.

Summer gave her a look. "How old are you?"

"Seventeen."

"Why can't you drive?"

"I have to tell you something." Ingrid glanced from side to side, looking guilty. "I Googled you."

"Do I even want to know what came up?" Summer braced herself for questions about the plane crash and Aaron and that one YouTube video she'd made a few years ago after a particularly rowdy night in Vegas.

"Are you really Jules Benson's daughter?"

"You've heard of him?"

"Of course!" Ingrid looked as though she was gearing up to ask for an autograph. "He's a literary genius."

Summer laughed. "He would agree with you there. And yes, I'm his daughter."

Ingrid lowered her voice as Alyssa got to work with the nail file. "I can't believe I'm sitting here getting my nails done with Jules Benson's daughter."

"Believe it." Summer yawned.

"But you're not a writer?"

Summer made a face. "God forbid."

"Really?" Ingrid looked incredulous. "You never wanted to be a poet?"

"Nope. I don't have a poetic bone in my body. Although I do know all the words to Jay Z's 'Ninety-nine Problems.'"

Ingrid flopped back, chagrined. "I wish *I* had a famous poet in my family."

"No, you don't. Trust me."

When it became apparent Summer wasn't going to elaborate, Ingrid shot her a knowing little smile. "So I heard about you and Dutch at the Whinery."

Summer froze. "What about me and Dutch?"

"You asked him out."

"Can't anyone in this town keep their mouth shut?" Summer lamented.

"Nope," Cori, Alyssa, and Ingrid chorused.

"Fine. If you must know, I did ask him out. He said no."

"He always says no." Alyssa gave a wistful sigh.

Ingrid's gray eyes sparkled. "You should try again."

"Why?" Cori asked. "He's just going to reject her again."

"And again and again and again." Alyssa pouted as she uncapped the cuticle oil.

"Don't take it personally," Cori said. "Dutch is just like that."

"He wouldn't even let the Friends of the Library auction off a dinner date with him," Alyssa grumbled. "And that was for *charity*."

"The country club has a big holiday party every winter, and he brought a date once. Once in, like, ten years. And she was some boring banker from Dover."

While Cori and Alyssa went on and on, Ingrid motioned Summer closer.

"Try again." She smiled down at her newly maroon nails. "Trust me."

"Fine." Summer slipped her feet back into her sandals and stood up. "I will."

"Where are you going?" Cori asked.

"I'll be right back. Don't spread any salacious gossip without me." She marched out of the salon and into the Retail Therapy boutique.

Beryl looked up from the stack of sweaters she was folding. "Back so soon? Good for you. Ready to move your wardrobe to the next stage?"

"We'll be skipping a few stages, actually." Summer strode over to the underwear display. "I need the most scandalous piece of lingerie you have. The smaller, the better."

Beryl browsed the display case, her lips pursed. Then she reached down and selected a tiny scrap of silk edged with lace. "Will this do?"

"Yes. Yes, it will."

"Do you have a color preference?"

"The time for subtlety has passed." Summer glanced down at her naked fingernails. "I'm thinking red. Dark red. The color of a nice Cabernet."

chapter 12

On Tuesday night, Summer wandered into the Whinery with a stack of fashion magazines, planning to set up camp at a café table and work her way through *Vogue* and a chilled glass of Chardonnay.

But a busload of heartbreak tourists had just arrived and Jenna was slammed, pouring reds and whites and rosés as fast as she could. Hollis was helping out, too, and Summer noticed that while Jenna had a clean dish towel tucked into the front pocket of her apron, Hollis had a paperback copy of *The Best of Dorothy Parker* tucked into hers.

Over the buzz of female chatter and the clinking of glassware, Summer could hear the harmonica solo at the end of Liz Phair's "Divorce Song."

"Need some help?" Summer stepped behind the bar and handed a clean goblet to Jenna. "What am I pouring first?"

"Thank you so much for offering, but you're not allowed to be back here." Jenna tilted her head toward the trio of framed health inspection certificates on the back wall. "You don't have your food handler's license."

"Neither does Hollis and she's back here," Summer pointed out. "Besides, I'm an excellent bartender."

"But you—"

"Let her help," Hollis told Jenna. She turned to Summer and said, "She's been on her feet all day and she's getting a migraine."

"I'm fine," Jenna insisted.

"Stand down. If I can mix amaretto sours at thirty thousand feet in major turbulence, I can handle a few glasses of Merlot." Summer washed her hands in the stainless steel sink.

As the song changed from Liz Phair to the Velvelettes' "Needle in a Haystack," Jenna and Hollis gasped.

"Don't look now." Jenna tightened the knot of her apron. "It's Miss Huntington."

Summer stood on tiptoe and craned her neck to catch a glimpse of the woman who'd just walked through the door. All she could see through the throng of sunburned, teary-eyed tourists was the back of a sleek, white pageboy haircut.

"Hattie Huntington." Hollis's face was even paler than usual.

"*That's* the biggest bully in Black Dog Bay? She's teeny tiny," Summer scoffed. "You could snap her like a twig."

"Think so? Go take her order and see for yourself," Hollis said.

"Yeah, go handle her the way you handled Mimi Sinclair." Jenna pinched the bridge of her nose. "I cannot deal with her. Not today."

Summer leaned over the bar, trying to get a better view. "That lady can't be over five feet tall."

Jenna produced a bottle of Advil and tapped a pair of pills into her hand. "She runs this town with an iron fist."

"She's been here for decades. Owns half the land up and down the shore," Hollis said. "And she's mean."

"Really mean."

"*So* mean."

The crowd shifted, and Summer finally got a good look at the wisp of a woman wearing lemon yellow linen and carrying a Hermès satchel. "She's all frail and birdlike."

"Ha! More like a pterodactyl," Jenna said. "She's bitter and sour and spiteful."

Summer had to smile at this. "Sounds like me."

Hollis shook her head. "No. Hattie Huntington has taken bitter to a whole new level. She's estranged from everybody she's ever known. Her sister, her cousins, her old friends—"

"Not the senator," Jenna said.

"True," Hollis said. "She managed to hold on to her old pal the senator, but only so she can terrorize the rest of us with his political influence."

Jenna tried to dry-swallow the ibuprofen, and Summer gave her a glass of water.

Hollis was on a roll. "She stopped speaking to both her parents before they died, even though they left her this enormous estate with all this money and land."

"And beach rights," Jenna said.

"Yeah. And for the last few years, she's been telling us all she's going to die any day."

"But she never does." Jenna crossed her arms. "She'll probably live forever."

"The bitter ones always do."

"She's immortal." Jenna resumed pouring glasses of wine. "Now that I think about it, she's probably an actual demon. It would explain a lot of things."

"Listen to you two." Summer tsk-tsked them. "Wishing death on a harmless old biddy."

"Pterodactyl," Jenna corrected.

"You're racking up some bad karma."

Hollis stopped serving long enough to do a shot of Shiraz. "No. Bad karma is constantly threatening to restrict beach access for half the length of the boardwalk."

"Bad karma is showing up at city council meetings and mentioning that you're thinking of selling off some of your downtown real estate and letting a big-box store come in and wipe out the local merchants."

"Bad karma is handing out lawsuits like they're Smarties at Halloween."

"But you know what's good karma? Waiting on the harmless old biddy." Jenna shoved a wine list and a pen into Summer's hands. "Good luck."

"I don't need luck." Summer tucked the pen behind her ear. "I've worked flights from Newark to Vegas. I once had an entire coach section full of slot machine enthusiasts over seventy. Watch and learn, ladies. Watch and learn." She waved the wine list at Hollis. "Hey! You can't watch and learn while you're rolling your eyes."

She made her way through the clusters of women drinking and laughing and crying and singing along to the Velvelettes.

"Good afternoon!" She put on her friendliest flight attendant smile as she sauntered up to the pterodactyl in yellow linen. "Welcome to the Whinery. Would you like to hear about our specials?"

Miss Hattie Huntington was even more diminutive up close. Although her white hair was thick and well coiffed, the face beneath it looked gaunt and pinched. Her skin was pale and thin almost to the point of translucency, and her suit, which couldn't have been bigger than a size two, hung off her bony frame. She met Summer's cheery greeting with a dour, flat-eyed sneer. "When, exactly, did this establishment turn into Fort Lauderdale during spring break?"

Summer smiled even wider and leaned in closer. "Pardon?"

"This is disgraceful." Hattie shuddered. "Ladies wearing shower shoes in a restaurant? Unseemly."

"Flip-flops aren't shower shoes when they're bedazzled and made in Spain," Summer said.

Hattie's gaze went glacial. "Are you contradicting me, young lady?"

"That's a lovely handbag." Summer offered up the wine list. "May I suggest a Chardonnay?"

"You may not," Hattie harrumphed. "I've got half a mind to leave right now."

Summer jerked her thumb toward the exit, her smile never wavering. "Door's right where you left it."

"You're very rude." But Hattie sat down at a table and settled her handbag on the chair next to hers.

"Part of my charm." Summer helped push her chair in. "So you're not leaving?"

"I'll go when I'm good and ready. And in the meantime, I suppose it's too much to ask for a half-decent red?" Hattie scanned the wine list. "Hmm. The Stag's Leap Cabernet will suffice."

"Coming right up." Summer grabbed the list back and be-bopped away. She could feel the old lady glaring at her back.

Jenna and Hollis were still distributing drinks as fast as they could.

"Well, you were right," Summer told them. "She hates me."

"Are you kidding?" Jenna elbowed Hollis. "She actually spoke to you."

"Miss Huntington doesn't deign to speak to just anyone," Hollis explained. "Half the time, she pretends the unwashed masses don't exist."

"You haven't really been snubbed till you've been snubbed by Miss Huntington," Jenna agreed. "You must have charmed the Hermès handbag off her. What's your secret?"

Summer shrugged. "Oh, I told her it's fine to wear flip-flops and to get the hell out if she didn't like the ambience. Same old, same old."

Hollis's jaw dropped. "And you're still alive?"

"Bossy people secretly liked to be bossed," Summer informed them. "All that scraping and bowing gets old. And she doesn't like me; I just took her off guard."

"If you're still alive, she likes you." Jenna blew out her breath. "So what did she order?"

"The Stag's Leap."

"*Of course* she did." Jenna rubbed her temples again. "I think we have one bottle left, but it's going to take me forever to find it."

"Have no fear. We've got you covered."

Fifteen minutes later, Jenna had located the wine, uncorked the bottle, and approached Miss Huntington with the demeanor of a wayward puppy expecting to get a rolled-up newspaper to the nose.

"I'm pretty sure she turned that wine into vinegar with her look of death," Jenna said when she retreated to safety behind the bar. "But at least she didn't talk to me. Thank God I'm part of the unwashed masses."

A few minutes later, Summer looked up and noticed that Hattie was no longer seated at the wrought iron table. The elderly lady was standing, swaying on her feet, both hands braced on the table-top. She wasn't sneering or berating anyone. She wasn't even breathing.

"Oh shit." Summer slammed down her wine bottle. "She's choking."

She vaulted over the bar, charged through the sea of customers, and placed her hand on Hattie's shoulder.

"Are you all right?" she yelled into the elderly woman's face. "Can you breathe?"

Hattie didn't respond, just kept clutching the table and gaping at Summer with wide, terrified eyes.

The crowd went silent for a moment, then erupted into a flurry of gasps and murmurs and worried questions:

"Is she okay?"

"What should we do?"

"Hang on—the bartender looks like she knows what to do."

And indeed, Summer knew exactly what to do.

"Brace yourself." She stepped behind Hattie, wrapped her arms around the old woman's rib cage, and made a fist with her left hand. She covered her fist with her other hand, then pulled sharply upward and inward on Hattie's sternum, hoping she wouldn't snap any brittle ribs.

Hattie made a low gurgling sound, then went back to silence. Summer positioned her hands for round two, but then Hattie's entire body shuddered with the force of a coughing fit.

A small, dark chunk flew out of Hattie's mouth and landed on somebody's bedazzled flip-flop.

Summer got right up in Hattie's face and again demanded, "Are you okay?"

Hattie shoved her away. "Yes! For heaven's sake, yes! Stop accosting me!"

Summer exhaled with relief. "Oh, good. I was really hoping I wouldn't have to do an emergency tracheotomy with a corkscrew."

"I've got half a mind to have you arrested for assault and battery." Hattie patted her ribs with a grimace. Her pallid complexion regained a touch of pink.

Summer offered her hand to Hattie. "You're welcome. Why don't you sit down and I'll bring you some ice water?"

"Not so fast." Hattie raised one bony index finger. "I want to know what I choked on."

The owner of the sequined flip-flop crinkled her nose and used a napkin to collect the evidence. "Here."

She passed the napkin to Summer, who unfolded it to reveal . . .

"Oh no," Summer murmured.

"A piece of cork!" Hattie snatched the napkin away and bundled it into her handbag. "I nearly died because of somebody's carelessness. Inexcusable." The crowd parted before her as she marched up to the bar.

"Who poured this drink?" She brandished her wineglass, spilling a few drops of the dark red liquid on her sleeve.

Jenna stepped forward. "I did."

"Do you make a habit of serving your patrons chunks of cork?"

"No, Miss Huntington. I am *so* sorry. It was an old bottle, and the wine was so dark. . . ." Even in the dim lighting, Jenna's cheeks glowed red. "But that's no excuse."

"It certainly is not." Hattie's eyes gleamed.

"Truly, I am so, so sorry."

"Don't blame her." Hollis stepped in front of her friend. "Blame me. I was distracting her with questions and jostling her and stealing her corkscrew since I dropped mine. That's why she didn't notice the bottom of the cork had fallen off."

"Gross negligence on both your parts," Hattie concluded with grim satisfaction.

Summer cleared her throat. "But luckily, it all turned out fine. And FYI, the next time someone asks you if you can breathe, and you can't, you should shake your head no. Takes the guesswork out of it."

Hattie kept glaring at the bartenders.

Jenna's lower lip trembled. "Please, let me pay for your dry cleaning."

"Oh, you'll pay for my dry cleaning," Hattie assured her. "You'll pay for much more than that."

Summer put her hands on her hips and asked Hattie, "Are you going to pay for that woman's flip-flops? Because you totally spat on them."

"You haven't seen the last of me," Hattie proclaimed, then stalked toward the door.

And before the door finished closing behind the biggest bully in Black Dog Bay, the mayor walked in.

"Well, well, well." Summer wound a strand of hair around her index finger. "Look who's back."

"Twice in one week?" Hollis said. "That has to be a record."

"Oh God. Why is he here?" Jenna launched into a second nervous breakdown. "He's going to cite me and shut the whole place down. Unless Miss Huntington beats him to it."

"No one's shutting the place down," Summer said.

"Miss Huntington will," Jenna predicted. "That's how she is."

"Should I go ask him if he wants a drink?" Hollis asked.

"I'll do it," Summer said. "As long as he's here, I might as well ask him out again."

Jenna stopped hyperventilating long enough to ask, "Didn't he turn you down before?"

"Yep."

"He's looking at us!" Hollis spun around so quickly, the paperback fell out of her apron pocket. "Be cool! Be cool!"

Jenna was still staring at Summer. "So all these women have asked him out, and he's said no. And *you* asked him out and he said no."

Summer nodded. "Correct."

"But this time, he's going to say yes?"

"Correct."

"And it will go differently this time because . . . ?"

"Because, um . . ." *Because I'm the girl who can always get the guy. I can't keep him, but I can get him.* "I heard from a reliable source that it was worth trying again. So break out your marshmallows and your sleeping bags, because this girl is on fire." She rummaged through her handbag until she located a small paper bag. "Jenna, would you kindly set the mood with some appropriate music? Something sultry and slow? Maybe Nina Simone?"

Jenna changed the soundtrack to "Call Me Maybe" and Hollis started lip-synching.

"I hate you both," Summer told them.

Dutch caught her eye and started toward the bar, but every few feet, he was waylaid by a friend or a concerned constituent.

Summer helped herself to a clean wineglass, added the finishing touch, then handed it over to Jenna.

"Give that to Dutch," she instructed. "Tell him it's compliments of the hot blonde on the other side of the bar."

Jenna looked at the glass and burst out laughing. "You really want to do this in front of everyone?"

"Hell, yeah. This is the Summer Benson school of courtship. Go big or go home."

Hollis whispered to the woman next to her, who exclaimed to the person next to her, and a crescendo of chatter swelled through the crowd. All eyes were on Dutch by the time Jenna arrived with the wineglass in hand.

The moment Jenna opened her mouth, all conversation ceased, though Carly Rae Jepsen kept singing in the background.

"This is, uh . . ." Jenna almost dropped the glass. "From her."

Dutch reached into the glass and pulled out the lacy red panties Summer had tucked inside.

He looked at her. She looked at him.

The registered voters of Black Dog Bay scrambled to clear the way as he strode across the room.

He stood directly in front of her, blocking her view of the bar and backing her up against the wall. She could feel tension radiating from his chest and shoulders. He was obviously struggling to keep himself in check. But she couldn't figure out if he was angry or exasperated or . . . something else.

Finally, he spoke. "Thanks for the drink."

Definitely something else. She caught the undercurrent of heat in his voice.

"Oh, you're welcome. I know you like reds." She tilted her head and smiled. "I considered writing 'Will you go out with me?' on them in glitter, but I thought that might be overkill."

His expression shifted just a bit. "You're a master of understatement."

"Exactly. So!" She glanced down at the undergarment clutched in his hand. "Ready to die of embarrassment yet?"

"Summer." He said her name low and rough. "Do I look like I give a damn what anybody else is thinking right now?"

She stopped sassing him and glanced down, feeling suddenly shy. "No, you do not."

"Okay, then. You want to go out?" His slate gray eyes darkened. "Let's go."

"Right now?" Her throat had gone dry.

"Right now."

"Oh, I . . . Okay." She started toward the door, but he pressed his palm against the small of her back.

"Allow me."

She let him lead the way, feeling more flustered with every step as they headed out into the night.

And as she fell into step behind the levelheaded, responsible small-town mayor, she knew that he was about to give her more trouble than all the bad boys she'd ever been with.

chapter 13

"So, um, where are we off to?" The air outside the Whinery felt cool and still. The town square was illuminated by only a streetlamp and the white moon over the ocean.

Dutch never took his gaze off her face. "You tell me—you asked me out. Or would you like me to take over from here?"

I love it when he tells me what to do.

Summer shook off the memory from the flight to Paris, determined to stay in the moment.

"No curfew?"

"Not tonight." He smiled. "My sister's at a sleepover."

"Ingrid," she said. "I met her."

"She may have mentioned that." Before he could say more, his cell phone buzzed. "Speaking of Ingrid, I'm sorry, but I have to take this."

"Of course; go ahead." Summer hung back to give him privacy, but she couldn't help overhearing bits of the conversation over the strains of music from the Whinery.

"Wait, *where* are you?" Dutch hunched over the phone. "I thought you were at Hayley's house. Ingrid, stop. Take a breath.

I can't understand what you're saying." He pulled his car keys from his pocket with his free hand. "Start over. You're *where*? Sit tight. I'll be there in fifteen minutes." He straightened up, his expression grim as he turned back to Summer. "Let me walk you to your car."

"Everything okay?"

"My sister, who is supposed to be at her friend Hayley's house, is apparently out with a bunch of college kids at some eighteen-and-over club in Ocean City."

Summer pulled out her own phone and started tapping away on the screen. "What's the name of the club?"

He rubbed his forehead. "The Cheeky Tiki."

Summer laughed. "I'm sorry. I know this is serious, but—"

He rolled up his shirt cuffs. "I should have known this was coming. All those years of straight A's and common sense had to end eventually."

Summer couldn't help noticing that Ingrid's inner problem child had emerged the week she'd met Summer. "Want me to come along? I can navigate."

Dutch jingled his keys, then nodded and led her across the street to a dark sedan. "Can you talk sense into a bunch of adolescents sloshed on Alabama slammers?"

"Like a professional hostage negotiator."

He opened the car door for her, and Summer slid into the passenger seat and buckled her seat belt.

"When I was seventeen, clubs like the Cheeky Tiki were my second home. Although I think the one I went to was called Risqué."

"She shouldn't even be there." Dutch backed the car out and turned onto the main road that led to the highway. "She's only seventeen."

The overhead sodium lights illuminated the car's interior

as they drove down the coastal highway. Although the radio was turned way down, Summer could make out the intonations of an NPR broadcaster reporting on mounting international hostilities. "She must have borrowed an ID from an older friend."

"My sister would never do that."

Summer hid her smile. "Maybe they didn't even check her ID. When I used to go to these places, they'd just take pity on me and wave me through."

Even as he fumed, Dutch abided by all posted speed limits and traffic signs. "That's illegal."

"That's reality." She checked their progress on her phone map as they crossed the state border into Maryland. "Although Ingrid doesn't strike me as a normal, rebellious teenager."

"She's not." Dutch scrubbed his jawline with the back of his hand.

A few minutes later, they located the Cheeky Tiki in a run-down strip mall bedecked with pink neon, blazing tiki torches, and real palm trees.

"Wow." Summer rolled down the window, the better to hear the Bob Marley cover band and smell the cigarette smoke wafting through the air. "I feel like I'm back in high school."

A tall, shaggy-haired boy lurched across the parking lot, pausing just long enough to throw up on Dutch's car headlights.

"Oh my God—I *am* back in high school."

Dutch opened the door and got out. "Back in a minute."

But as Summer scanned the teens milling in front of the club's entrance, she spotted a slender, shuddering silhouette near a trio of tiki torches. "I see her. She's right there." She stuck the upper half of her body out the window and waved. "Ingrid!"

Ingrid jerked to attention and hurried toward the car, stumbling over every crack and pothole in her high heels. Her hair seemed different than the last time Summer had seen her, but Summer couldn't be sure because she couldn't stop focusing on the teenager's outfit.

"What the hell is she wearing?" Dutch said.

"Don't say anything," Summer instructed. "It'll only make it worse. Let me do the talking."

Dutch reached into the car's backseat and grabbed a box of tissues, which Ingrid seized as soon as she was within arm's reach. She was crying and ranting and shivering all at once.

No surprise, given the amount of exposed skin.

"Hayley left without me, and Mattie's making out with her boyfriend on the patio, and . . . and . . ." She blew her nose and turned to Dutch. "I lied to you."

He nodded and indicated she should get into the car.

"I know I'm not supposed to be here." *Honk, sniffle.* "Are you going to have them shut down for letting me in when I'm not eighteen?"

Dutch slid into the driver's seat and rolled up the car windows. "No."

"Thank you."

Summer shifted in her seat and gave Ingrid a sympathetic look.

"Go ahead and yell at me." Ingrid hung her head. "I deserve it. I know you're disappointed."

At this, Dutch turned off the ignition and gave his sister his full attention. "I'm not disappointed. I always told you to call me if you need a ride home, and you did. I'm proud of you."

"You are?"

"Yes. Plus, Ocean City's not my jurisdiction." He started the car again, drove out of the parking lot, and pulled into the gas station across the street.

"Why are we stopping?" Ingrid asked.

Dutch swore under his breath as he unbuckled his seat belt. "I have to wash off the headlights."

"So? What's his name?" Summer twisted around in her seat and grinned at Ingrid.

Ingrid was going through three tissues at a time. "What're you doing here?"

"Dutch and I were just . . ." Summer narrowed her eyes. "Oh, no you don't. I'll be asking the questions tonight, missy. What's his name?"

Ingrid scrunched up her body even tighter. "Whose name?"

"The guy you got all tarted up for." Summer reached back and patted Ingrid's knee. "Please. I know that no woman puts on heels that high and a skirt that short unless she's man hunting."

Ingrid gazed down at her neon pink halter top, zebra-print miniskirt, and S&M shoes. "I look ridiculous."

"You don't look ridiculous. You look . . ." Summer struggled to find the right word. "Listen, ain't nothing wrong with flashing a little flesh. But it's an art form. You have to feel good about yourself. Own it."

Ingrid tugged at her skirt hem. "These aren't my clothes."

"I figured."

"I borrowed them from my friend Mattie." Ingrid tossed another crumpled tissue to the floor mat. "And his name is Maxwell."

"Okay, well, tonight we're going to go home and get you cleaned up, and tomorrow we're going to go shopping and find you something to wear next time you're on a man hunt." Summer felt an unexpected burst of energy and purpose. "Something sexy that you'll still feel comfortable in. We'll also do a walking-in-heels tutorial." She couldn't stop staring at the dark rings around Ingrid's sweet gray eyes. "And an eyeliner tutorial."

"It won't make any difference." Ingrid sighed. "I'm hopeless. I can't even do a shot right. I took one sip of a Swedish Fish shooter and almost threw up."

"Well, I can't even hear the words 'Swedish Fish shooter' without wanting to throw up, so don't feel too bad about that." As an afterthought, Summer added, "Oh, and, you know, underage drinking's bad, mmm-kay?"

"Boys like Maxwell never want girls like me." Ingrid swiped at her smeared eye makeup. "I'm too boring and quiet and brown-haired."

That's when Summer finally noticed the follicular fallout. She squinted, trying to assess the damage through the shadows. "Ingrid Jansen. What did you do?"

Ingrid started sobbing again. "The box said ash-blond."

"The box?" Summer's heart sank. "Oh, no. You tried to dye your own hair? Without any supervision? *Whyyyyyy?*"

"I followed the instructions exactly." Ingrid hiccuped. "Well, I added a few minutes to the processing time. They said leave it on for twenty minutes, so I kept it on for thirty. For good measure."

"Oh, honey." Summer brushed her fingers against the formerly glossy chestnut locks that were now brittle, lank, and . . . gray.

"I followed the directions!" Ingrid repeated. "The box said ash-blond!"

"Yes, and your hair is now the color of ash. Literally."

They stopped talking when Dutch opened the driver's seat door. He started to get in but, upon seeing two sets of panicked female eyes peering back at him, backed away. "You two need a moment?"

Summer went into damage-control mode. "I need M&M's right now. Big bag, please—it's an emergency. And Ingrid needs . . . what do you need?"

"Cheetos," Ingrid quavered.

"Cheetos. And we need to stop at a drugstore on the way home." She held up a hand when Dutch opened his mouth. "Yes, it's a girl thing, and no, you may not ask any questions."

Two hours later, Summer padded down the staircase from the top floor of the Jansen home. "Well, she finally stopped crying. And her hair is . . . Well, it'll have to do until the salon opens tomorrow."

Dutch's house had probably been built a hundred years ago, and the simple, rustic decor reflected this. The floor planks, window casings, and banister were old, hand-carved wood that had been refinished. The furniture looked sturdy and no-frills, but Summer had been in enough trust fund babies' Nantucket summer homes to recognize heirloom-quality antiques when she saw them. There were photographs everywhere—the walls, the side tables, the edges of the built-in bookshelves. Black-and-white portraits and fading color snapshots of a huge extended family that had dwindled over the generations to these last two siblings.

Dutch sat on a dark blue sofa, his expression shell-shocked, a man who'd unwittingly stumbled into a minefield of neon and hormones. "What was all that about?"

"A boy." Summer perched on the sofa arm. "Some strapping lacrosse player named Maxwell. Sound familiar?"

"No." His brow creased.

"Well, apparently, she's pining away for this guy, and he goes for blond cheerleader types."

He covered his eyes. "I don't want to hear this."

"Have some M&M's. It'll help." She poured a few candies into his palm.

He threw back his head and swallowed them like they were prescription painkillers. "I can't handle this."

"You're handling it just fine," she assured him. "You're a great brother."

"Exactly—I'm her brother. Not her dad, not her mom." He unknotted his tie. She watched the light blue silk slide through his strong, tan fingers, let her inappropriate thoughts take over for a moment, and then remembered the distraught teenager who could descend upon them at any moment.

Dutch snapped her back to reality with, "Our parents both died when she was six. Boating accident." Finished with his tie, he unbuttoned his shirt cuffs. "I was in college at the time, so I was named legal guardian."

"How old were you?"

"Twenty." He smiled at her surprise. "Yeah, Ingrid was kind of a midlife surprise for our parents. My mom used to call her the 'bonus baby.' Anyway, one day I was living in the basement of a frat house, and the next, I was making funeral arrangements, moving into my old bedroom, and learning how to iron a Brownie uniform."

"Hang on—you look like that, and you garden, *and* you iron?" Summer said. "But you don't date? That is a crime against all womankind."

"I tried to do everything I was supposed to. All the parent-teacher conferences and piano lessons and soccer games, but obviously I missed a few things."

Summer smiled at the mental image. "I bet you were the golden boy of every PTA meeting. All the cougar moms must've loooved you."

"Oh, I never went to PTA meetings. But I did sell a lot of Girl Scout cookies."

"I can imagine."

"I don't mean to brag, but Ingrid and I set the troop record."
He finally relaxed a bit. "Plus, it was good training for door-to-door
campaigning."

"So you always knew you wanted to be mayor?"

He shrugged. "It wasn't really a choice—it's family tradition.
My dad would have wanted me to do it, so I did."

"But you never really got to experience your twenties."

"I don't think I missed that much." He settled back against
the cushions. "I went to class with my friends, then came home
and studied with Ingrid. We used to sit at the kitchen table together, doing our homework. She'd be working on spelling words
and punctuation and I'd be trying to write a paper on the Bolshe-
viks."

"That explains a lot. You're so lucky I asked you out." She shot
him a knowing look. "You have a decade's worth of wild oats
to sow."

He tensed up again. "Yeah. About that—"

"I know, I know." She reached out and nudged him back into
the cushions with her fingertips. "You don't date. You don't have
fun. You don't have scandalous flings with alluring out-of-towners
you meet in a bar. Until now."

He gave her his full, focused attention. "I'm listening."

"I get it. You have a sister to support. You have a job and a
reputation to think about."

"My life has never sounded more scintillating."

"It could be," she promised. "For the next week or so. You
don't do relationships. I just came off a bad breakup. We're perfect
for each other!"

"Because we're not perfect for each other."

"Exactly. It doesn't have to be a whole big thing. We can just
have a grand old time and then go our separate ways. No drama,
no expectations. Just fun."

"Fun. I think I have a vague memory of that from college."

"We'll make a pact." In the absence of a Bible, Summer put her hand on his coffee-table copy of *The History of Black Dog Bay* and prepared to make her oath. "Two weeks, then I'll pack up and ship out."

He raised an eyebrow. "You want to specify a cutoff date?"

"You seem to like rules and regulations."

"Two weeks." He put his palm next to hers on the book. "No drama, no expectations."

Summer lifted her other palm. "So help us God."

"And then we just walk away?"

"I walk away," Summer clarified. "You can stay here."

"Deal." He tossed the book aside and started to close the distance between them. She parted her lips and waited.

Both of them startled as Ingrid called, "Summer? Summer, could you come here for one more second?"

Summer pulled back with a sigh. "Duty calls."

Dutch trailed his fingers along her shoulder, arm, and hand as she rose to her feet. "Damn kid."

"This is the most interesting first date I've ever had." On an impulse, she leaned back down and planted a quick little kiss on his cheek.

His fingers wrapped around hers. "So we're all squared away with the rules and regulations? We can move on to the fun part now?"

"I thought you'd never ask."

"Okay, then. Have dinner with me on Saturday. It's a country club dinner thing. Fund-raiser. Pick you up at six."

"A country club fund-raiser? That's not what we agreed on!" She tried to pull her hand away, but he held on. "We said fun!"

"It will be fun."

"No, it won't."

"You strike me as the adventurous type." His gray eyes flashed, challenging. "Give it a try."

"But you . . . I can't . . ." She took a deep breath. "I don't have anything to wear to a fund-raising dinner."

He glanced down at the red silk panties still tucked into his blazer pocket. "I'm sure you'll think of something."

chapter 14

. . . Upon information and belief, you or your employee did, with reckless disregard and utter contempt for the well-being, health, and safety of my client, leave a foreign object in the wine served to my client. . . .

"That vindictive old hag is suing me." Jenna slapped down a piece of stationery emblazoned with a law office logo. "I'm going to lose the bar. I'm going to lose everything."

"This is ridiculous." Summer skimmed the letter again, her eyes widening with every line. "It was an accident."

"An accident that's going to cost me my business and my bank account." Jenna blew her nose into a pink paper napkin. "I'm going to have to live in my car at the beach. Except I won't have a car once she's done with me. I'll have to live under the dock."

"Slow down. Don't go all 'Rock Lobster' yet." Summer squeezed her arm. "She can't do this."

"She already did." Jenna grabbed a fresh napkin and dabbed at her eyes. "I told you, she lives for stuff like this. How am I going to fight this? She has an entire team of bloodthirsty lawyers on retainer."

The door flew open as Hollis raced in, her body silhouetted in the blazing noon sun. "I just heard. Are you okay?"

"It was a tiny piece of cork." Jenna gave up wiping her cheeks and let the tears flow.

"Do you think it would help if we apologized again?" Hollis nibbled her lower lip. "Maybe sent a fruit basket or something?"

"It won't do any good." Jenna shook her head. "Remember when she went after Jim Renard?"

"What happened to Jim Renard?" Summer asked.

"Nobody knows, because he left town in despair and never came back." Jenna appealed to Hollis. "Can I come sleep at your bookstore when I'm homeless?"

"Of course."

"No, no, no." Summer planted her hands on her hips. "We are not conceding defeat."

"Hattie Huntington's got nothing but money and free time," Jenna pointed out.

"And spite," Hollis added. "An abundance of spite."

Jenna nodded. "She can keep this up forever."

Hollis read the attorney's letter for herself. "It's not about the money; it's the principle. She always has to be right. She always has to win."

"Well, this time she's met her match." Summer got to her feet and collected her purse. "You can't have a breakup town without a bar. That's madness. Wine is an integral part of the recovery process."

Jenna looked dubious. "How are you going to stop her?"

With no M&M's in sight, Summer grabbed a sugar packet from under the counter, ripped it open, and poured the contents into her mouth. "I'll show *her* a thing or two about reckless disregard and utter contempt."

———

The purple mansion was even uglier up close. Miss Huntington's sprawling Georgian Revival estate was surrounded on three sides by brick patios and lush green lawns, behind which the surf pounded on the shore. This was the biggest house, on the best-situated lot, and was clearly the crown jewel of Black Dog Bay real estate.

Or at least, it would have been if it hadn't been painted a mottled shade of violet. Summer remembered Jenna and Hollis saying that Hattie had chosen the color out of stubbornness and malice.

Evidently, Hattie did a lot of things out of stubbornness and malice.

And as the daughter of a poet who blamed all his bad behavior on an "artistic temperament," Summer could work with that. Her father had locked himself in his office for days at a time, swilling scotch, dallying with a series of increasingly young and unsuitable girlfriends, alternating between rage and despair with no apparent trigger. She remembered coming home from her last day of first grade, curling up on the rug by his study, and pressing her ear against the closed door. She could hear the clacking of typewriter keys interspersed with the clinking of ice cubes in a glass. The shadowy hallway had felt cavernous, and all she could think was: *Who's going to take care of me all summer?*

Her next thought: *I'll do whatever it takes to get his attention.*

She'd been thrilled when he'd married Georgia, Emily's vivacious mother. Together, Summer and Emily had planned an idyllic future for their blended family. There would be road trips, home-cooked meals, holiday traditions.

But as much as the daughters craved stability, their parents craved drama. Jules and Georgia's marriage lasted less than one year. Their divorce lasted more than two.

Summer knew her father had once been capable of great love. He'd spent her entire childhood penning beautiful, agonized, award-winning poems inspired by her mother. The wife he'd lost without warning. The woman who had loved him, but not enough.

The absence that had only felt bigger and emptier as Summer grew up.

She parked her red convertible under the purple portico, climbed the white marble steps, rang the doorbell, and waited.

And waited.

And waited.

Finally, a ruddy-cheeked man with a close-clipped gray mustache, a seersucker jacket, and an actual bow tie opened the door.

"Hey," Summer said before Mr. Seersucker had time to utter a word. "I need to speak with the lady of the house."

Seersucker gave her a look of disdain that should have been accompanied by a monocle and a top hat. "I'm afraid Miss Huntington is not at home."

"Bullshit." Summer cupped her hands around her mouth and yelled into the entry hall, "Hey, Hattie! Our Lady of Litigation! I'd like a word!"

Seersucker tried to close the door, but Summer wrapped her hand around the doorjamb.

"If you mash my fingers, I'll sue!" she cried. "I'll take you to court for pain and suffering."

Seersucker's bushy gray brows snapped together. "See here, young lady—"

"Step aside, Turner. I'll handle this." Hattie's voice echoed off the polished marble floor. "Kindly leave us for a moment."

The butler retreated down the hallway as Miss Huntington took his place in the doorway. As always, she was impeccably turned out in a crisp white shirt and white pants with orange loafers and a narrow orange belt. Despite the stifling humidity outside, the house's interior was cool . . . and much more tastefully decorated than the exterior. Summer could glimpse fresh flowers, bright fabrics, and huge barrel-vaulted hallways beyond the expanses of white marble in the entryway.

She leaned against the doorjamb with great nonchalance and wished she had a piece of gum to snap. "Nice digs."

Miss Huntington's expression didn't even flicker. "Are you threatening to sue my butler for injuries you purposefully sustained?"

"Why not?" Summer asked. "Turnabout is fair play."

A faint smile played on the old lady's lips. "You'll never make it to court. My attorneys will bury you in paperwork."

"I save your life and this is the thanks I get." Summer drummed her fingers on the doorframe. "If I had known you were going to sue Jenna, I would have let you die."

"You've got quite a mouth on you, Miss Benson. Oh yes, I know your name. I've had my staff look into your, shall we say, *colorful* history."

Summer refused to get sidetracked. "Jenna got distracted for two seconds and made a mistake. Could've happened to anyone."

"But it happened to *me*."

"So what? You're more valuable than anyone else because you have boatloads of money?"

Hattie inclined her head. "Yes."

"Seriously? You didn't even earn your fortune!"

"I *beg* your pardon."

"Guess what? I did a little research into *your* colorful history. You got lucky. You happened to be born to rich parents, and instead of being grateful for all this"—Summer threw out her arms to encompass the mansion, the beach rights, the inlaid marble and fresh flowers and priceless antiques—"you waste it on frivolous lawsuits and petty grudges. You should be ashamed of yourself."

Hattie's frail, knobby fingers curled into fists. "No one speaks to me that way."

"Let me tell you something. I grew up with the trust fund crowd. I went to boarding school—well, I went to five, actually. They kept asking me to leave. But I know how this game works. I'm not afraid of you." She locked gazes with Hattie. *"I see you."*

Hattie surprised her by looking away first. The tiny tyrant in white linen relaxed her posture, looking almost amused. "My. You're quite the spitfire."

"You have no idea."

Hattie made Summer wait another few seconds, then relented. "Very well; I'll drop the lawsuit."

"Thank you." Summer opened her arms. "All is forgiven. Let's hug it out."

Miss Huntington promptly closed the door on Summer's foot, then opened the door back up.

"Ow!"

"A thousand pardons." Hattie's eyes gleamed. "An accident, of course."

"I'm bleeding." Summer stared down around her red, swelling toenail.

"I wasn't finished." Hattie addressed Summer the same way she did her live-in help.

"With what? Living up to your reputation as a—"

"With my offer." And that polite smile turned sinister. "I'm willing to drop the lawsuit . . . on one condition."

"Her paid companion?" Forty minutes later, Jenna stared at Summer, her brow creased in bewilderment. "What does that even mean?"

"Sounds very nineteenth-century." Hollis pulled her hair back into a bun. "Like something from a Henry James novel."

Summer unwrapped a 3 Musketeers bar. "It means I'm her bitch, as far as I can tell. Did Henry James write about that?"

"It's probably just snob-speak for personal assistant." Hollis brought up a Web browser on her cell phone. "Okay, according to the Internet, paid companions are expected to provide entertainment and conversation. They aren't responsible for household chores."

"So I don't have to scrub her solid-gold toilets?"

"No. You're supposed to help with things like threading her embroidery needles and serving tea. And keeping up with her correspondence."

Summer rolled her eyes. "That anything like e-mail?"

"And you don't get a salary; you get an 'allowance,'" Hollis continued.

Jenna pretended to shudder. "Salaries are so vulgar."

"As long as the check clears, call it whatever you want," Summer said.

"You know, she wouldn't need a paid companion if she weren't so awful." Jenna scrubbed the bar top with renewed vigor. "When you have to pay people to be your friend, it's time to reevaluate your life."

"Oh, but I'm not her friend," Summer said. "Friends can call you out on your shenanigans; employees cannot. This way she can lord her power over me." She drew herself up. "Well, this should be an interesting few months."

"I still don't understand why you'd even consider working for her." Jenna passed Summer a glass of Sauvignon Blanc.

Summer put the glass to her lips and inhaled the fresh, fruity scent of the wine. She didn't want her new friend to feel guilty or responsible for her indentured servitude, so she'd decided not to share the details of Hattie's ultimatum. "Don't worry, I can handle her. I talked her out of the lawsuit, didn't I?"

Jenna wadded up her dish towel. "And *how* exactly did you do that?"

Summer waved this away with a secretive smile. "She's a peach compared to some of the passengers I've put up with over the years. Besides, the bed-and-breakfast's getting pricey, and she's offering me a huge suite with ocean views."

"Not worth it," Hollis said.

"Deal with the devil," Jenna agreed.

"Maybe, but if I stay here for the rest of the summer, I could keep hanging out with you guys . . ."

"And Dutch Jansen," Hollis finished for her.

"I didn't say that."

"You didn't have to." Jenna unwrapped a miniature peanut butter cup. "Get it, girl."

Hollis was still shaking her head and calling for caution. "Miss Huntington has never had a companion—paid or otherwise—in all the time I've been here."

"How bad could it really be?" Summer shrugged. "I'll cut the crusts off her cucumber sandwiches and hold her parasol while she plays the occasional game of croquet."

"Schedule her conference calls with all her lawyers," Jenna muttered.

"Taste her food in case one of her many enemies tries to poison her," Hollis said.

"You know, if you want a job, you can bartend here with me," Jenna offered.

"Too late." Summer peered down at her big toe, which was still smarting and red. "But the good news is I'll be in town for the rest of the season."

"Poor Dutch won't know what hit him."

Hollis giggled, and for a second, Summer glimpsed the naive, fresh-faced girl that had set off for Hollywood once upon a time. "I'll tell Beryl to stock up on skimpy underpants."

"You guys, no. Dutch and I are not a thing."

"Really. That's not what it looked like when he dragged you out of the bar the other night."

"Nothing happened." She tried to look innocent. "Scout's honor."

Hollis scoffed. "Uh-huh."

"You can tell us," Jenna said.

"Yeah, we can keep a secret."

"*No one* in this town can keep a secret," Summer said. "Besides, for real, there's nothing to tell. Dutch and I are not dating. We're not having sex. We're not even kissing." *Yet.*

"Really?"

"Really."

"That is so disappointing."

Summer wound a lock of hair around one finger. "Well."

Hollis leaned in. "Yesss?"

"We might be having dinner on Saturday."

"I knew it!"

"It's no big deal. He just needs a plus-one for some stuffy country club thing, and I need a suitably boring cocktail dress. Do you think Retail Therapy is still open?"

"No, but let me make a call." Jenna picked up the phone. "Hi, Beryl." She paused. "Wow, word travels fast, huh? Yeah, that old witch was going to sue, but Summer Benson convinced her to call off the dogs. Yeah, I know, she's my hero, too. Speaking of which, she's actually at the Whinery right now, but I'm sending her your way. I need you to give her the First Lady treatment."

chapter 15

"First you want a muumuu, then a red thong, now this? You're all over the road, aren't you?" Beryl unlocked the back door of the boutique and ushered Summer in as she flicked on the overhead lights.

"Yep," Summer said.

"I knew I liked you."

"So I'm going to this super-stodgy dinner."

"Really? With who?" Beryl put one hand on her hip and waited. "Dutch?"

"Funny—I thought the sign out there said 'boutique,' not 'interrogation room.'"

Beryl grinned. "I try to give my customers a full range of services."

"Whatever." Summer scowled. "I need to look . . . I believe *dainty* is the word. No cleavage, no sequins, no leather." She felt the life seeping out of her just saying the words.

"Well, you do have dainty bone structure." Beryl studied her face. "Look at those cheekbones."

Summer waved this away. "Just make me look like I'm a

lobotomized lady who lunches. On something other than grilled cheese."

"This is all so exciting!" Beryl made a beeline to the sale section, and indicated Summer should follow her. "Dutch never takes anyone anywhere. He must really like you."

"The old panties-in-the-wineglass." Summer laughed weakly. "Works every time."

"I mean, he's taking you to a fancy dinner! At a country club! As his official girlfriend!"

Summer stopped laughing. "Whoa, there. I'm not his official *anything*."

"If he's taking you to a fund-raiser, you're official." Beryl genuflected. "Oh mighty man-wrangler, I bow to thee!"

Summer focused her attention on the racks. "My best friend almost got married last summer and strong-armed me into this tasteful mint green tea-length deal, so I thought I might be able to wear that. But then I remembered that I threw it in the garbage the second the ceremony was over."

"Just as well—you don't want to wear a bridesmaid's gown to a political fund-raiser. I have the perfect thing in mind. . . ." The hangers clicked against the metal rack as Beryl flipped through the inventory. "Now, where did I put that lilac chiffon?"

Summer caught a glimpse of her expression in one of the dressing room mirrors. She looked pinched, anxious, pale. "That sounds like an ice-skating costume."

"It's going to look fabulous with your skin tone." Beryl plucked a demure lavender cocktail dress from the rack. With a modest bateau neckline and a full, filmy skirt, it was the polar opposite of everything else in Summer's wardrobe.

Summer shied away as Beryl tried to hold the dress up to her shoulders. "I have a strict policy against pastels. I should have mentioned that earlier."

Beryl gave her a little push toward the dressing rooms. "Stop stalling and go try it on."

Four minutes later, Summer was staring at a version of herself she almost didn't recognize. The light purple fabric was formfitting without being clingy and the hemline hit midknee.

"Too stunned to speak?"

"Stunned isn't the word. I look . . ." Summer paused to tamp down the dry heave rising in her throat.

"Appropriate for a fund-raiser at a country club?"

Summer shook her head. "It just screams . . ."

"'I'm dating the hottest mayor in Delaware'?"

"I feel like this should come with white gloves and a flowered hat. And a chastity belt."

"You do need accessories." Beryl rushed to the shelves by the cash register, then rushed back with a slim silver headband, which she arranged in Summer's choppy blond hair. She stepped back to assess the effect and smiled. "There."

"I'm wearing a headband," Summer informed her reflection. "Next up, the apocalypse."

"You look like a punk rocker pixie at charm school!" Beryl gushed. "I die."

Summer yanked at the material brushing her collarbones. "I feel like I'm choking in this neckline."

"A V-neck would be better with your face, I agree, but you want to play it safe. Trust me."

Summer ripped off the headband. "Why did I agree to this, again?"

"Because Dutch is the hotness and you want to get him into bed?"

"Oh, yes, that's right."

Beryl hummed a happy tune. "So a few hours in pastels will be worth it. Give me your credit card, and I'll ring it up while you're changing."

Summer looked down at the lavender frock. "I don't suppose there's any way you'd let me keep the tags on and return everything after the dinner?"

Beryl just laughed.

"Please? I'll be careful. I won't eat or drink or dance."

"Oh, that reminds me: You're buying some dainty shoes to go with your dainty dress."

"I have shoes," Summer said.

Beryl raised one eyebrow. "You don't have country club shoes, and don't even front like you do. Now hand over your card and let me do my job. If you're going to be with Dutch, you'll be doing this a lot, so you better get used to the charm school look."

"For the last time. I'm not with him."

"Whatever you say."

"No, I mean it." Summer reached both hands behind her back and yanked at the zipper. "We have rules. Deadlines. Clear-cut expectations. It's all very orderly."

"You're wearing a silver headband for him. You loooove him." A few minutes later, Beryl had bundled everything up in tissue paper and shopping bags. "Come back when you're ready to buy a wedding gown!"

Summer stuck out her tongue. "You're dead to me."

"Have a great time! Oh, and here." Beryl grabbed the black version of the lacy red panties and threw them in the bag. "For good luck. Enjoy your deadlines and your rules, you crazy kids!"

chapter 16

On the evening of the fund-raiser, Summer barricaded herself in the bed-and-breakfast's attic and tried to psych herself up for all that lavender and tulle by blasting old-school hip-hop on her iPod. With the resigned air of a martyr donning a hair shirt, she pulled the chiffon dress over her head.

When she checked her reflection in the tiny oval mirror in the corner, she had to turn off the music right in the middle of Run-D.M.C.'s "It's Tricky" because the contrast between the downbeat and the dress design was bringing on a headache.

She looked like she was getting ready for prom. In 1958.

Horrified, she snatched up her cell phone and dialed Emily, who refused to treat the matter with the solemnity it deserved.

"What are you so worried about?" Emily asked. "I thought you hobnobbed with politicians on the regular."

Summer stepped away from the mirror, bonking her head against the sloped ceiling. "If by 'hobnob' you mean that I pour them gin and tonics and then fend them off when they try to snake their hands up my skirt in the middle of meal service, then yes, I routinely hobnob with politicians. But fund-raisers?

Small talk? Rhetoric and platforms and whatever? Not my scene."

"Well, look on the bright side. You're not thinking about Aaron anymore."

Bonk. "Aaron who?"

"Exactly." Despite being inundated with scheduling difficulties and studio demands, Emily sounded chipper and cheery. "This guy must be quite the charmer if he can sweet-talk you into lilac chiffon."

"That's the problem, Em. He's not a charmer." Summer paused. "Well, sort of. He's charismatic, but it's not all practiced and manipulative. He's . . . nice."

"Okay. I'm waiting for the bad part."

"No, I mean he's *really* nice."

Emily laughed. "And that's a problem because . . . ?"

"You know how I am with men. I like to play a little rough."

"Are we talking about *Fifty Shades of Grey* stuff? 'Cause if we are, I'm going to need a margarita before we continue."

"No, no, that's not what I'm saying." Summer gnawed the inside of her cheek. "I'm used to master manipulators. Take-no-prisoners psychological warfare followed by hot sex. 'Nice' puts me off my game."

There was a long pause on Emily's side of the line, so Summer kept blathering.

"I mean, I'm offering to be his dirty little secret, and he's taking me out to a country club to meet all his fancy friends? Who does that?"

Emily sighed. "You know you have serious emotional problems, right?"

"Of course I know that. Everyone knows that." Summer started brushing her hair with renewed vigor. "Let's stay focused. What am I going to do?"

"Here's an idea: Why don't you go meet all his fancy friends and have a good time?"

Summer's stomach churned. "I should probably cancel. I think my spleen might be acting up." She glanced down at the white-washed floorboards. "And I have a splinter."

Emily laughed and quoted their favorite line from *Pretty Woman*: "'Call me when you're through. Take care of you.'"

"You know, when you were going through a romantic crisis, I didn't laugh at you," Summer said. "I listened. I helped."

Emily snorted. "You forced me to go to a male strip club."

"Exactly. I *helped*."

At six o'clock, she heard a knock on the door, but couldn't bring herself to open it.

"Summer?" Marla's voice drifted up from the landing. "Your date's here."

Summer dropped the hairbrush.

A few moments later, she heard another light rap.

"Keep knocking," Marla's voice urged. "I know she's in there."

"Summer?" Dutch sounded both concerned and amused.

She forced out her breath in a dry cough. "Yeah?"

"You okay in there?"

"Absolutely! Almost ready." She grabbed the sparkly silver headband and set her jaw.

But she could not bring herself to actually put it on. So she stood there, clutching the row of rhinestones, for what felt like forever. The sharp little prongs bit into her palms.

"Do you need a few minutes?" Dutch called. "I can wait down-stairs."

"I made iced tea!" Marla exclaimed.

"No, I'm ready," Summer replied. "I just . . . uh . . . Any min-ute now."

Dutch's voice changed from concerned to cajoling. "I can't tell if you want me to take the door off the hinges or leave and never call you again."

Both. She sidled closer to the door and said, "I don't want you to leave."

"So I should go find a screwdriver, then?"

She took a deep breath, shoved the headband into her hair, stepped into her ivory shoes, and, without glancing in the mirror, flung open the door.

Dutch took a step back and smiled at her. "You look . . ."

Marla actually said the word "Squee!" then skedaddled back to the lobby.

"You look beautiful," Dutch finished.

She had no idea how to respond, so she volleyed back with, "I have to tell you something. There's been a slight change of plans, and I'm going to be in town a little longer than two weeks."

"Okay." He seemed to be staring at her headband.

"I'll be here at least another month, maybe longer. Which I know is a violation of our pact." She went to fluff her hair, then realized that the headband was in her way. So she pivoted, grabbed her clutch (ivory, beaded, borrowed from Hollis), and marched toward the stairs. "But we can still stick to the original agreement: two weeks. I don't want you to think that—"

"Summer." He said her name quietly but firmly and reached for her hand. "Let's go have dinner."

"Two weeks is what we agreed on." She clutched her clutch until her knuckles went white.

"It's fine. Don't be nervous."

"I'm not nervous." She cleared her throat. "But our pact also specified fun, and this whole thing sounds like the opposite of fun."

"I promise you, we'll have fun." He took the lead as they started down the stairs. "I won't bring you back until we do."

"You say that now, but I'm wearing lilac chiffon and you're wearing a blue blazer. 'Fun' is going to be kind of a tall order."

He looked over his shoulder at her, his eyes gleaming. "I love a challenge."

"I'm drinking water," Summer pointed out during a five-second break between introductions to people whose names she forgot immediately. "I want full credit for my restraint."

"It's called 'cocktail hour' for a reason," Dutch said. He looked completely at ease in the country club ballroom, surrounded by crystal chandeliers and servers in black bow ties. The faint strains of jazz music played in the background, and though they'd rotated through countless conversation partners, the small talk was always the same. "Have a glass of wine. Have two. You'll be glad you did, come speech time."

"No way. I'm on my best behavior, and wine doesn't go with that. Trust and believe."

"It's dinner, not purgatory. The goal is to have a little fun, remember?"

Summer took another sip of water, trying to imagine it was vodka. "That's what I'm trying to tell you—with me, there is no such thing as 'a little' fun."

"Well, then, let's try to make it through dinner," he murmured into her ear, "and then we'll get out of here and go take off your . . . headband."

She stared at him, deliberating. "Are you being inappropriate?"

Before he could reply, Mimi Sinclair swanned into the room, pausing in the doorway so everyone could take note. She was perfectly turned out in a black-and-white bouclé cocktail suit with sparkly buttons . . . and several inches of toilet paper trailing from the heel of one of her black pumps.

Her dramatic entrance caused quite a stir—the amount of snickering and whispering would have been more suited to a middle school assembly than a room full of elected officials. But the terrorist in tweed was oblivious to the commotion. She sashayed toward Dutch, then stopped in her tracks when she noticed Summer by his side. "*You're* here? With him?"

"Kind of." Summer grinned. "Unofficially."

"You look"—her icy gaze raked over Summer's lavender dress—"different."

"Don't I?" Summer squeezed Dutch's hand and stepped away from him. "May I have a word?"

Mimi sniffed. "I have nothing to say to you."

"But I have something to say to you."

"If you're trying to apologize for the scene you caused at the nail salon—"

"Don't worry, I'm not." Summer put her arm around Mimi's shoulder and steered her back to the ladies' room. "We'll be right back."

"I am humiliated!" Mimi's voice came out as a strangled little squeak as she sagged against the wall of the white wooden bathroom stall. "Positively *mortified*."

"Oh, relax. It's no big deal." Summer plucked the last bit of tissue off the socialite's shoe. "Happens to everyone."

"But it didn't happen to everyone—it happened to me. People were laughing at me. The lieutenant governor was laughing at me!"

Summer's forehead creased. "I don't even know what that is. Is that a real job?"

"Yes! An important job!" Mimi looked as anguished as her Botox would allow.

"Well, I'm sure the lieutenant governor has walked around

with toilet paper stuck to his shoe, too." Summer appropriated Mimi's handbag and started reapplying the traumatized woman's powder. "I know I have. In fact, this exact thing happened to me at my dad's Pulitzer Prize luncheon."

Mimi looked at Summer with new interest. "Your dad won a—"

"That's not the point of this story. The *point* is, I made people laugh with me instead of at me." She winked. "Not to boast, but agents and publishers in New York still talk about that day. I've dined out for years on that story."

Mimi accepted the lipstick and hand mirror Summer offered. "What'd you do?"

Summer shrugged one shoulder. "Since everyone was already talking about me, I figured I'd give them something worth talking about. So I went back to the restroom, bided my time, and waited until the speeches were about to start."

"And then?"

"Then I gave my encore." Summer crouched down and liberated a spare roll of toilet paper from the metal dispenser. "Here. You'll need at least two more of these."

Ten minutes later, in the lull after the band stopped playing while diners were taking their seats, Mimi traipsed back into the ballroom. She'd tucked the ends of three rolls of toilet paper into the waistband of her skirt. The rolls unfurled behind her like a two-ply bridal train.

The crowd laughed. Mimi laughed. The lieutenant governor and his wife got up from their seats and went over to greet her. And after she'd schmoozed and simpered her way through all the VIPs, Mimi beamed at Summer and informed Dutch, "Chip and I will be writing you a check for your next campaign."

"Mrs. Sinclair likes you now?" Dutch turned to Summer, his voice lowered in awe.

"Yeah. And bonus, now you can spring for the fancy, four-color campaign leaflets." She toasted him with her water glass. "Enjoy."

"First Ingrid, now Mrs. Sinclair." He kept staring at her. "How do you do it?"

Summer smiled and straightened her headband. "I have my ways."

As Dutch had predicted, Summer was regretting her water-only policy halfway through the speeches. She'd had better entrées and more comfortable seating on transatlantic flights. She'd heard more engaging oration on the talking-heads portion of *Real Housewives of Orange County*. But she kept herself in check with her ankles crossed, her hands folded, and her eyes on the podium.

Then, after the servers cleared the dinner course, Dutch pulled a pen and a stack of business cards out of his suit jacket pocket, drew a tic-tac-toe grid on the back of a card, placed an "X" in the center of the grid, and slid the card over to Summer.

"Your move," he murmured as the audience broke into applause.

"Game on, buddy, you're digging your own grave." Summer drew an "O" in the upper right corner.

For the next hour, they played increasingly cutthroat rounds of tic-tac-toe, then moved on to hangman. And all night, she was acutely aware of her posture, her expression, and the headband pressing into her scalp. Though she felt like a fraud, she looked like a lady. And Dutch always looked thoughtful and engaged, even as he tried to provoke her with tic-tac-toe effrontery. She realized the two of them weren't so different: They both spent their lives hiding their true feelings and putting up a good front in public.

Halfway through dessert, he leaned over and murmured, "Are we having fun yet?"

And she was stunned to realize that the answer was yes.

chapter 17

"Let the record show that I didn't have a single drop of alcohol." Summer sighed with relief as Dutch accepted his car keys from the valet at the end of the night. Her toes were numb from standing on carpet over concrete, her fingers felt grimy after countless hand-shakes, and her cheeks ached from forcing a smile while making inane chitchat.

Basically, she felt the way she did after working nine hours in first-class. All she had to do now was collect newspapers and plas-tic cups and stow the little oblong pillows in the overhead bins.

"You're the picture of restraint." Dutch opened the car door for her.

"But let the record *also* show that I desperately wanted to play a political fund-raiser drinking game where every time somebody said the words 'progress,' 'future,' or 'leadership,' I'd do a shot." She slid into the passenger seat and kicked off her shoes.

"Maybe next time." He settled into the driver's seat and pulled the car around the hedge-lined circular driveway.

"And if I *had* played such a drinking game, I'd be in the emer-gency room with acute alcohol poisoning."

"Well, you're off duty now, and you did great." He reached over and patted her knee through two layers of chiffon.

"So did you." She inched the hem up a few inches to see if he'd try for skin-on-skin contact. "I can see why everyone votes for you."

"Not everyone," he corrected, putting on the brakes as they waited for the long line of cars in front of them to turn left.

"Don't be modest. My sources tell me that you won the last election by a landslide. Like, ninety-nine point nine percent."

He laughed. "With Hattie Huntington being the very vocal dissenter."

"Let's not talk about Hattie Huntington right now." Summer made a face. "In fact, let's not ever talk about Hattie Huntington."

"We'll add that to our pact." He settled his hand back on her bare knee. She responded by reaching over and loosening the knot of his silk tie.

He upped the ante by edging out of the line of cars, executing a U-turn over the country club lawn, and pulling into the dimly lit parking lot by the service entrance.

Summer's jaw dropped as he reached across her to unbuckle her seat belt. "Oh my God, you left tire tracks on the grass."

"I guess we both have problems driving while we're distracted." He caught her hand in his and brushed a kiss over her knuckles.

"You rebel, you." Summer continued to work on his tie with her free hand. Once she'd undone the knot, she grabbed both ends of the tie and tugged him closer. "Admit it: You have a fetish for tea-length skirts. Lavender to you is like a red flag to a bull. You have problems."

"*I* have problems?" He hauled her up and settled her into his lap. "You can't control yourself around cuff links and two-button blazers."

"It's true." She leaned down and licked his bottom lip. "I had no idea an oxford shirt could be so clean and so dirty at the same time."

He brushed her bangs back and yanked off the sparkly headband.

"That feels so good." Summer threw her head back and shook out her hair like a shampoo commercial. "I'm pretty sure I—yep, I just came."

He laughed and cupped her cheek for a moment, then ran his hands along her bare feet, her ankles, her calves, her—

They both startled as a blinding beam of light appeared on the other side of the driver's window.

"Police. Step out of the car, please."

Summer clapped her hands over her mouth. Dutch gripped the steering wheel for a second, swore under his breath, then rolled down the window.

"Hi, Sean." He raised his palm in greeting. "It's me."

The baby-faced sheriff's deputy dropped his flashlight, picked it up, and dropped it again. "Oh, hey, Dutch. I mean, Mayor Jansen. I mean . . ." He backed away from the car, tripping over his own feet.

"We were just leaving." Dutch rolled the window back up and started the car. He turned to Summer with a rueful expression. "*Everyone* is going to hear about this. The sheriff's department gossips more than a quilting bee."

She tossed her headband into the backseat and reiterated her words of wisdom from earlier that evening. "Well, if everybody's going to be talking, we might as well give them something worth talking about. Let's go parking by the boardwalk."

Summer arrived at Hollis's bookstore early Monday morning with a spring in her step and a box full of doughnuts from the Eat Your Heart Out bakery.

Beryl and Hollis were lying in wait with a French press full of coffee and the latest edition of the town newspaper.

"Well, well, well. If it isn't the star of the *Black Dog Bay Bulletin*'s police blotter."

Summer dodged Snidely Whiplash's attempt at assault and placed the pastry next to the cash register. "What are you talking about?"

Hollis rolled her eyes at Beryl. "Look at her, acting all wide-eyed and innocent."

"I think we know who this little item is referring to." Beryl pointed out a block of text on the newspaper's back page:

> *Saturday, 8:41 a.m.: A caller on Oceanside Drive reported a possible theft after she was unable to locate her grocery list.*
>
> *Saturday, 6:35 p.m.: A caller on Bayshore Crescent reported that a pair of "belligerent seagulls" were trespassing on her second-story balcony, refusing to let the caller's husband use the barbecue.*
>
> *Saturday, 10:27 p.m.: Adult male and female engaged in amorous activities in a parked vehicle in the Gull Points Country Club parking lot were issued a warning by the sheriff's department.*

Summer scanned the newspaper, then read it again. "Holy shit. Someone seriously called the police because she couldn't find her shopping list?"

"Oh, that's probably Mrs. Ledbetter," Beryl said. "She needs a lot of attention."

Hollis nodded. "Last month, she called the sheriff because she couldn't get the price she wanted at a garage sale."

"But there you lovebirds are." Beryl tapped the page. "Right next to the gangster seagulls. I see the lilac chiffon worked its magic."

"Making out in a car at the country club? Hot," Hollis decreed. "Put down the doughnut and tell us everything!"

"Well." Summer dabbed a sprinkling of powdered sugar off her lip. "We did get a little carried away."

Hollis and Beryl nudged each other and giggled. "And when you say 'carried away,' you mean . . . ?"

"He took off my headband . . . and I loved it."

"Oooooh!" They all laughed.

"And then?" Beryl pressed.

"And then the police shut us down and blabbed to the media, apparently. Political scandal!"

"Are you guys going out again?" Hollis demanded.

Summer was saved from having to answer this by Hattie Huntington, who tapped her huge cocktail ring against the bookstore's plate glass window and beckoned her paid companion out to the sidewalk.

"She is such a piece of work," Beryl muttered.

"Here." Hollis pressed a paperback titled *Coping with Difficult People* into Summer's hands. "You'll be needing this."

Summer marched outside and greeted her employer with a snappy salute.

Hattie was not amused. "What time will you be moving in today?"

"Oh, right, I guess it's Monday. I don't know. A few hours?"

Hattie glanced at the book in Summer's hands. "I'll expect you at noon sharp."

Summer squinted in the sunlight glinting off the ocean waves. "You know, I don't seem to recall signing any sort of contract or employment agreement."

"Noon, Miss Benson."

This time, Summer responded with a curtsy. "As you wish." She straightened up. "Is that better, Your Highness?"

Hattie inclined her head. "Inestimably so."

Summer spotted Ingrid walking out of Rebound Salon, so she flashed Miss Huntington the peace sign and hurried across the street.

"Looking good!" She fell into step beside the teenager, noting that Ingrid had reverted to her usual baggy jeans and reddish brown hair.

"Thanks." Ingrid ducked her head to hide her face. "I had to go in twice for restorative color. Cori called in a master stylist from Baltimore to help." She hugged herself with both arms. "I just forked over a month's pay."

"And it was worth every penny." Summer steered her toward the bronze dog statue in the town square. "Blond washes you out. Now you know."

"Yeah, yeah." Ingrid shot an envious look at Summer's platinum layers. "Some of us are doomed to boring brown hair."

"Boring is an attitude, not a hair color," Summer informed her. "Which reminds me, I did promise to take you shopping, so let me know when you're ready."

"I'm going to need more than new clothes to get Maxwell to notice me." Ingrid plopped down on the gazebo steps with a sigh. "I need, like, a new personality and massive amounts of plastic surgery."

Summer sat down next to her. "I'll only ask this once: Are you sure this dude is worth it?"

"I dyed my hair gray. What do you think?"

"I think that, if nothing else, shopping will cheer you up. Rumor has it there's an outlet mall in Rehoboth Beach."

"Can't." Ingrid heaved a world-weary sigh. "I just spent all my fun money on restorative color."

"I thought you had all these jobs. Teaching swim lessons, babysitting, whatever. And you clearly don't spend anything on gas, car insurance, or cute outfits. How do you have no money?"

"Oh, I have money," Ingrid said. "But I invest most of it."

"You invest it?"

"Yeah." Ingrid scratched a mosquito bite on her elbow. "Municipal bonds and index funds. High-interest CDs. Nothing crazy."

Summer narrowed her eyes. "*How* old are you?"

"Old enough to know that money is better off compounding interest in the market than wasted on some overpriced tank top."

"Really. Says who?"

"Dutch."

"Of course. I should have known. This is crazy. This is like an episode of *Scooby-Doo*." Summer tugged at a lock of Ingrid's restored russet hair. "Take off your mask. Admit you're a sixty-five-year-old tycoon."

Ingrid laughed. "I'm just practical, okay? I like to plan ahead and think about the future."

Summer shook her head. "Then we really have no business being friends."

"Oh, we're not friends," Ingrid said with the same sense of authority that Dutch often displayed. "You're my mentor."

Summer kept shaking her head. "Uh, no."

"Yes."

"No."

"*Yes.*"

"Nuh-uh."

"Yuh-huh." Ingrid got to her feet, rubbed the bronze dog's nose, and started toward the drugstore down the block. "Can you at least help me pick out some lipstick and mascara?"

"Open your ears. I'm done giving you advice."

Ingrid ignored this. "Would you say I'm more of a winter or a spring?"

Summer stood up and rubbed the bronze dog, too. The metal felt warm from the sun. "I'd say you're a nut job." She couldn't help herself from adding, "Who should be wearing pinks with copper undertones. And just so we're crystal clear: I'm not and never will be your mentor."

"Please?" Ingrid turned around to face Summer, her eyes wide and earnest. "You saw me at the Cheeky Tiki. I need help."

Summer couldn't refute that. "Fine. *Fine.* I'll give you five minutes' worth of dating advice, but that's it." She opened the door to the drugstore and stepped into the air-conditioning.

Ingrid followed, rolling her eyes. "I know the drill already: Be yourself. Don't play games."

"What?" Summer yanked off her sunglasses. "Who the hell told you that?"

"All the women's magazines in the library."

"Child, what misguided crap are you reading? *Single and Bitter Weekly?*" Summer paused. "I should probably subscribe to that, myself. Anyway, no. Never listen to anyone who says don't play games. You should always play games."

Ingrid's clear gray eyes got even wider. "But isn't that manipulative?"

"It's *strategic.*" Summer threw up her hands. "Not playing games and being yourself is the worst possible thing you can do."

"Okay, got it." Ingrid pursed her lips. "What am I supposed to do, then?"

Summer tried to figure out how to word this. "Hold back part of yourself. It drives men crazy. They can't get enough."

"That doesn't sound very healthy."

Summer perused the candy counter. "No matter how much time you spend with him, no matter how much you talk or how physically intimate you are, keep part of yourself off-limits. Ooh, peanut butter Twix."

"Which part?" Ingrid asked.

Summer snapped out of her candy-induced reverie. "What, now?"

"Which part of yourself do you keep off-limits?"

"Your soul. Your heart. Whatever you want to call it." Summer lit up as she spied Rolos. "You just withhold a little bit. They want it, but you never give it to them."

Ingrid looked dubious. "Hmmm."

"Don't 'hmmm' me. I know what I'm talking about."

"But if you're holding part of yourself back, then you can't really be in love," Ingrid argued. "And your boyfriend's insane, because you made him that way."

"Which means, when you break up, you just dust yourself off and move on to the next prospect."

"That just sounds so . . ." Ingrid flipped through a fashion magazine and slapped it back on the wire rack. "How about if you just find a really nice guy that you love, and he loves you back, and you both trust each other enough to be honest? How about that?"

Summer snorted with derision. "Oh, to be seventeen again."

"What? There are some really nice guys out there, you know."

Summer gave her a look. "Guys like Maxwell, you mean?"

Ingrid flushed.

"I've been around the block. Hell, I've been around the world. I know how this works." She could hear her voice getting louder, knew she should shut up, but added, "And I'll let you in on a little secret: Nice guys can leave you, too."

Ingrid stared at her.

Summer slipped her sunglasses back on. "Now, where's the latest issue of *Single and Bitter Weekly*?"

Ingrid touched Summer's arm. "Maybe you just haven't found the right one yet."

"When it comes to men, play the law of averages." Summer shook off Ingrid's hand. "Hope for the best, prepare for the worst. You'll get the hang of it. It's just a matter of setting boundaries. In the meantime, we can start with practical, concrete steps."

Ingrid pulled her phone out of her pocket, her finger hovering above the screen. "Like what?"

"For starters, you might want to start wearing makeup every day. You never know when you're going to run into someone at the gas station or the grocery store, especially in a town this small."

Ingrid tapped away at the screen. "Okay. What else?"

"Are you seriously writing this down?"

"Yeah."

"You're very detail-oriented."

Ingrid grinned. "You noticed."

"So what kind of makeup do you usually wear to school or work?"

"None whatsoever. Oh, wait, does ChapStick count?"

"A little piece of my soul just died."

"I work in a swimming pool!"

"No excuses!" Summer headed over to the cosmetics section. "They make waterproof mascara!"

"That sounds like so much work." Ingrid put down her phone. "You know, maybe it's not just my social weirdness that's stopped me from having a boyfriend."

"You're not weird," Summer said.

"I'm a little weird." Another world-weary sigh. "I can't help it. But growing up in this town, you kind of get cynical about love."

"From the constant influx of heartbreak tourists like me?"

"Well, yeah. It makes you think, you know?" Ingrid browsed the selection of mascaras. "Lots of the women I see at the Better Off Bed-and-Breakfast are beautiful, smart, successful—we've even had a few celebrities—but they still get their hearts broken."

Summer perked up. "Which celebrities?"

"I can't say. They have a right to privacy."

Summer held open a magazine page filled with paparazzi shots. "Just point at a picture."

Ingrid closed the magazine. "If you lived in a honeymoon destination, it'd probably be the opposite. You'd probably just want to fall in love and get married."

"Demi Moore?" Summer pressed. "Jennifer Aniston?"

"You're wasting your time," Ingrid said. "I'll never talk." She stepped back and crossed her arms. "All this stuff about setting boundaries and holding back . . . is that what you're doing to Dutch?"

Summer opened and closed her mouth a few times. "If we're going to hang out, we can't talk about Dutch."

"He likes you." Ingrid's posture got even more defensive. "A lot. He talks about you. He never talks about anyone." She cleared her throat. "And I read the police blotter."

"You and everyone else." Summer sighed and broke into the Twix bar. "Your brother is a grown man. He can handle his business just fine."

Ingrid, usually so shy and tentative, looked positively fierce. "He's not playing games with you. So you better not play games with him."

chapter 18

Summer stepped over the threshold into her new bedroom and felt as though she'd teleported to the swankiest retirement community in West Palm Beach.

Last week's glimpse into the Purple Palace's opulent foyer had in no way prepared her for the rest of the house. Every room was filled with priceless paintings and objets d'art and frail-looking furniture that should probably be cordoned off in a museum somewhere. The place might as well have been carpeted with hundred-dollar bills.

But she'd maintained her poker face while Hattie led her up the grand staircase to her quarters. This bed and bathroom suite, which was easily three times the size of her apartment in New York, featured vibrant green silk wallpaper accented with a white chinoiserie pattern. Green and pink drapes pooled on the varnished hickory floorboards, and a massive white scrolled chandelier hung from the ceiling. But all this finery only served to set off the view of the bay directly outside the balcony.

Summer tossed her garbage bag of belongings onto the pristine white eiderdown. "This is it? *Pfft*. I've stayed in Best Westerns nicer than this."

Hattie didn't deign to respond.

Summer indicated a slim green sofa in the corner. "Is this a fainting couch?"

"It's a chaise longue." Hattie's every syllable oozed condescension.

"For swooning? Or eating bonbons?"

"I leave it to your own discretion."

"Ooh." Summer brightened. "Can I get actual bonbons to eat while I'm lounging on my chaise? Fancy French ones?"

Hattie couldn't tear her gaze away from the garbage bag. "Turner can fetch whatever you require."

"I'm guessing M&M's are too lowbrow for this place." Summer flung herself down on the mattress, which was big enough to petition for statehood. "So do I have to make my bed in the morning? Because I have to warn you: I haven't made a bed since MTV played actual music videos."

Hattie folded her hands in front of her yellow printed shift dress. "I thought you said you were well brought up. Boarding schools, et cetera."

"It didn't take." Summer snuggled deeper into the puffy white linens. "This is a pretty nice room for a servant."

"You're not a servant, Miss Benson. I believe we've established that. I would never tolerate such insolence from a servant."

"You can always fire me," Summer suggested hopefully.

"I can." Hattie smirked. "But I won't. Not until I'm good and ready."

"Why do you even want me here?" Summer sat up and got to her feet. "You're rich enough to hire someone who would at least *pretend* to like you."

"You're to be my companion, Miss Benson, not my psychoanalyst."

"Or here's an idea: Stop suing people and painting your house hideous colors for spite. Use your powers for good. I bet you could be the most popular girl in all of Black Dog Bay if you just put your mind to it." Summer gave her two thumbs-up.

"I'll leave you to unpack and get settled. Tea will be served at three." Hattie walked out of the room and closed the door firmly behind her.

Summer threw the door open again and yelled down the hall. "You know, getting laid would solve a lot of your problems!"

Hattie never faltered in her stride, but Summer heard a surprised bark of male laughter from downstairs.

"Turner thinks I'm funny!"

All she heard in reply were the staccato clicks of high heels on marble.

Much to Summer's disappointment, tea at Hattie's house did not include cucumber sandwiches with the crusts cut off. But, as with everything else in the Purple Palace, the fare was upscale and fussy: pastry puffs with sun-dried tomato and asparagus, Scottish smoked salmon with lemon butter, and a delicate chicken and fruit salad.

Summer took a seat across from Hattie at the round dining table in the sunroom and unfurled her linen napkin. "You eat like this every day? How are you so thin?"

"It's unspeakably rude to comment on someone's personal appearance." Hattie nodded as Turner approached with a pair of green teacups.

"Even if I'm saying you look good?"

"Have a biscuit, Miss Benson, and try not to talk with your mouth full."

They regarded each other across the table in silence for a few moments.

"So is this where the companion thing comes in?" Summer asked. "I'm supposed to entertain you while you eat finger food? Dance, monkey, dance?"

Hattie thanked Turner and added a cube of sugar to her tea with sterling silver tongs. "Let's start with the art of polite conversation."

"Fair enough." Summer grabbed a biscuit, slathered on some strawberry preserves, and crammed half of it into her mouth. "So this entire house has central cooling, huh? Your electric bills must be obscene."

Hattie pretended not to notice the crumbs scattered across Summer's side of the table. "We do not discuss money. It's vulgar."

"Says the woman who owns four houses and a ton of beachfront property." Summer paused for another huge bite. "News flash: Some of us have to work for a living. Sorry if that offends your delicate sensibilities."

Hattie finally cracked. She returned the teacup to its saucer with a clatter. "You're very impertinent, Miss Benson."

"You're just now noticing this?"

"And who on earth told you I have four houses?"

"The unwashed masses." Summer laughed at Hattie's expression. "Oh, come on. You practically own this whole town. Of course people talk about you."

"Idle gossip and falsehoods." Hattie reached across the table and swept aside some of the crumbs. "I do not own four houses."

"How many, then?"

"That's none of your business."

"Give me a hint," Summer said. "Three? Five? Higher or lower?"

"This is not conversation, nor is it polite." Hattie signaled to

Turner, who whisked away the pastry plate before Summer could help herself to another biscuit.

"You're so touchy." Summer attacked the salmon with her fork. "With your blood feuds and your lawsuits. Hattie, honey, look around and lighten up!"

Hattie gasped. "You do not refer to me as 'honey.'"

"You have fancy artwork, an undisclosed number of houses, high tea every afternoon. You get to wake up and see the ocean every morning. You're living the life!" Summer's eyes widened as she glimpsed a patch of shimmering turquoise on the far side of the patio. "You have a swimming pool, too? Because your private beach isn't chlorinated?"

"I also have a tennis court," Hattie informed her. "We'll play tomorrow morning."

Summer shook her head. "I haven't touched a racket in at least fifteen years."

"You'll pick it up again quickly enough."

"But I don't want to."

At this, Hattie's smile returned. "It's not your job to want to. It's your job to do it. And with your experience in air travel, I assume you're accustomed to doing things you aren't in the mood for with a smile on your face."

Summer took her time considering her response. "I suppose that's true."

"Now." Hattie settled back into her chair, as much as her perfect posture would allow. "I'd like to hear about your travels. I've never left the States."

"Really? I'd figure you for summers in Saint-Tropez and winters skiing in Gstaad."

The stern lines in Hattie's face slackened just a bit. "When I was young, it was considered somewhat improper for a woman of my social standing to travel alone."

"I heard you have a sister; couldn't you go with her?"

The facial lines tensed up again. "*Had.* Past tense."

"She died?" Summer stopped teasing. "I'm sorry to hear that."

"She may as well have." Hattie took a slow sip of tea. "We do not discuss my family, Miss Benson."

"Hang on." Summer pulled her phone out of her pocket and opened the notes section. "I'm going to have to start making a list of all the topics we can't discuss."

"Put that away," Hattie commanded. "This instant."

"But I—"

"I don't want to see or hear a cell phone in this dining room. *Ever.* I may have to suffer such boorishness at a restaurant, but not in my home. Do I make myself clear?"

"Yes, Lord Vader."

"Excellent. Now, tell me about France. Have you been to—"

Summer's pulse sped up. *Please don't say Paris, please don't say Paris.*

"—the Grasse region? I've done extensive reading on the perfume industry in Provence, and I've always wondered if the flower fields are as breathtaking as the photos make them out to be."

"Oh, I don't know anything about flowers," Summer said. "But you know who does? Dutch Jansen. He grows roses. Fancy ones. Ask me how I know."

"We do not discuss the Jansen family."

Summer whipped out her phone again and held up her hand to stem Hattie's protests. "Boorish or not, my short-term memory can hold only so much. There's no way I'll be able to keep track of all the things you hate."

"I don't *hate* the Jansens, Miss Benson." Hattie gazed out the window toward the ocean, her expression hard but her eyes soft. "At least, I didn't used to."

"But you do now?"

"This town got its reputation as the gathering place for heartsick women for a reason. You'd do well to remember that." And without another word, the stately old lady pushed back her chair and swept out of the sunroom.

chapter 19

"*It's* pain and suffering over there, I tell you." Summer pounded the bar at the Whinery, rattling the ice in her water glass. "And no matter how hard I try, she won't fire me!"

Jenna couldn't suppress a smile. "Yes, it certainly does sound like hard labor."

"It is! She makes me get up at the crack of dawn and play tennis. And golf. Golf!" Summer turned to Hollis, who was sipping iced tea and making sympathetic noises. "She forced me to play nine holes with her at the country club. And the whole time, she lectured me about my swing and my grip and my joints."

"Here." Hollis dug a child's activity book out of her woven straw beach bag. "Some kid ripped half the pages out of this, so I can't sell it. Try the word search—it's oddly therapeutic."

"Ooh, can I have one of the dot-to-dot pages?" Jenna peered over their shoulders. "I used to love those."

"Help yourself." Hollis passed the pages around. "I'll take the maze."

The three of them lapsed into silence for a moment and focused on their tasks. Though the awning shaded their seats, a slice of warm golden light filtered in through the window. Then Summer circled the word "MAD" and launched into a fresh rant.

"Let me tell you something about golf—it *hurts*! My entire upper body aches. I haven't been that sore since Rocco—he was a personal trainer from Chicago with eight-pack abs and full-blown narcissism—talked me into going to a CrossFit class with him." She rubbed the back of her neck.

"I hate to be the one to point this out," said Hollis, "but Hattie Huntington is more than twice your age."

"Yes, but she's very spry. I thought we'd be spending all day playing canasta and taking naps." Summer circled another word. "But no! It's golf and tennis and swimming and sailing all the livelong day. Like . . . like prison camp with monogrammed polo shirts. And a butler to bring you lunch on the patio."

Hollis pulled a pack of crayons from her bag and tossed it on the bar. "Sounds brutal."

"Ugh. I'm all sassafras to her, and she pretends to be appalled, but I think she secretly likes it." Summer grimaced. "I can't keep going like this, you guys. For real. I'm going to have a heart attack and die."

"On your fancy private beach with your butler." Jenna pretended to wipe away a tear.

"Well, it doesn't sound like prison when you say it like *that*."

They were all laughing and topping off their iced teas when Dutch walked in. Although he wasn't wearing a suit, he had the crisp shirt and tie thing going on, and Summer snapped to attention.

He took in the activity pages and the facial expressions and the iced tea before asking, very slowly, "What are you doing?"

"Connecting the dots," Jenna said.

"Coloring a frog," Hollis said.

"Making this word search my bitch," Summer said.

Dutch glanced behind him. "Is this . . . am I missing something here?"

"It's kind of soothing," Summer told Dutch. "You should try it. Here, want the hidden pictures?"

"I was hoping I might talk you into a quick lunch date." He held up his wrists, which glinted in the sunlight. "I wore cuff links."

"Like Kryptonite to Superman." Summer hopped off her barstool and hustled him toward the bar's kitchen exit. She called back over her shoulder, "I'll be back shortly, ladies. Or not."

As soon as they pushed through the heavy metal fire door into the alley, Dutch rounded on her, crowding her up against the building's brick wall. He held up the silver headband she'd worn to the country club dinner. "I found this in the backseat of my car."

"Thanks." She tossed the headband into the Dumpster across the alley and wrapped her arms around his neck.

He rested his chin on top of her head and murmured into her hair, "You haven't returned my calls."

"I didn't get any of your calls." Summer laughed. "Miss Huntington confiscated my cell phone."

"She did?" He ran the backs of his fingers up her neck and tilted her chin up. "Did she ground you, too?"

She reached up to touch the simple square cuff links. As he brushed his lips against hers, she could feel the cool bricks against her back and the warmth of his body against her chest. "You hoping to end up in the police blotter again?"

"A man can try."

He tugged down the neckline of her shirt to kiss her shoulder, exposing the strap of her newest bra.

He slid one finger between the strap and her skin. "Lavender."

"And nails to match." She fanned out her fingers, then twisted her hair up and let it fall.

"Forget the police blotter—I'm probably going to get thrown out of office. But it'll be worth it." All pretense of self-restraint went into the Dumpster along with Summer's headband, and they spent a few glorious minutes panting and kissing and laughing like teenagers at the Cheeky Tiki. And then . . .

"Mayor Jansen!" A shrill, panicked female voice echoed down the alley. "There you are! I've been looking all over town."

Summer gave Dutch's earlobe one last nibble and whispered, "You might want to get your hand off my ass." Then she ducked out from his embrace and waved to the agitated woman. "Well, you found him."

Dutch straightened up, his crisp white shirt now rumpled. "Mrs. Bucciol. How nice to see you."

Mrs. Bucciol wore a dirt-smudged gardening smock and wide-brimmed hat. "Dora and Frank Post are putting their beach chairs on my property. They're supposed to carry them back to their own house every night, but instead they just lean them against my fence. On *my* property."

"Dun dun *dunnn*," Summer murmured.

"I have tried to be a good neighbor—you know me, Mayor—but they simply won't cooperate. Frank says the beach side of the fence is public property."

Dutch shifted back into mayor mode, calm and unflappable. "I appreciate you voicing your concerns."

Mrs. Bucciol narrowed her eyes. "There are rules about the beach dunes, you know."

"There are." Dutch nodded.

"And their folding chairs are on *my* side of the fence."

"So you've said."

"I already called the sheriff's department. But I want you to talk to them personally. Make them see reason—that I am right and they are wrong."

Dutch tried to hand the woman his business card. "I'd be more than happy to—"

"Right now." Mrs. Bucciol addressed Summer. "This is the marvelous thing about a small town like Black Dog Bay. You're on a first-name basis with your city officials, and they'll drop everything to help their neighbors."

Summer straightened Dutch's tie and patted his shirtfront. "Have fun."

He growled low in his throat. "I hate my job."

She stepped back toward the bar's door and threw a saucy wink at him. "Until we meet again, Mayor Jansen."

He grabbed her hand and reeled her back in. "Before you go, I wanted to ask you something."

"Well, you're in luck," she murmured. "I'm in the mood to do your bidding."

He cleared his throat and glanced at Mrs. Bucciol, who was watching them with rapt attention. "I want you to . . ."

"Yes? Don't be shy." She cupped a hand to her ear. "It's impossible to shock me, you know. I'm shockproof."

But nothing could have prepared her for his request.

"I want you to teach Ingrid to drive."

The next day, Summer helped stage a vehicular intervention in the Jansens' blue living room. Tensions were running high, with Dutch making his stand by the coffee table and Ingrid holding her ground at the piano.

Summer positioned herself between the two siblings and attempted to open negotiations. "Why am I here, again?"

"I have no idea." Ingrid launched into an angry concerto.

"Yes, you do." Dutch had to raise his voice to be heard over the pounding from the piano. "She needs to learn to drive and she refuses to let me teach her."

Summer turned to Ingrid. "Your rebuttal?"

Ingrid ignored her, pouring her energy into dark, turbulent chords and echoing pedal work.

Summer crossed over to the piano and closed the wooden key lid. "Stop showing off and use your words, punk."

Ingrid snatched her fingers back and slumped down on the bench with a sullen expression. "Would you want him teaching *you* how to drive?"

"Um . . ." Summer fought to stay on task as her mind flooded with images from the country club parking lot. "Why not? I'm a hundred percent sure he's a better driver than I am."

"That's why I don't want him teaching me. He'll be all, 'You didn't check your blind spot' and 'You didn't come to a complete stop.'"

"I would not be like that." Dutch looked offended.

"Please," Summer scoffed. "You totally would."

"It's fine." Ingrid reopened the keyboard and flexed her fingers. "I don't need to drive yet."

"Yes, you do," Dutch said. "For your own safety. What if—let's just say—you're out with a friend who drinks too much and you need to get home from some seedy club? What if I'm at work and there's an emergency? What if—"

"Wait, wait. Why are we talking about all these dire scenarios? You're seventeen!" Summer cried. "Did you pass the test to get your learner's permit?"

"Yes," Ingrid admitted. "But only because he made me."

"How can you *not* want to learn to drive? Doesn't everyone want to drive? Does not compute."

Ingrid examined a hangnail. "Driving is scary."

"Driving is awesome!" Summer said. "Sweet freedom! Wind in your hair! Music on the radio! World at your feet!"

"Eyes on the road," Dutch added.

"A car is a huge, heavy, dangerous machine." Ingrid's eyes were solemn and dark. "One wrong move, one lapse in attention, and you could kill someone. Or yourself."

Summer had no idea how to respond to this because her own perspective at seventeen had been the polar opposite. "Is this, like, some deep-rooted trauma thing?"

"There's no trauma." Dutch glanced at his phone as his text alert beeped. "She's just being difficult."

Ingrid clutched the edge of the piano bench. "So now I'm difficult because I don't want to be responsible for steering a two-ton hunk of metal around hairpin turns at high rates of speed?"

"Hang on. Do my ears deceive me?" Summer leaned forward, blinking in disbelief. "Little Miss Responsible doesn't want to be responsible?"

Ingrid's knuckles went white as she clenched her fingers tighter. "Not for other people, no." And Summer recognized that tone and that body language: Ingrid didn't trust herself. She had no faith in her own instincts.

That, Summer could understand. She also understood that the only cure for self-doubt was swift and decisive action.

"You know what? I'm not going to stand here arguing. This isn't debate club." Summer pulled her car keys out of her bag. "Front and center, Ingrid."

"I told you, I'm not—"

Summer nodded at Dutch, and together, they grabbed Ingrid, pried her off the piano bench, and carried her kicking and screaming out to the driveway.

"This is kidnapping!" Ingrid screeched. A pair of seagulls screeched back. "You can't make me!"

"Welcome to adulthood," Summer announced, "where you have to do all kinds of crap you don't feel like doing. I had to play tennis at dawn this morning. Do you think I felt like doing that?"

"Oh, boohoo." Ingrid made a break for the porch, but Dutch cut her off.

Summer yanked open the driver's side door of her little red convertible. "Get in."

Beth Kendrick

Ingrid dug her heels into the white gravel. "No way. I'm not wrecking your Mercedes."

"Calm down. I learned to drive in this thing; you think it hasn't been wrecked before?" Summer tossed the keys to Ingrid, who instinctively caught them. "Good girl."

"I'm not going to be responsible for wrecking it again."

"You're right—you're not going to wreck it. You're going to drive it like a normal human being. Get. In."

Ingrid sat in the driver's seat, but refused to put the keys into the ignition. "I'm not driving."

"Oh, yes you are."

"Says who?"

"Me." Summer played her trump card. "Your mentor."

"But you said—"

"Changed my mind. I'm officially your mentor now. And as your mentor, I'm ordering you to shut your mouth, adjust the mirrors, and put the keys in the ignition."

Ingrid complied, sulking as only a teenage girl can sulk. "You're going to be sorry."

"I already am."

"Good luck." Dutch rubbed the back of his neck. "If anyone needs me, I'll be inside having a nervous breakdown."

"Have one for me, too, while you're at it." Summer buckled her seat belt, opened a fresh bag of M&M's, and focused her attention on Ingrid. "Okay, now put your foot on the brake, put the car into gear, and move your foot to the gas pedal. Here we go."

"How was the driving lesson?" Dutch was waiting on the porch with a glass of red wine when Ingrid pulled the car back into the driveway.

Summer's jaw muscles still ached from trying not to scream. "So great."

"Summer says I'm a natural!" Ingrid slammed out of the car, bounded up the porch steps, and practically pirouetted. "I made a few mistakes, though."

"Oh, honey, don't worry." Summer followed her in, clutching the porch railing for support. "Everyone goes the wrong way down a one-way street once in a while. Sometimes on purpose, if traffic is really bad." She coughed. "I hear. The important thing is, we didn't get caught."

Ingrid beamed. "That's true. And I only hit one trash can."

"And you braked for the cat." Summer shuddered at the memory. "Like I said, a natural." She tried to accept the wineglass Dutch offered, but her hands were shaking too much.

"Ooh! Next time we should go on the highway! Let's go tomorrow. Can you come over to the country club? I have a lunch break at noon."

"No can do." Summer staggered into the living room and collapsed on the sofa. "I'm playing golf against my will at eleven."

"That's okay. We can go after you finish golfing. And then you can teach me how to parallel park."

Summer lifted up her head from the plaid throw pillow. "Are you nuts? *I* don't even know how to parallel park."

"You must." Ingrid placed the car keys on the table next to Summer's bag. "You have to parallel park to pass the test to get your license, don't you?"

"Not if you flirt with the test instructor."

"It was amazing," Ingrid gushed to Dutch. "Wind in my hair, music on the radio, sweet freedom! I can't believe I didn't want to try this. Pretty soon I'll be driving at night, with headlights and everything!"

"Oh, I'm sure your brother wants to teach you that," Summer said. "Night driving can be tricky, and you know he's very protective."

Dutch leaned down and patted her ankle. "Yes, but thanks to you, I'm trying to loosen my iron fist of tyranny."

She gave his knee a little kick. "Aren't you supposed to be a control freak?"

"I'll make an exception for you."

"Aw. You guys are so cute. Want me to leave so you can have some"—Ingrid lowered her voice dramatically—"alone time?"

"Yes," Dutch said. "Get out."

"Have fun, you crazy kids." Ingrid picked up her earth-friendly reusable tote bag and headed out the front door.

"Next lesson, you're driving to the store to buy a real handbag!" Summer yelled after her.

The screen door slammed.

"Shouldn't we ask where she's off to?" Summer asked.

Dutch shook his head. "She'll be fine. Probably going to the movies or the library or—"

"What seventeen-year-old goes to the library on a Friday afternoon?"

"I'll be at the bookstore!" Ingrid called from halfway down the driveway. Summer heard the crunch of footsteps on the gravel.

Dutch lifted up Summer's ankles, then sat down on the couch with her feet in his lap. "How was the driving lesson, really?"

She put the back of her hand to her forehead. "You know how I almost died in an air disaster? This was worse."

"You're a good mentor."

"I'm not right. I'll never be right again."

Dutch picked the wineglass off the table, took a sip, then handed it back to her. "You need this."

She waved him off. "I'm beyond wine at this point. I need, like, street drugs."

"I don't think you're going to find many of those in Black Dog Bay."

"Even down by the boardwalk?"

He thought this over. "Maybe you could score some NyQuil.

Possibly a cigar or two, but you can't smoke in public areas, so you might get fined or arrested."

"You're running a police state here."

"I'll be sure to bring that up at the next council meeting."

"Well, if I get arrested buying black market NyQuil, does that mean I don't have to do any more driving with Ingrid?"

He laughed. "Was it that bad?"

"It was like Grand Theft Auto with Beethoven in the background. Your sister likes to listen to classical music even while she's tooling around in a convertible. She says it helps her concentrate."

"You two are good for each other. She really looks up to you. She says you're her—"

"Do not even say the word." Summer fell silent, listening to the waves and the gulls and a wind chime in the distance.

"We've got a few hours to ourselves." His hand slid up her shin. "We could go out."

"No way. I'm never getting in a car again."

His hand inched under the hem of her skirt. "We could stay in. You won't even have to get off the couch."

"Seriously? This isn't high school." She shifted, her skin sliding against his. "I am not going to spend the whole night making out with you on the couch." Then she pounced, straddling him. "Not when there's a perfectly good bed right upstairs."

He kissed her. "Being a grown-up rules."

She kissed him back. "I know, right?"

They heard the porch boards creak, and then a familiar voice: "Mayor Jansen?"

Summer and Dutch stared at each other, eyes huge, bodies shaking with silent laughter.

"Yoo-hoo! Mayor Jansen?" The doorbell rang. "Dora Post's beach chairs are on my fence again."

Summer pulled back a fraction of an inch and whispered, "Do you need to get that?"

Dutch undid her top button. "No."

"I know you're in there." Mrs. Bucciol was sounding less neighborly by the second. "Your car is right outside. Open the door!"

Summer let herself tumble sideways onto the couch cushions. "You really need to reconsider your career choices."

Dutch tossed his shirt on the floor. "We're locking the door and going upstairs."

Summer slid her hands along his shoulders and pressed her cheek against his back. "Don't you get tired of bossing everyone around all day? Making all those decisions? Solving all those problems?"

"Sometimes."

"I thought so. That's why I'll be calling the shots tonight. First, I'm going to—" Her sultry-voiced promise was cut short by the doorbell ringing five times in succession.

"Wait your turn!" Mrs. Bucciol cried. "I was here first!"

"I wouldn't have to be here at all if you weren't such a fussbudget!" hissed a new female voice. "I'm supposed to be on vacation!"

"Let me guess," Summer said. "Dora Post?"

The porch sounded like it might collapse as the two women jostled each other and yelled, "Mayor Jansen!"

Dutch set his jaw and yanked his shirt back on. "To be continued."

"Promises, promises." Summer buttoned up and saw herself out the side door.

After she got into her little red convertible, she glanced up at the house and saw Dutch pacing around the living room, brokering a peace agreement over lawn chairs like it was the Treaty of Versailles.

She was sorry she had to leave—and not just because she was missing out on what promised to be some truly great sex.

cure for the common breakup   167

She was missing out on his company. Yes, she liked making out with him, but she actually wanted to talk to him, too. He made her laugh. He made her think. He made her want to stay.

Oh no.

She sat in the driver's seat, belted in, hands positioned at ten and two, perfectly safe and immobile. But when she closed her eyes, she was back in the jump seat while the plane plummeted through the dark—her mind blank with terror, her lungs burning, her heart opening up at exactly the wrong moment.

Never again. She'd sworn to herself she'd never allow herself to endure another free fall. She'd retreated, she'd refused to fly, but here she was all over again.

Bracing for impact.

chapter 20

"This isn't going to end well," Summer told her best friend the next day. "Mark my words, Em."

"I don't know—sounds pretty juicy to me." Static crackled on Emily's side of the phone connection.

"Which is why all my rational logic is useless." Summer stacked her bare feet on Hattie Huntington's desk. The Purple Palace had a designated office outfitted with antique furniture and cutting-edge computer equipment, but since Hattie never stepped foot in the room, Summer had appropriated it for her own use. "Okay, you know how I love dark, handsome alpha males?"

"You love arrogant assholes with more looks than brains," Emily decreed. "Not that I'm judging."

Summer didn't bother refuting the truth. "Well, Dutch is the opposite of that. He's restrained and well-mannered. But there's something else underneath all that. He has this, like, raw, masculine, commanding . . ."

Emily laughed. "You sound like you're reading the back of a bodice ripper."

"I don't know what it is about him." Summer realized her

forehead was dotted with perspiration, despite the arctic air-conditioning. "After all these years of guitar players and soccer stars, I'm suddenly drooling over gray flannel and cuff links. Cuff links, Em."

"I don't even know who you are anymore."

"And I burned all of my fancy black European lingerie—another story for another time—and replaced it with lavender."

This got Emily's full attention. "You're wearing lavender again? Voluntarily?"

"I can't get enough of it! And neither can he! Madness, I tell you!" Summer swung her feet down to the Tibetan rug and sat up straight. "He and I made a pact. We had an agreement, and it did not include hanging out in broad daylight and meeting each other's friends and families. But now I'm teaching his sister to drive, and it was his idea!"

"Wait. You ran down his rose garden, and he's letting you give driving lessons?" Emily whistled. "This guy has more twists and turns than a bagful of weasels."

Summer braced her elbow on the desk and let her head drop into her palm. "I have to leave before someone gets hurt."

"You don't have to leave."

"Yes, I do."

"No, you don't. Perpetual motion is not the answer to all of life's problems." Emily took a deep breath. "You don't always have to walk it off, or whatever your mother used to say."

Summer still associated those words with her mother, Nicola, though Nicola had never once uttered the phrase. An amateur painter who grew up in privilege, Nicola had been a big believer in fate.

Love was a calling, not an obligation.

Summer had been five years old when her beautiful blond mother had hired an afternoon babysitter to care for Summer while Jules taught and wrote on campus.

"Have fun, darling." Nicola would give Summer a hug as she prepared to depart for her new studio—a mysterious loft that Summer never visited. The leasing of the studio coincided with other changes in her mother; Nicola seemed distracted and smelled of a new floral perfume. "Mama's going to go work for a few hours."

Kristi, a jocular, ruddy-cheeked softball player, was the kind of babysitter Summer wished could be her older sister. She took Summer to the park to ride her bike and climb the jungle gym. When Summer fell down, her lower lip trembling as blood appeared on a scrape on her knee, Kristi would clap her hands and cry, "Walk it off! Walk it off!"

And Summer did. She learned that cuts stopped bleeding if you ignored them. Pain lessened if you kept pedaling.

One evening, while Jules gave a poetry reading, Nicola buckled Summer into the car and drove across town to a fancy restaurant Summer had never been to. An unsmiling, handsome man was waiting at a table.

"Summer, I want you to meet someone." Nicola's voice sounded lilting, supplicating, and Summer knew that her mother was nervous.

When Summer looked at the man, she could tell from the way he looked back that he didn't like children. He didn't like her. But her mother wanted him to like her, and so she tried. She sat still and said "please" and "thank you" and put her napkin on her lap. She was careful, oh so careful, but when she reached for the bread basket, she spilled her orange soda all over the table.

The man's expression didn't change, but his eyes did. And Summer knew, as the icy wetness seeped into her dress, that she had ruined everything.

Her mother left two weeks later. Summer came home from a trip to the pumpkin patch with Kristi sporting a fresh Band-Aid on her shin, anxious to show off her new battle scar, to tell her mom that she had walked it off.

Nicola had smiled and nodded, but Summer could tell she wasn't really listening. "I'm going to be away for a few days." Nicola's hands had twisted together. "Just a little while."

"Where are you going?" Summer asked. "Can I come?"

"I'll be back soon, but I want you to be good while I'm gone." Nicola gave Summer a kiss on each cheek. "I love you, I love you, I love you, my baby girl."

Summer pulled away, frightened by the panic in her mother's voice and the tears glistening in her eyes. "Why are you crying?"

"I'm in love." Nicola had looked miserable about this, but she still left, stacking her suitcases in the trunk of her car and driving away before Jules got home.

Over the next few weeks, when Summer asked or cried for her mother, her father stormed into his study and locked the door, so she stopped crying. She stopped asking.

Her grandmother came to stay through the holidays and predicted, with grim satisfaction, "She'll be back. Wait and see. She'll come crawling back."

But Nicola never came back. She sent postcards and paintings, she called every night at first, but then her contact tapered off. For years, Summer remained convinced that she'd lost her mother because she'd spilled a soda.

Later, of course, she realized that life wasn't that simple. Her parents had unknowable pasts and inner lives she would never be privy to. Fate trumped commitment. Love lasted until you fell in love again.

And Summer had been walking that off, across six continents, for almost three decades.

"Hello?" Emily sounded a little panicked. "Are you still there?"

Summer snapped back to the here and now. "I'm still here."

"Sorry if that was out of bounds. I just—"

"It's fine." Summer paused. "But I do have to leave." She paused again. "We have an agreement."

"Well, I say enjoy the cuff links while you can. And the bodice-ripper sex."

Summer said good-bye as Miss Huntington walked into the room. "Gotta go. Cruella calls."

Hattie never left her bedroom looking anything less than impeccable, and this morning, she was decked out in a simple black blouse, coral pedal pushers, and matching coral loafers. Her snow-white hair was pulled back into a silver clip at the nape of her neck. She made no mention of the fact that Summer was still in pajamas, but her expression conveyed her displeasure. "Miss Benson, may I ask why you're lounging around my personal office?"

"You never use it," Summer pointed out. "Somebody should. Do you have any idea how fast your Internet connection is? It's like military-grade."

Hattie narrowed her eyes and studied Summer's face. "You look tired."

"I'm fine." Summer fought back a yawn.

"You're tired." Hattie thinned her lips. "And when you are tired, you are of no use to me on the tennis court or the putting green."

"I'm of no use to you, anyway," Summer pointed out. "Yesterday, you said my serve looked like a chimpanzee hitting a melon with a baseball bat."

"I don't want you coming home so late. I like to think of myself as a fair-minded and generous employer—"

Summer laughed out loud.

"When I'm not in need of your companionship, you're free to come and go as you please. But I expect you to exercise good judgment and self-control, and if you won't, I will. Henceforth, your curfew is ten o'clock."

Summer's jaw dropped. *"P.m.?"*

"Of course, p.m. You need to be well rested for our morning outings."

"I'm thirty-two," Summer pointed out. "You can't give me a curfew."

"I'm your boss," Hattie shot back. "I can do whatever I please."

Summer put her bare feet back on the desk, enjoying a little stab of satisfaction as Hattie winced. "I know you refuse to fire me, but can I quit?"

"No."

"Why?"

"Because I said so. You accompany me at my pleasure."

"I demand a union rep."

Hattie shrugged. "You're free to leave whenever you choose. Just as I'm free to pursue my lawsuit with the wine bar. Now put your shoes back on and get your feet off my furniture."

Summer eyed the stack of mail on the corner of the desk. "Do you even know how to turn this computer on?"

"No. And I have no intention of learning."

"It'd make your life much easier." Summer powered up the system and marveled at the crisp, clear resolution on the monitor. "I can teach you how to pay bills and manage your money online—"

"I have people for that."

"How to check the weather and surf conditions."

"I have people for that."

"How to organize all your correspondence and thank-you notes."

"Miss Benson, a well-brought-up lady would sooner die than send a thank-you by electronic mail."

"E-mail," Summer corrected. "That's what the kids are calling it these days. And I'm not saying you should send the actual notes by e-mail. I'm saying you could keep all the addresses and contact information in a nice, orderly spreadsheet." She opened the Web browser and clicked through the highlights of cyberspace. "You could post pictures of your chauffeured Rolls-Royce and your fancy-schmancy pool on Facebook."

Hattie sniffed. "Facebook is a bastion of vulgarity."

"You could Google-stalk all the people you hate and laugh at their misfortunes." At this, Summer detected a spark of interest in Hattie's eyes. "You have no idea what you're missing."

"Thank you, but no."

Summer brightened. "There's this newfangled thing called 'online dating.'"

Hattie couldn't have looked more stricken if Summer had physically punched her. "Never."

"Yes! You'll stay out past curfew, I'll stay out past curfew—everybody wins." Summer pulled up a dating site. "A few nights out with some silver fox would do wonders for your disposition. Give you something to look forward to besides frivolous lawsuits. Who knows? You might even enjoy yourself."

Hattie took a step back toward the door. "I don't want to enjoy myself."

"That's your problem right there. We're totally signing you up for eHarmony. Or maybe you're more of a Match.com girl? Screw it, we'll sign you up for both. You can afford it." Summer started clicking away with the mouse. "Give me back my phone and we'll get started. First, you take some selfies in your bathroom mirror—pink tube top optional—and then you—"

"I don't comprehend a single syllable you just said."

Summer rolled her eyes. "Fine. You can take your selfies in the mirror over the mantel at the country club. And you can wear a St. John jacket instead of a tube top. Then we'll write up a profile and you can specify what you want in a guy."

"I don't want a guy." Hattie practically spit the word out.

"My bad. You can specify what you prefer in a *gentleman*. I'm thinking we're targeting the Ebenezer Scrooge crowd—am I right? Introvert? Pessimist? Lots of disposable income?"

"Miss Benson, your impertinence is breathtaking."

"Thanks; I get that a lot." Her fingers flew over the keyboard as she started compiling a list.

"Cease and desist," Hattie snapped.

"Is that a legally binding order?" Summer asked. "Should I be expecting a strongly worded letter from your attorney?"

"I have no interest in sifting through the chaff of humanity in some bizarre and impersonal imitation of courtship." Hattie turned toward the bay window and stared off toward the ocean. "There's no other man who will ever do."

Summer pushed back from the desk. "I knew it! So there was a man?"

Hattie ignored her.

"What happened? Was it tragic?"

"It's none of your affair."

"One of the Jansens, right? Is that why you have it out for Dutch?"

"I'd drop the subject, Miss Benson, unless you want me to book a seven a.m. tee time tomorrow. Eighteen holes."

Summer ceased and desisted. "Fine. Let's set you up with some live-streaming music, at least." She browsed through the music offerings. "Maybe they have an all-jitterbug channel."

Hattie's nostrils flared. "Exactly how old do you think I am?"

"Beats me. A lady never reveals her age or her weight, right?"

"Seven o'clock tee time it is. I suggest you retire early tonight."

Miss Huntington skipped afternoon tea and sent word through Turner that she'd be "dining out" for supper, so Summer changed into a navy sundress, hopped in the red convertible, and headed over to the Jansen house to see if Ingrid wanted to try driving again.

When she parked on the white gravel driveway, she noted that the wooden trellis had been repaired and the run-over rosebushes had been replaced with tiny, sparse brown seedlings. No one answered the doorbell, but she heard rustling from the other side of the house, so she followed the wraparound porch to the backyard, which sloped down to the beach.

The last time she'd been over here, she'd been too busy making out with Dutch on the couch to notice the view. What had probably once been the perfect lawn for hosting barbecues and parties was now a huge rectangular rose garden framed by white paving stones. A sea of blossoms stretched out from the porch to the edge of the ocean. The roses were arranged by color—stripes of red, yellow, pink, and white against a blue background of sky and water—and the visual effect was breathtaking. Summer braced herself for an overpowering olfactory assault, yet there was only a trace of floral perfume mingling with the salty sea breeze and the tang of pine.

And in the middle of all those blooms and thorns and earth and sky, Dutch was hard at work.

He had his back to her, and for a moment, she leaned against the side of the house and watched him.

Over the last few weeks, she'd gotten used to seeing him in collared shirts and ties. Spotless shoes and shiny watches. Close shaves and combed hair and always, always, the right words on the tip of his tongue.

But now, he looked the way he had the day she first met him: jeans, a sweat-soaked gray T-shirt, and calfskin gloves. His forearms were tan and his brown hair glinted bronze in the fading sunlight. As she changed position, she could see the muscles shifting in his back. He was in his element here, kneeling in the dirt with the cool breeze blowing in from the ocean and the sun-drenched earth radiating warmth. She could tell, even without seeing his face, that he was happy.

She hung back for a moment, relishing the silence and the fleeting sense of balance.

Finally, she pushed off the wall and started down the stone path past a white picnic table. "I like your outfit."

He looked up, then took in her short, ruffled dress with a smile. "I like yours, too."

"I'd ask what you're doing, but I'm guessing you don't want me anywhere near your roses."

He raised one gloved hand and beckoned her closer. "I'll take my chances."

She stepped into the field, careful not to trample the rosebushes in various states of growth. Some were truncated outcroppings of brown sticks, some had just started sprouting green leaves, and some were in full bloom.

Her sandals sank into the loamy ground, and she winced as pine needles and thorns pricked her bare toes. "I'm no expert, but aren't you supposed to plant in spring?"

"Not really. You want them to bloom pretty much continuously, except for the dormant season." He waited for her, hand still outstretched. "And since I had to replant everything by the driveway, I decided to try out some new strains back here, too."

"Driveway?" She batted her eyelashes, the picture of innocence. "What happened to your driveway?"

He grinned. "These new ones don't have much of a scent, but they're disease-resistant and salt-resistant. Bulletproof."

Summer glanced at the pocketknife in his hand and the clippers by his feet. "Don't you need a shovel if you're ripping things out of the ground?"

"Nope. You don't need to replant the whole bush. You can keep the rootstock intact and just graft new buds."

"I'm new to this," Summer reminded him. "Talk slow and use small words."

"The roots can survive a lot of trauma, even if the branches are damaged. Just cut the stems down, below the broken part, and it'll grow back healthy. You can transplant new buds onto the old growth." He handed her the tiny, super-sharp knife. "Want to give it a try?"

She peered down at the mounds of dirt. "Won't that ruin my manicure?"

"It'll be worth it. Come on." He wrapped his soft leather glove around her fingers and tugged her down next to him.

"I take it Ingrid's not here?" She knelt down next to the smallest seedling.

"Nope." He moved behind her, guiding her hands. Together, they selected a rose in full bloom, excised a slender branch, and cut off all the leaves, exposing three tiny green buds.

"I feel like I just committed rose murder," she said. "Again. This is just a stick now. Not even—it's half a stick."

"Six weeks from now, you'll be able to get a bouquet out of this stick." He showed her how to slice the buds off and tuck them into little pockets of bark in another bush.

"What color are these going to be?" she asked.

"Red, mostly. I like to keep the color ratio even."

"Of course you do." She nestled into the contours of his body. "But theoretically you could, like, make a pattern or write a message with different colors? 'Dutch was here'?"

She could feel the rumble of his laugh against her back. "If you were so inclined and had an infinite amount of patience, I guess you could."

"I can't get over this garden," she marveled. "And I can't

believe you work all day in your office and then come home and work in the yard."

"I like it." He kept moving, readjusting her grip on the knife. "No debates, no arguments. Sometimes you just want to pull up weeds without taking it through eighteen committee meetings."

"I could see that."

"You put in the work, you see the results."

She lifted her head. "And you don't have to listen to fights about beach chairs or a bunch of women drinking wine and cursing their exes?"

He brushed his cheek against hers. "And I don't have to wear a tie."

Summer could feel him smiling, and she smiled, too. "These roses are magic. They make me not care about anything." She closed her eyes. She could still see the golden glow of the sun and feel the warmth on her cheeks. "I'm trying to give a damn, and I just can't. I'm physically incapable."

"See? It's the perfect antidote to a city council meeting."

He wrapped his arms around her waist and they tumbled onto the ground. Summer yelped as thorns and pine needles pricked her bare arms. "Ow. Ow! Ow."

The little bursts of pain made her realize how much she *hadn't* been feeling. The all-consuming sorrow that had threatened to drown her those first few days in Black Dog Bay had subsided to . . . nothingness. She'd been distant and detached and blessedly numb.

But not right now.

Right now, surrounded by green leaves and sharp thorns and pops of red and yellow roses and blue sky, she couldn't suppress a rush of emotion. Her brain understood that this was temporary, that the euphoria she was feeling right now was nothing more than an artificial high that would wear off and leave her even emptier than before. Her heart was still untouchable. But her body craved contact.

Dutch got up and hauled her to her feet. "Sorry about that."

"Don't be." Summer dropped the knife. "I'm kind of having a hard time keeping my hands off you right now."

"I don't remember asking you to restrain yourself." He straightened up, smiled slow and sexy, and kissed her.

She ran her hand along the inside of his arm, where his skin was hatch marked with raised, red lines. "These are from the rosebushes?"

"Mm-hmm."

"So all day long, while you're chairing zoning committee hearings or whatever, you're all scratched up under your suit?"

"Yeah."

She threw both arms around his neck. "Take my clothes off."

He started to take off his work gloves, but she stopped him.

His gray eyes darkened with intensity. "I'm going to get you all dirty."

"Yes, please."

He backed her up a few steps and lifted her to sit on the edge of the white picnic table.

The old wood creaked as she shifted her weight. "I hope this thing can hold me."

"It will," he assured her. "I built it."

Summer braced her hands behind her and looked up at him. "You put this together yourself? With, like, tools and sweat and the gloves you're wearing right now?"

He lowered his mouth to her ear and murmured, "Sawed the lumber myself."

She grabbed a fistful of his damp T-shirt. "Oh my God, I— yep, I just came again."

He shucked off his gloves and ran his bare hands along the undersides of her arms.

"Mmm. You smell all woodsy and delectable." She shivered at the feel of his calluses against her smooth skin. "I didn't know men like you existed in real life."

He brushed a lock of hair back from her forehead. "I didn't know women like you existed."

"Oh, I don't." She hooked one ankle around his waist. "I'm an optical illusion. A figment of your imagination. For a limited time only."

He rested his hands on her hips and nibbled her earlobe. "Then we better make every second count."

Heartbreak happy hour was in full swing at the Whinery when Summer dropped by. The crowd at the bar was three deep and "Someone Like You" was playing in the background.

When it was finally Summer's turn to place her order, Jenna took in the dirt-smudged cheeks, tousled hair, and blade of grass stuck to the front of the sundress. "You look like you've had quite a day." She pulled out vermouth and champagne and started mixing a Cure for the Common Breakup.

Summer took a sip and closed her eyes as the sweet, sharp tastes swirled together on her tongue. "Hey, did you switch to a different brand of champagne?"

Jenna shook her head. "Nope."

"Different vermouth?"

"Everything's exactly the same as always. Why?"

"Because this is, like, the best drink I've ever had in my entire life." Summer took another sip, marveling at the harmony of flavors. "It's just so . . . so fizzy and orangey and delicious!"

Jenna furrowed her brow. "Are you okay?"

"I'm better than okay. I am fan-fucking-tabulous." Summer sighed in contentment. "Can we change the music? I love Adele, but this song's a downer."

"Sure. What would you prefer?" Jenna handed over the iPod.

Summer scrolled through the song options. "Katy Perry. 'Teenage Dream.'"

"Oh. My. God." Jenna slammed down the bottle of vermouth and grabbed Summer's arm. "You and Dutch are totally doing it."

Summer grinned. "Can't a girl pick out a pop song without being harassed and accused?"

"Not around here." Jenna's expression cycled between delight and disbelief. "You love him. You love him and he loves you and you're going to settle down here and be the First Lady of Black Dog Bay forever."

"Not forever," Summer corrected. "Just until Labor Day. For a limited time only."

chapter 21

"Tell me about Italy," Hattie commanded the next morning after she finished torturing Summer on the tennis court. "Have you been to Florence? Capri?"

Summer braced her hands on her knees, gasping for breath and dripping sweat. The only thing keeping her from collapsing was sheer stubbornness.

She took her sweet time catching her breath and gulping from her water bottle. "Well, I've been to Florence, but I had such a good time, I don't really remember much. If you have questions about limoncello, though, I'm your girl."

Hattie folded her spindly arms over her tennis whites, which still looked fresh and crisp. "I hear you've disregarded my advice and consorted with the Jansen boy again."

Summer wrung out her ponytail and looked longingly at the pool on the other side of the yard. "I'm surprised you got the gossip so fast. Who are you still speaking to around here?"

Hattie just glared at her. "So you admit it?"

"That we, um, consorted? I guess." Summer turned away to hide a secret smile. "Although we were outside on a picnic table and

covered with dirt, so 'consorted' seems a little fancy." She tossed a
tennis ball in the air and caught it. "How about if we just say I hit
that?"

"Why?" Hattie tossed her racket down on the clay. "*Why* must
you delight in being so déclassé?"

"I thought we were talking about Capri. Instead of asking me
about some new city every day, why don't you just go?"

"Don't be absurd. I'm too old."

"You just whipped my butt at tennis. You're healthy, you're
wealthy, but you're not going to live forever."

Hattie sniffed, but didn't argue, so Summer persisted.

"You've been badgering me all week. First Dublin, then Bath,
and now you want me to describe Capri in lurid detail? I'm not
your travel-porn purveyor! Just hop on a plane, already."

"It's not that simple."

"Actually, it is. You can book tickets online. Give me an Internet connection and a credit card, and I'll take care of everything."

Hattie hesitated so long that Summer thought the old lady
might actually agree. But then Hattie bounced a tennis ball on the
ground and asked, "While you were pickling your liver in Florence, did you happen to stagger through the Uffizi?"

"Enough!" Summer kicked off her shoes and peeled off her
shirt. "I'm melting!" She dived into the deep end of the pool clad
in socks, her tennis skirt, and a sports bra.

She took her time coming up for air, relishing the silence and
the chill of the water against her flushed skin. When she splashed
back to the surface, she waved to Hattie and yelled, "Come on in!
I dare you!"

Hattie glowered. "Put your clothes back on this instant, or
I'll . . . I'll . . ."

"You'll what?" Summer filled her cheeks with water and
spouted into the air like a Florentine fountain. "Fire me?"

"Don't you wish, Miss Benson." Hattie looked around, at a loss. "Now get out of that pool immediately or I'll confiscate your cell phone for the rest of the month."

"Coming, Mom." Summer sloshed over to the side and hoisted herself up the ladder with the very least amount of grace she could muster. When Hattie handed her a towel, Summer debated hip-checking the old bat into the shallow end, but chickened out at the last second.

Breakfast awaited them on the back porch, the table set with embroidered linens, sterling silver, and fresh flowers. Hattie perched on one of the hand-carved white chairs and lifted an eyebrow at Summer. "I'll wait while you change into something dry and presentable." She glanced pointedly at the array of warm foods cooling on the table. "Take your time."

Summer did, stopping to check Facebook, Twitter, e-mail, texts, and a trio of celebrity gossip blogs before she returned to the table in a faded T-shirt emblazoned with her airline's corporate logo.

Hattie helped herself to a tiny portion of fresh melon. "Don't you get tired of traveling, Miss Benson? All those time zones, all those airports?"

"Nope. I love it." Summer snagged a croissant and took a bite before she'd even sat down. "I love seeing new things, meeting new people, trying every single cultural variation on chocolate. I'm really not cut out for long-term commitments."

"I see. Then you're not planning to stay in Black Dog Bay permanently?"

"'Permanently' isn't part of my vocabulary." Summer took a sip of freshly squeezed lemonade. "Wow, that's delicious. Do you lace it with crack, or what?"

"I believe the chef puts in a few sprigs of fresh lavender."

Summer could feel her expression change at the word

"lavender," and Hattie must have noticed, too, because she asked, "What, precisely, are you doing with Mayor Jansen?"

"Um, defiling his picnic table?" Summer glanced from side to side. "Is this a trick question?"

Hattie pushed her plate and silverware aside. "I can't tell if you're trying to deceive me or yourself."

"I'm not deceiving anybody. I was *there*, lady." Summer turned sideways in her chair and hooked one arm over the back. "When I defile a picnic table, I do a thorough job."

"You love him." It was a statement, not a question.

Summer swallowed her bite of pastry the wrong way and started hacking and wheezing. Hattie didn't lift a finger to assist or even summon Turner.

After she finally managed to clear her airway by guzzling the rest of her lemonade, Summer glared at Hattie. "You know, when you were choking to death, I tried to help."

"Yes, and look how that worked out for you."

Summer rested one elbow on the table and made a point of chewing with her mouth open.

Hattie responded by signaling Turner to clear Summer's plate. "Now. Back to you and the object of your undying devotion."

Summer plucked a few strawberries straight out of the serving dish. "First of all, I don't have undying devotion for him. I'm faithless and fickle—you can ask anyone. And P.S., he's not an object, Miss Huntington. He is a *human being*."

"Of course." A tiny smile played on the old woman's crinkled lips. "How crass to imply otherwise."

"Us plebs are people, too."

"I'll make every effort to remember that." Miss Huntington repositioned her chair to remain shaded as the morning sun rose higher over the horizon. "Why do you love him?"

Summer ignored the bait and countered with, "Why do you hate him? What'd he do to you?"

"Nothing."

"Then what's your problem?"

Hattie stared out at the ocean. "The Jansen men are also faithless and fickle, Miss Benson. My advice to you is to guard your heart."

"Fine. What about my body, though? Can I at least check 'have hot sex with an elected official' off my life list before I stop speaking to him?"

"Are you trying to shock me?"

"Is it working?"

"Hardly. I may look doddering and frail to you, but I lived through the sixties."

Summer pulled her knees up to her chest, nearly upending the table. "Finally, we get to the juicy stuff."

"The 'juicy stuff,' as you put it, never changes," Hattie said. "Love, lying, loss. Every generation thinks they've invented scandal."

"Well. My generation did invent sexting."

Hattie took her sweet time finishing a bite of fruit. "And mine invented miniskirts and birth control pills."

"Touché."

"I know you don't want to listen to an old woman. I wouldn't have when I was your age. But I recognize myself in you."

Summer threw up both palms. "No, you don't."

"Yes, I do." Hattie leveled the tines of her fork at Summer. "And mark my words, Dutch Jansen is going to break your heart."

"Oh, you don't have to worry about that." Summer waved her hand dismissively. "My heart's already broken. It's shriveled up like a putrid black raisin."

"You'll heal soon enough. That's why you're here."

"Wrong again. I'm here because I didn't have to board a plane to get here. I'm here because eating boardwalk fries on the beach beats running up medical bills in the ICU. I'm here because . . ."

Summer struggled to remember what *had* prompted her to head to the Delaware shore. "I got a sign from God by way of a booze-hound musician. But enough about me! Who broke your heart? I'm guessing he's connected to Dutch Jansen somehow." She tapped her temple. "Psychic."

Hattie, who had just moments ago been radiating vigor and stamina, now looked exhausted and frail. "Dutch is named after his grandfather, Mies Jansen."

"Let me take a wild guess: He was passionate, spontaneous, and searingly hot?"

"He was a duplicitous philanderer," Hattie spit out. "Who asked me to marry him."

"But it didn't work out." Summer tapped her head again and mouthed, "Psychic."

Hattie fumed in silence for a moment. Summer could practically see black smoke coming out of her ears, like a polyester wedding gown burning in a bonfire. Finally, the older woman spit out another two words: "My sister."

"Double betrayal." Summer grimaced. "Brutal. Hey, you want to go to the Whinery?"

"It's not even ten o'clock. The Whinery's not open, and besides—"

"You can't have this kind of conversation without a drink. Fact."

Hattie didn't refuse outright, so Summer dashed into the house, grabbed a crystal decanter from the liquor cabinet, and spiked the lemonade with some unidentified spirit.

"Ah, much better." Summer abandoned the table for the white wicker settee. "Now. Who broke your heart more: the guy or your sister?"

Hattie's ramrod posture never slackened, but she sipped the spiked lemonade. "They both betrayed me equally."

"Not buying it." Summer shook her head. "Who do you still miss? Who do you want to drunk dial when you're listening to the Andrews Sisters and throwing back shots of—what does a woman like you do shots of? Sherry? Liquid platinum with a chaser of pulverized diamonds?"

"I will hate them both forever," Hattie adjusted the delicate gold chain around her neck. "But for different reasons."

"And you're *sure* this guy was related to Dutch?"

"Spitting image."

Summer slipped off her sandals and tucked her bare feet under her. "That explains why you couldn't keep your hands off him."

"Mies Jansen broke my heart, dallied with my sister, and once he'd ruined our family forever, he went and married some"—Hattie's upper lip curled—"two-bit chippie who came out for a week to visit her sorority sister."

"Dutch's grandmother," Summer said.

"Sloe-eyed Jezebel," Hattie corrected. "Gold-digging little tart."

Summer watched Hattie's face, looking for any trace of sorrow or softness. But all she saw was anger, still going strong after half a century.

"Okay." She turned up her palm. "So the guy's a tool. But don't you think it might be time to let it go? Head to Vegas for a girls' weekend and hook up with an Aussie rugby player with some interesting scars and an accent? I promise you'll feel a thousand percent better."

"Never." Hattie wadded up her cloth napkin in her fists. "I will *never* forgive him."

"Oh, I'm not suggesting you forgive Mies." Summer paused. "Isn't he dead, anyway?"

"Yes." Hattie smiled with savage satisfaction.

"But your sister . . . I mean, you guys were, like, twenty when this all went down?"

"Eighteen and nineteen."

"You were children! It was fifty years ago!"

Hattie took a deep breath and another sip of lemonade. "I take it you have no sisters, Miss Benson."

"I have a stepsister. Well, former stepsister. It's complicated."

"Have you and your stepsister ever shared a man?"

Summer pretended to be scandalized. "Miss Huntington, are you asking about threesomes?"

"NO!"

Summer laughed. "Sometimes it's just too easy. Anyway, no, we've never fought over a guy. But if we did, I'd just let her have him. And knowing Emily, she'd probably just let me have him."

"Well, how lucky for you that you have the perfect sisterly relationship." Hattie tossed her napkin on the table. "Try to have a bit of compassion for those of us who don't."

"I never said we had a perfect relationship. I just said I would never break up with my sister over a man. It's not worth it."

"Everyone always liked Pauline better. My parents, my schoolmates, my fiancé . . ."

"Hold on, hold on," Summer said. "I thought you said he ran off with some floozy."

"Ha! Running off would have been the decent thing to do. No, he had the gall to settle down with her, which was infinitely worse."

"Okay, but he didn't run off or settle down with Pauline, right?" Summer clarified. "You guys should have banded together and gotten revenge! Put sugar in his gas tank! Spelled out obscenities on his lawn with salt!"

Hattie laughed mirthlessly. "Pauline was far too fragile for anything like that. *She* was so heartbroken that she couldn't even set eyes on Mies without crying. *She* was so devastated that she threatened to kill herself when the engagement announcement was published. So my parents sent her off to California, while I had to stay here and molder."

"Why didn't you take off for California? Or Florence or London or Madrid?"

"Someone had to take care of my parents. I wasn't their favorite, but I'm the one who saw them through illness and old age. And I had to grit my teeth and bite my tongue every time I saw Mies and his bride and their ill-mannered children."

"And look at you now: grand marshal of the bitter parade." Summer shook her head. "Seriously, Hattie, it's been long enough. You have to at least try to move on. Isn't that what this town's all about?"

"I don't want to move on." Hattie set her jaw. "I don't ever want to feel that way again."

This is what happens, Summer realized. *This is what happens when you wallow too long, when you keep picking at the scab. You fester. You get infected. You feed the fear and numb the pain until you don't have the option to heal anymore.*

She gazed at the stately old lady who had wasted her whole life wishing she could change the past. Who cherished old grudges like family heirlooms.

Whatever Hattie saw in Summer's expression seemed to enrage her further. "Stay away from Mayor Jansen. That's not a request."

Summer didn't bother to hide her irritation. "Do you really not see how dumb this is? I get that you have a blood feud with his grandfather, but Dutch didn't actually *do* anything. You're single; you're powerful; you're filthy stinking rich! If I had your money, I'd enjoy every dollar. I'd be partying like the Great Gatsby every night."

"You're not me, Miss Benson." Hattie arched one eyebrow. "I believe we've established that."

"Haven't you ever heard that old saying: 'Resentment is like drinking rat poison and waiting for the rat to die'?"

"I don't mind dying, as long as I can take the rats down with me. Stay away from him or you'll be sorry." Hattie's vengeful smile tightened. "And so will he."

chapter 22

Summer's heart had nearly resumed its normal rhythm by the time Ingrid parked Scarlett near the porch steps.

"Good job today," she managed to say. The afternoon was damp and cloudy, and her cheeks were freezing from driving around in the wind with the top down.

"Really?" Ingrid handed back the car keys.

"Really. But let's set some goals for next time." Summer reminded herself to breathe. "Number one, the sign says 'yield,' not 'surrender.'"

"I was just being cautious." Ingrid bristled. "I didn't want to cause an accident."

"Which leads us to goal number two: If you don't want to cause an accident, bear in mind that a stop sign is not merely a suggestion."

"I told you, I didn't see it because you were distracting me with the radio."

"I cannot listen to any more Mozart," Summer countered. "And besides, when you turn up A Tribe Called Quest high enough, you can't hear that engine noise."

"What's wrong with your engine?" Dutch asked, rounding the corner from the backyard. He'd spent his morning working in the garden, and had the sweat, dirt smudges, and fresh scratches to show for it.

"It's making weird scraping noises," Ingrid reported.

Dutch turned to Summer, hand outstretched. "Give me your keys."

Summer shot Ingrid a look. "It's fine."

"Keys."

"It's fine."

Dutch took off his work gloves, pried open Summer's hand, and took the keys from her. She looked at his hands and his gloves, and when she glanced up at his eyes she could tell he was also remembering their romp in the rose garden.

He cleared his throat. "You're risking life and limb in a car with a new driver and an engine making, quote, 'scraping noises.' It's not fine."

"She is not risking life and limb." Ingrid put her hands on her hips. "I'm a very safe driver." She paused. "Well, except for that one stop sign."

Dutch popped open the convertible's hood and disappeared into the engine cavity. "I'm taking this into the shop."

"Here, let me give you my credit card." Summer dredged through the receipts, pens, and loose M&M's at the bottom of her purse.

Dutch waved the card away. "Forget it. Go have a glass of wine and decompress. Are you free tonight? Let's have dinner."

"Oh, I can't." Summer pouted. "Hattie says I have to—"

"Seven o'clock?" Ingrid asked.

"Make it eight," Dutch replied.

"Jeans or little black dress?" Ingrid asked.

"Little black dress. Better yet, little lavender dress."

"She'll be ready." Ingrid saluted. "And, bonus! I'm going to the movies tonight, so you guys can have the house to yourselves after dinner."

"You just doubled your allowance for the week," Dutch told Ingrid as he walked around to the ignition and started the car. To Summer, he said, "See you at eight."

Summer followed Ingrid into the house with her mouth hanging open and her hands flung wide. "Did you two just railroad me into a dinner date? Hattie's going to be pissed." She brightened. "Maybe she'll fire me."

"It's nice, huh?" Ingrid tugged Summer's purse strap. "Having some nice guy do nice things for you? I bet you could really get used to it."

"He's not doing it for me." Summer took off her sweater as she stepped into the foyer. "He's doing it for you. You're the one learning to drive."

Ingrid continued as if Summer hadn't spoken. "I mean, I'm sure guys fall all over themselves doing nice stuff for you all the time. Flowers, fancy dinners, jewelry . . ."

Summer laughed. "I live quite the life in your imagination."

"But I'll bet none of them were as nice as Dutch."

"That's true." Summer sighed. "I haven't dated many nice guys. Just one. And that didn't turn out so well."

"I've decided I'm only going to date nice guys," Ingrid announced with great authority.

"I'm glad to hear that. Makes perfect sense since you're such a nice girl."

"Once I get Maxwell out of my system." Ingrid grinned and darted into the kitchen.

Summer stayed right on her heels. "Excuse me?"

"Don't worry; I know I'm never going to be his girlfriend." Ingrid opened the refrigerator, pulled out two bottles of water, and handed one to Summer. "I know he's out of my league. I just really want to sleep with him before he leaves for college. Is that so wrong?"

Summer grabbed a bottle of water, twisted off the cap, and chugged half the contents while she tried to strategize her arguments. "Yes, it's wrong!"

"Why?"

"Because . . . because . . ." *Chug, chug, chug.* "Listen, I don't know this guy, but I *know* him. I know the type. *You* are out of *his* league, and don't you forget it."

"Oh, God." Ingrid scrunched up her face. "Here we go with some lecture about how I'm so smart and such a good person and I should wait for someone else who's such a good person."

"That's right! Here we go with that lecture!" Summer pounded her bottle on the counter, splattering drops of water across the floor. "Sit down and make yourself comfortable, missy."

But Ingrid was having none of this. "I don't want anyone else. Yeah, he's shallow. Yeah, he's superficial. Yeah, okay, he can barely fill in his name on standardized test bubbles. But guess what? I don't care! I just really, really want to know what it's like to kiss him." Ingrid lifted her chin. "Haven't you ever felt like that about a guy?"

"Um. Maybe."

Ingrid's expression went from defiant to desperate. "Why does being smart mean I have to be boring and lame?"

Summer sighed, combing her fingers through her windblown hair. "It doesn't. But—"

"You have to help me get his attention." Ingrid snapped her fingers. "Ooh, I know! I'll take off my underpants and send them to him in a glass!"

"What? No!"

"Yeah, I guess we don't really use glasses at high school parties. Okay, I'll send them to him in a red Solo cup!"

"No. No way!"

"Why not?" Ingrid gave her a look. "*You* did."

Summer sputtered. "How did you hear about that?"

"Are you kidding? The whole town heard about that."

"Well, erase that image from your mind." Summer strode to the other end of the kitchen.

"Too late; I'll be talking to my therapist about it for years."

"Then talk to your therapist. But don't waste your time and energy on some mouth-breathing troglodyte in a lacrosse jersey. You deserve better."

Ingrid got right up in her face. "Why is it okay for you to do it, but not for me?"

Summer put her hands on Ingrid's shoulders. "Because, honestly, you're better than me. You're brilliant and beautiful and destined for greatness."

"So are you."

Summer wasn't about to get sidetracked arguing that point. "You don't need validation from some jackass who doesn't see what a gem you are."

"I don't want validation." A note of whiny exasperation crept into Ingrid's voice. "I want to make out with him. Just once."

"Oh, boy. I know that face. I've seen it in the mirror many times." Summer glanced at the cabinet doors. "Where do you keep the Advil?"

"Here." Ingrid rummaged through a drawer by the dishwasher.

"Thanks." Summer pressed her hands to her forehead. "Fine. *Fine.* Make out with him if you must, but don't have sex with him. I'm begging you."

"Why not? It's just virginity. Don't be such a slave to the patriarchy."

Summer sagged back against the countertop. "I'm having a

heart attack and dying right now. You may not be able to see it on the outside, but trust me, inside, my circulatory system is screeching to a halt. You have no clue what you're saying. You're seventeen. A child! A toddler! An infant!"

Ingrid gave her a knowing look. "So you were still a virgin when you were seventeen?"

"I, uh . . ." Summer waved her hands. "That's not the point!"

"Try to remember what it felt like to be seventeen," Ingrid pleaded.

"I don't have to remember," Summer said. "I *still* feel seventeen."

"I'm so sick of being smart and responsible. I'm tired of thinking about how my behavior reflects on my brother and my family name and all that shit." Ingrid looked a bit terrified as she cursed.

"Did you just say 'shit'?" Summer had to laugh. "You *are* in a rebellious mood."

"I just want to be pretty and fun for once. I want to do something exciting."

"Then apply to study at the Sorbonne. Join the Peace Corps. Go heli-skiing. Don't swap bodily fluids with some guy who makes you feel like you have to bleach your hair and pretend like you don't know the difference between 'there,' 'their,' and 'they're.' And yes, I'm aware of how hypocritical I sound. But that's why I'm your mentor—you can learn from my mistakes!" As she said the words, Summer realized that Hattie had said the exact same thing to her.

Ingrid stuck out her jaw the same way Dutch did when he got obstinate.

So Summer played her trump card. "Guys like that aren't even good in bed. Trust and believe. Sure, he looks hot on the outside, but that's not going to do you any good once the lights are off. You're looking for excellent concentration and attention to detail."

She raised an eyebrow. "Does Mr. Mouth Breather have excellent attention to detail?"

Ingrid looked away. "I don't know."

"Then it's a pass." Summer swept back into the living room to indicate that the subject was now closed. "I mean, ultimately, it's your decision."

"That's right." Ingrid nodded.

"I can't physically stop you."

"That's right."

"But. I can tell your brother."

Ingrid gasped. "You wouldn't."

"I would." Summer touched up her lip gloss while Ingrid pitched a thirty-second temper tantrum. "So make the right decision. Be responsible for your actions. Now let's go. I have to buy a little lavender dress before eight o'clock."

By the time Summer and Dutch returned from dinner in Rehoboth Beach ("Where no one will interrupt us to rant about whose beach chairs are touching whose fence—I hope"), a light drizzle had started to fall.

Dutch took off his jacket while he walked around the car to open Summer's door, and when she stepped out into the rain, he draped it over her shoulders.

Summer, shivering in her lavender blouse and black skirt (all she could find on short notice), tried to hand the jacket back. "I'm okay."

He smoothed the silk-lined wool over her back. "Would you please let me take care of you?"

She stumbled as her high heels got caught in the white gravel lining the driveway. "I don't need you to take care of me."

He placed his hand under her elbow to steady her. "I'm well aware."

"But you—"

"I'm being a gentleman," he said.

She shut up for about three seconds. "Well, I'm just saying. You don't have to be careful with me. I'm not some delicate flower."

He guided her up the wooden stairs to the porch, where she could smell the faintest trace of blooming roses and fresh soil. As the rain fell faster and thunder rumbled in the distance, he tilted up her chin and looked down into her eyes.

"Summer?" His lips were inches from hers.

"Yes?" she breathed.

"Do you want to stand out here and pick a fight, or do you want to come inside?"

She realized that it was too late to make a choice—she'd already let down her guard. She felt safe with him. She trusted him. She wanted to stay up all night, laughing and talking about nothing with him.

This was the best part of falling: the rush, the high, the illusion that it could go on forever.

But it wouldn't go on forever. And she didn't want him to be careful with her because that would only compound the heartache when he inevitably stopped being careful and she had to pick up all her baggage and walk it off again.

"I want to come inside."

chapter 23

"The world is a better place when you take your shirt off." Summer stretched her arms over her head and let them fall back against the pillows. "I'm serious. You should get humanitarian awards every time you undress."

She rolled onto her stomach, propped herself up on her elbows, and faced Dutch, who was sprawled next to her in the bed. The curtains were open and the porch light cast a cold, pale glow into the room. She trailed her index finger along his stubbled jawline. "You still breathing over there?"

"Barely." He sat up, his brow furrowing as he touched the shiny red burn marks on her back. "Does this hurt?"

Summer swung one foot up and traced circles in the air with her ankle. "Not at all. I can't even feel it. Nerve damage."

"Permanent?"

She glanced over her shoulder long enough to confirm that he was still touching her skin. "No idea. I had so many doctors explaining so many things that I kind of lost track of what's temporarily jacked up and what's permanently jacked up."

"I'm guessing you're supposed to follow up on that."

"Probably," she agreed. "But sometimes I think a fully functioning nervous system is overrated. I mean, there's worse things than *not* feeling, right?"

"I don't know." His hand slid down to rest on the curve of her lower back. "You're pretty sensitive for someone who claims not to feel anything."

She gave him a little kick in the shoulder. "Take that back or you'll never see me naked again."

He laughed. "What's wrong with being sensitive?"

"Would *you* like it if I called *you* sensitive?"

"Go right ahead."

"Whatever." She let her foot fall back onto the mattress with a *thunk*. "You're just saying that because you're all swarthy and secure in your manhood."

They listened to the steady patter of rain on the roof and the muffled thump of a loose shutter banging against the house.

Finally, he broke the silence. "Why did you come to Black Dog Bay?"

Summer stared at the wooden headboard. "You watch the news. You have Internet. Hell, you have the Whinery and a working pair of ears. You know why I'm here."

He didn't move, but his hand went from resting to pressing against her back. "I have a feeling your version is slightly different from the one they reported on CNN."

"Pillow talk: You're doing it wrong."

He waited.

She sighed and pulled away from him. "You're the Mayor of Breakup Town, Dutch. I'm sure you've heard my story a million times. It's boring. There was this pilot; there was this plane crash; blah, blah, blah."

Even in the shadows, she could see the intensity in those gray eyes. "It's the 'blah, blah, blah' part that interests me."

"You really want the blah, blah, blah?"

"I really do."

"Ugh. *Fine.*" She looked at the rumpled white sheet while she gave him the bullet points on her upbringing, her job, her restlessness. She looked at the floorboards while she told him about the emergency landing. She looked at the ceiling while she talked about the hospital, the ring, the note of regret in Aaron's voice when he acknowledged the truth that Summer had always sensed: *I love you . . . but I don't love you enough.*

Finally, she stopped talking and looked out the window at the moonless night.

"Summer." His voice was low. "Look at me."

She tossed her hair and glanced in his general direction.

He waited until she finally met his gaze.

"I'm still here," he said. "I'm not going anywhere."

She forced a smile. "That's because I'm lying in your bed naked."

He smiled back. "Not entirely."

She tucked the sheet up around her shoulders. "Okay, then it's also because I left out all the parts that make me look bad. You just got the highlight reel."

"Know what I think? I think you're secretly very, very sensitive." He brushed his lips against the nape of her neck and tugged on the sheet as he made his way down between her shoulder blades. "Do you feel that?"

Summer's breath hitched. "Maybe."

He ran his tongue along the valley of her spine. "How about that?"

"Hmm. Possibly a tiny tingle."

He tossed the sheet to the floor and nipped the swell of her hip. "Tingling's a good start. Let's see if we can bring some of these nerve endings back to life."

Summer wakened with a start at the first light of dawn. She'd been dreaming about the plane crash, the terror of plummeting through the darkness, the acrid smell of smoke filling her lungs. She must have shifted position in her sleep, because although she'd fallen asleep next to Dutch, now she was all snuggled up with her cheek against his chest. His arm was draped across her shoulder, anchoring her to him. She felt warm and peaceful and . . .

She wanted to stay like this forever.

That one word, "forever," was enough to get her out of bed and back into her clothes. The warmth pooling inside her turned icy.

She eased out the bedroom door and crept down the hall, pausing as a floorboard creaked.

She held her breath, counted to ten.

Just the wind. Just an old house settling after a storm.

She exhaled and tiptoed down to the landing.

"You are so busted." Ingrid whispered from the top of the staircase.

Summer whirled around to face the bleary-eyed teenager. "I . . . You . . . You missed curfew last night, young lady."

"And I see you took full advantage." Ingrid yawned and tied the sash of her ratty plaid robe. Her hair looked frizzy and disheveled.

"It's not what you think," Summer insisted. "We were just, um, talking."

"Really? Then why do have lipstick smeared all over your cheeks?" Ingrid squinted down at her. "And a hickey?"

"Oh my God." Summer clapped her hand to her neck. "I have a hickey?"

Ingrid grinned. "Gotcha."

Summer could feel her cheeks flushing. "Listen, I'd love to stay here and match wits with you, but I've got to go."

Ingrid's grin vanished. She glanced at the door to the master bedroom. "Does he know you're leaving?"

"Um." Summer rubbed her ankle with the toes of her other foot. "No. I didn't want to wake him up because he's got a breakfast meeting with—"

"Uh-huh. So you're nailing and bailing?"

"Since when do you even know phrases like 'nailing and bailing'?"

Ingrid's expression darkened. "Answer my question."

"Of course I'm not nailing and bailing!" Summer "yelled" this as loud as she could while still whispering. "But I missed curfew, too, you know! Hattie Huntington's going to be on your porch with the FBI and a pack of bloodhounds any second now."

Ingrid looked incredibly intimidating for a seventeen-year-old with bedhead and pink striped socks. "You better not mess this up."

"I won't."

"You better call him."

"I will." Summer held up one palm.

Ingrid leveled her index finger at Summer. "This afternoon."

"I *will*."

Ingrid gazed down at her for a few beats before nodding. "I'm trusting you to stick around. So is he. Don't you dare let him down."

The beach was chilly and deserted as the first pale streaks of dawn crept over the horizon. Summer dashed barefoot past houses and hotels toward the hulking purple mansion around the curve of the bay.

She didn't worry about muggers or jellyfish or even sand crabs. From the moment she'd first arrived, she'd known that Black Dog Bay was the kind of town where a woman could run around by herself at four in the morning. There was an unshakable, almost mystical sense of security here.

As she jumped over a pile of seaweed, Summer saw a huge black dog lumbering toward her. She scanned the shoreline, looking for a jogger or fisherman, but saw no sign of the dog's owner.

"Hey, buddy." She crouched down and held out her hand. "Are you lost?"

The shaggy dog dropped down into a play bow, wagging his tail. His eyes were partially obscured by wiry tufts of fur, and a drool-drenched pink tongue lolled from his mouth. When Summer took a step forward to check for a collar, the dog darted out of reach and galloped back across the beach, leaving a spray of sand in his wake.

She watched him go, staring at the spot where he disappeared over a dune. The early glow of dawn gathered into a golden ray of morning sun and she felt the light pierce her heart and soul, as though she'd just witnessed a miracle.

chapter 24

"*D*o you know if anyone around here is missing a dog? A giant black furry one?" Summer sat down at the Whinery after another grueling day of paid companionship. Turner had busted her shimmying up the porch columns to get back into her bedroom before breakfast, and he'd ratted her out to Hattie, who had punished her by extending her cell phone ban and forcing her to play several rounds of croquet.

Jenna jammed along to Rihanna's "Breakin' Dishes" and scooped fresh ice out of the cooler. "What?"

Summer had to repeat the question twice to make herself heard over the chatter and music: "Black dog! Big as a pony! Does he have an owner?"

Jenna exchanged a look with Beryl, who was sitting next to a burly guy in a baseball cap.

"Hi, Summer." Beryl rested her hand on the guy's arm. "This is my boyfriend, Scott. He's in concrete."

Summer wasn't entirely sure what that meant, but she extended her hand. "Nice to meet you. I'm Summer."

Scott responded by grunting and glancing at his watch.

"Sorry." Beryl finished the last of her drink. "I promised we'd go somewhere he could watch the baseball game. He's an Orioles fanatic." She collected her purse and looked longingly at the candy dishes and pink napkins. "Jenna, have you ever considered putting in TVs with ESPN?"

"God, no." Jenna grimaced. Then she returned her attention to Summer. "So you saw a black dog at the beach."

"Yeah. I was coming home from Dut—I was, uh, out for a walk this morning on the beach, and this ginormous dog ran up to me. I didn't see a collar."

Beryl toasted Summer with the icy dregs of her cocktail. "That's great. We're so happy for you!"

"Why?" Summer looked from Jenna to Beryl.

"How were you feeling?" Jenna poured a glass of Moscato. "When you saw the dog?"

"I don't know." Summer shrugged. "Cold and wet and covered in sand?"

"No, I mean emotionally." Jenna passed the glass to a waiting patron. "Would you say that you were feeling peaceful? Hopeful?"

"Warm and fuzzy?" Beryl said.

"I don't remember," Summer hedged. "I hadn't had my coffee yet."

"You guys! Can I have your attention, everyone?" Jenna paused the music and announced to the entire bar, "Summer saw the black dog!"

Cheers erupted and glasses clinked. "Congratulations, honey!" A dozen bed-and-breakfast guests descended upon her in a group hug.

Summer elbowed her way out of the embrace and demanded answers from Jenna. "What's the deal with the black dog?"

"This *is* Black Dog Bay," Beryl said, as if this explained everything.

"It means you're turning a corner." Jenna poured a glass of Shiraz and held it up to the lights before serving it. "I always double-check for cork chunks now."

"You saw Lavinia's black dog," Beryl explained.

Summer scanned the crowd, exasperated. "Who's Lavinia?"

"Oh, she's dead. But her dog still patrols the beach."

"If you're all trying to drive me crazy, mission accomplished." Summer put her hands on her hips. "Would someone please start making sense?"

"Go to the bookstore tomorrow morning," Jenna advised, then went to change the music as a tourist offered her twenty dollars to put on Iris DeMent's "God May Forgive You (But I Won't)." "Hollis will explain everything."

. . . In 1878, after being deserted by her husband, New York socialite Lavinia Leighton built a huge house on the Delaware shore and founded the town of Black Dog Bay. "When I first came to the ocean," Lavinia told her biographer, "I was drowning in despair, pulled under by the jaws of the 'black dog' of depression. One summer night as I sat by the water, I saw him: a ghostly black beast romping on the sand in the moonlight. The apparition capered and ran, playful as a pup. I realized he hadn't come to submerge me; he'd come to save me."

Shortly before her death in 1909, Lavinia commissioned an artist in Italy to create a large bronze statue of the phantom dog, which has since acquired a black patina in the salty sea air. The statue stands today in the Black Dog Bay town square, overlooking the boardwalk and the sand dunes. Passersby rub the dog's nose for luck. The statue features an open mouth and a hollow interior, and local legend holds that if you write down your worries on a scrap of paper, Lavinia's black dog will "swallow your sorrows" and leave you free to start a new life unencumbered by past disappointments. . . .

Summer glanced up from the pages of *The History of Black Dog Bay*. "So you seriously expect me to believe there's a phantom dog galloping around the beach?"

"Believe it or don't believe it." Hollis hummed as she watered the potted plants by the cash register. "But the ghost dog is real."

"Come on, you can tell me." Summer closed the book and set it aside. "You guys made this up for tourist purposes, right?"

Hollis put down the watering can and fixed her gaze on Summer. "You know it's real. You saw for yourself."

"I saw a dog," Summer corrected. "An *actual* dog. Not a magical, woo-woo phantom dog."

"Uh-huh."

"He left footprints in the sand! Ghost dogs can't leave footprints."

"Whatever you say." Hollis resumed humming. Snidely Whiplash the cat purred along.

"What kind of dog is it, anyway? Labrador? Poodle? Giant schnauzer?" Summer pounded her fist into her palm. "I need specifics!"

"I'm not sure. We once had a dog show judge come through town, and when she saw it, she said it looked like an Irish wolfhound." Hollis brought over a dog breed guidebook.

Summer flipped through the breed descriptions until she found a photo of an Irish wolfhound. "Okay, well, that *does* look like the dog I saw. But aren't ghosts supposed to come out at night? This dog is a rule breaker!" She returned her attention to *The History of Black Dog Bay*. "Who fact-checked that book?"

"I did." Hollis pointed out her name on the front cover. "I wrote the whole thing, actually."

"You did? Oh." Summer flushed. "Well, in that case, I'll buy ten copies. It's just . . . a dog ghost? Really? I'm sure you understand my skepticism."

"How do you think this town got its name and reputation?" Hollis asked. "Lavinia Leighton is like the patron saint of broken hearts. Her husband deserted her for another woman, and Lavinia was left with nothing."

"Except piles and piles of money." Summer considered this. "She and Hattie Huntington have a lot in common, actually."

"Yes, but what good did all her riches do her without love?" Hollis sighed. "Without the husband she adored?"

Summer tucked her hair back behind her ear. "I know plenty of women who'd be thrilled to exchange their husbands for piles of money."

"Well, Lavinia wasn't one of them. And because of the legal system of the time, she was stuck. Her husband had left but wouldn't actually divorce her, and she couldn't show her face in New York society—that's why she moved down here. The black dog saved her life, and it's saved countless others over the last century."

"So one night she saw a dog playing on the beach, and suddenly, she's fine?" Summer snapped her fingers. "Just like that?"

"Well, that's the official story." Hollis motioned her in. "The truth is a little grittier."

"Ooh, I like gritty." Summer perked up. "What happened?"

"Lavinia was going to kill herself," Hollis said. "She tried to drown herself in the ocean, and the dog saved her. Literally dragged her back to shore and up on the sand."

"Why didn't you put that in the book?"

"Lavinia wanted to be remembered a certain way, and we respect that. That night by the ocean was her rock bottom. We've all been there."

Summer thought about her last day in the hospital. Her first day at the Better Off Bed-and-Breakfast. "Yes, we have."

"And the very next morning, she started putting her life back together and facing the future. That's what Black Dog Bay is about. It's about starting over. The Lavinia who went into the ocean was not the same Lavinia who came out."

"Because a gigantic ghost dog saved her."

Hollis thought this over, then shook her head. "She saved herself. And she founded a town that saved lots of other people."

"So my seeing the dog means . . . what?" Summer asked. "All my problems are magically solved, too?"

"Let me ask you something," Hollis said. "What were you trying to get away from when you came here? What were you saying to yourself that was so unbearable you needed the ocean to drown it out?"

I'm hard to love and easy to walk away from.

"Big changes are coming your way." Hollis looked as sure and smug as the cat flicking his tail on a pile of paperbacks. "You'll see."

chapter 25

Summer spent the next day attending to Hattie's every whim, fetching and fussing and making an extra trip to the study, where she used a silver Cartier letter opener to jailbreak her phone out of custody.

"I want to go to the beach," Hattie declared after lunch.

"Well, then . . ." Summer nodded at the expanse of pristine golden sand across the lawn.

"I want to go to those dunes over there." Hattie indicated a patch of sand half a mile away. "I want to bring towels, an umbrella, and a picnic hamper. And I want you to carry it all."

Summer rolled her eyes. "You're just doing this because you're mad I consorted with the grandson of your archnemesis on a picnic table. And a bed. And the floor. And the—"

"No."

"Okay, then, you're just doing this because I broke your drainpipe trying to climb back into the house."

"When I'm punishing you, Miss Benson, you'll know it." Hattie adjusted a wide-brimmed straw hat on her head. "Requiring you to act as a pack mule for a single afternoon will hardly suffice as retribution for ignoring my clear instructions. *That* will come later."

After hours of angling Hattie's umbrella for maximum shade and refreshing her iced tea with just the right amount of fresh mint, Summer hauled everything back to the Purple Palace, where a sleek black Town Car idled in the driveway.

"Who's that?" Summer let the wooden umbrella pole drag on the grass.

"I'm expecting a visitor this afternoon." Hattie's clipped tone did not invite further questions. "You may leave the beach equipment by the stairs, right here."

Hattie took off her sun hat, smoothed her white hair, and climbed the stairs to the front door, where Turner greeted her with even more gravitas than usual.

"Your guest is waiting in the living room, Miss Huntington."

"Thank you, Turner." Hattie glanced back at Summer and made a little shooing motion with her hand. "Run along, now."

"Delighted to oblige." Summer dropped the umbrella, beach chairs, and picnic basket in a heap and headed back to the shoreline. Sunburned and weary, she strolled around the bay to Dutch's house, wended her way through the rosebushes, and let herself in the side door.

She found him sprawled out on the couch in the family room, reading. He put the book on his chest when he saw her and made room for her on the cushions.

"Hi." She curled up next to him and tucked her head into the space between his chin and his chest.

"Hi." He kissed the top of her head. "You smell like the sun."

She nestled into him for a moment, listening to the steady thud of his heartbeat under his thin cotton T-shirt and feeling the rise and fall of his breathing.

"What're you reading?" she asked.

He glanced at the book's cover. *"The Nature and Properties of Soils."*

"Sounds like a page-turner."

"It's pretty interesting, if you're into that kind of thing."

She smiled. "Well? Don't leave a girl in suspense."

He wrapped his free arm around her. "You want to hear about soil?"

"If you're the one telling me about it."

He read a few pages to her, the timbre of his voice deep and soothing. She didn't realize she'd fallen asleep until the screen door slammed again. Ingrid bounded into the room, carrying a white paper bag stamped with the Eat Your Heart Out logo.

"I'm back and I brought brownies." When she saw Summer and Dutch on the sofa together, she beamed.

"Oh good," she said. "You're home."

Halfway through the brownies, Dutch had to take an emergency work call, leaving Summer and Ingrid in the family room.

"Hey, why aren't you wearing any of that makeup we bought?" Summer asked.

"Oh." Ingrid touched her bare cheeks, her expression sheepish. "I wanted to, but . . ."

"But what?"

"I put it all on this morning. Foundation, blush, eye shadow, everything."

Summer waited.

"And then I washed it all off before I left the house."

Summer considered the implications. "Does this mean you gave up on your one-night stand with the sex god in the lacrosse jersey?"

Ingrid ducked her head. "For now."

"So wait—I actually talked some sense into somebody?" Summer held up her hand for a high five.

"No, it's more . . ." Ingrid nibbled her lower lip. "Okay, you probably won't get this since you didn't grow up in a tiny town where everybody talks about everybody else."

"I worked for an airline, which is basically an intercontinental gossip mill."

"Well, I have to be careful. My brother is the mayor. And he's been raising me by himself. So if I go out looking all"—Ingrid rubbed her cheek again—"trashy, it reflects on him. Everything I do reflects on him."

"In what world is wearing beige eye shadow trashy?"

"I have to err on the side of caution. Same with dating and drinking and everything else."

No wonder the poor kid was so angst-ridden all the time, Summer thought. Throughout her entire childhood and adolescence, Ingrid had been framing every action and decision in terms of what it would say about her family. That's what it meant to be the mayor's sister—constant scrutiny and criticism.

Everyone in Dutch's life had to consider how her actions reflected on him. Especially his girlfriends.

"What?" Ingrid prompted.

"Nothing." Summer blew out a breath and shook out her hair. "But you've got to let go and live a little. Otherwise, you'll be one of those overly sheltered kids who goes crazy and flunks out after freshman year of college because you're all drunk on freedom and cheap beer."

Ingrid shook her head. "Can't go wild in college, either."

"Why not? That's what college is for."

"I'm just going to Wilmington." Ingrid announced this with glum resignation. "That's where kids in Black Dog Bay go. Half the people from my high school class will be there, reporting back to their parents."

"Hold the phone. I thought you were some frighteningly gifted supergenius."

Ingrid laughed. "Don't exaggerate. I just have a high GPA."

"Then you can go to school anywhere you want. I refuse to let you spend your life identifying yourself as 'the mayor's little sister.'" Summer tried to pinpoint the perfect blend of academia and cultural enrichment. "Have you thought about UCLA? Columbia? Tulane? Let's swing by the bookstore and see if Hollis has any college guides."

"Great idea. I'll drive." Ingrid's smile dimmed as she remembered Summer's car was still in the shop. "Oh, crap. We'll have to take Dutch's car. Maybe you should drive."

Summer threw up her palms. "I'm not driving his car!"

"Well, I don't want to wreck it!"

"Well, I don't want to, either!"

"I guess we're staying home, then," Ingrid said.

"Guess so." Summer popped the last bite of brownie in her mouth. "So what do you want to do?"

"I know!" Ingrid jumped to her feet. "It's my turn to be your mentor."

"Take it from the top." Ingrid turned a page of the magazine she was reading.

"Seriously?" Summer squirmed on the piano bench. "More scales?"

"Yep." Ingrid put down the article on jewelry trends and repositioned Summer's hands on the piano keyboard. "Do 'em all again. And keep your wrists up this time."

"My wrists are up!"

"Your wrists are like overcooked linguine. Posture, please." Ingrid tapped Summer's back to remind her to sit up straight. "Scales. Let's go."

"But I just did them."

"You have to play them over and over. Your fingers are learning." Ingrid put on her most superior expression. "Muscle memory."

"So that's it? I'm just going to sit here all afternoon, playing a bunch of scales over and over?"

"Yep."

Summer slouched and let her wrists go limp. "When I said I wanted to learn to play piano, I meant I wanted to play actual songs. Not just scales."

"We'll get there," Ingrid promised. "What, did you think we'd jump right in with sonatas and concertos the first day?"

"A little 'Heart and Soul' never hurt anybody." Summer played the opening notes, trying to entice Ingrid to join in.

"No. No 'Heart and Soul,' no 'Chopsticks,' no nothing." Ingrid pointed imperiously at the keyboard. "Scales. Middle C is right there."

"This sucks." Summer flexed her fingers, launched into a new set of scales, and mentally revised her bucket list:

Have a garden.
Have hot sex in a garden.
Learn to play piano.
Learn to pole dance.

"Wrists!" Ingrid cried. "Wrists!"

Dutch strode down the stairs, jingling his car keys in one hand. He'd changed into crisp navy pants and a light blue button-down shirt. "I'll be back in a few hours."

"More beach chair intrigue and sand dune scandal?" Summer's smile faded as soon as she made eye contact with him. "What's wrong?"

He turned his face away and straightened his shirt cuffs. "Nothing."

"Liar." She stood up and crossed over to him. "Something's wrong."

Ingrid put down her magazine. "Yeah, what's up?"

"Nothing." He pulled away when Summer tried to take his hand. "Sorry, I'm distracted. I have to go put out some fires." An electronic ringtone sounded upstairs. "Damn. I left my phone."

He loped back up the stairs. Summer and Ingrid looked at each other.

"This is bad," Ingrid whispered. "Really bad."

"Okay, let's think. What could have happened in the last twenty minutes?"

"I don't know." Ingrid tucked her long brown hair behind her ears. "What should we do?"

"Well . . ." Summer perched on the back of the sofa. Getting information from taciturn men was not her forte. She was used to men who slammed doors, called names, raised their voices, and made empty threats. But Ingrid looked so worried, so certain that Summer had the answers.

So Summer climbed up the stairs and knocked softly on the bedroom door. She could hear Dutch's voice, muffled and low on the other side. When he went silent, she knocked softly. "Hi. Can I interrupt for one second?"

He opened the door, his face and demeanor betraying nothing.

"Ingrid's all freaked out down there, and honestly, so am I."

"Sorry." He pocketed the phone and rubbed his forehead. "I'm in mayor mode."

"And that's fine, seeing as you are in fact the mayor. But your jaw is all clenched and your eyes are all flinty." She glanced downstairs and lowered her voice. "And you're kind of . . . overenunciating."

He blinked at her. "Overenunciating."

"Yeah. I've noticed guys tend to do that when they're really worked up about something."

He opened the door wider and brushed past her. "I'm fine. Everything's going to be fine."

"Tell me." She wrapped her hand around the doorjamb. "Whatever it is, just tell me."

He didn't look back as he ran down the stairs. "I wish I could."

chapter 26

"... So I have no idea what's going on, and he won't tell me." Summer drained the last of her fresh-squeezed orange juice, slammed her empty glass on the bar, and signaled Jenna to pour another.

"Maybe he can't." Jenna took the pitcher out of the refrigerator. "Maybe it's super-secret mayor stuff."

"Maybe." Summer sighed. She grabbed some M&M's out of the communal candy bowl.

"But whatever's going on, I think it's adorable that you want to take care of him."

Summer's head jerked up. "What?"

"You worry about him, you want to smooth his furrowed brow, all that stuff."

"Um, no. If anything, he's taking care of me. Against my will, but still." She told Jenna about the car engine.

"Aww. That's nice of him."

"I know."

Jenna refilled the juice glass and topped off the dish of M&M's. "So I guess the days of begging him to go out with you are over?"

Summer grinned. "They were over the first time I made out with him."

"And you're still teaching Ingrid how to drive?"

"I'm doing my best. And she's repaying me by teaching me to play piano."

"Well, there you go." Jenna flipped a pink dish towel over her shoulder. "The three of you are a cozy little family."

"No." Summer nearly spit out her M&M's. "No, no, no. We're only temporary. Not to mention dysfunctional and crazy."

"All the best families are."

"Don't even joke about that." The sweet taste of chocolate soured in Summer's mouth. "We're not a . . ." She couldn't even force out the word.

"Call it whatever you want, but we all know the truth. And we're all rooting for you." Jenna excused herself from the conversation to rock out as Joan Jett's "I Hate Myself for Loving You" came on the stereo.

The smell of Chanel No. 5 and filthy lucre drifted in as Mimi Sinclair walked through the door. She made a valiant effort to hide her disdain for the tourist trap of a bar, but couldn't quite suppress a little shudder. "Summer, I've been looking everywhere for you!"

Summer swiveled on her wrought-iron stool and raised her glass in greeting. "Hey, girl. What's up?"

"Don't you look cute today." Mimi leaned in to deliver a kiss on each cheek. Jenna paused her air-guitar solo long enough to roll her eyes. "I've been looking all over town for you."

"Next time, check the bar first," Summer advised. "Save yourself some time."

Mimi giggled and clutched the chain strap of her quilted leather purse. "Well, I'm so glad I found you. My husband and I have the white and green Cape Cod down by the dunes?"

"Okay."

"And we'd just love to have you over for dinner one night next week. Shall we say Friday night?"

"Ooh, Friday night's not going to work." *I'll be busy doing filthy, sweat-drenched things to Dutch.* "I think I have a prior engagement with Miss Huntington."

The perfect white smile never wavered. "Saturday, then? Or perhaps Sunday brunch. I make a mean eggs Benedict." Mimi gave Summer a playful swat. "And when I say 'I,' I mean my housekeeper, of course."

Summer swatted right back. "Of course."

"So Sunday, then?" Mimi didn't give Summer a chance to object. "It's a date! We'll see you two next Sunday at noon." She bounced off, her sporty tennis skirt and shoes as white as her teeth.

Summer watched her go, bewildered, then turned to Jenna. "What was that all about? I mean, we had a little moment of bonding at the country club a few weeks ago, but . . ."

Jenna patted her hand. "That was about Dutch. Note how she said she'll see 'you two' on Sunday. Word's gotten out that you two are an item. So you're the one to schmooze if they want to get to him."

Summer laughed. "Be serious. I can't make Dutch do anything."

"One make-out session and he's putty in your hands," Jenna reminded her.

Summer smoothed back her hair. "What can I say? I'm a good kisser."

"Welcome to small-town politics. People who want favors, people who want publicity, people who want special treatment . . . they'll be knocking on your door."

Summer heard Ingrid's words echoing in her mind: *Everything I do reflects on him.* She chewed on the end of her straw. "Dutch and I don't talk about his job. I couldn't care less about that stuff, and anyway, he's very discreet. Not to mention, I have better things to do in bed than play lobbyist."

"Mimi Sinclair is the tip of the iceberg," Jenna warned. "Prepare yourself."

Sure enough, over the next few days, Summer found herself propositioned by both summer and year-round residents, many of whom she'd never met:

"We'd love to have you as a guest of honor at our charity luncheon."

"Some of the girls are getting together for drinks at the country club. Care to join us?"

"You simply must come to the caviar clambake." This last one was accompanied by an actual engraved invitation.

"What the hell is a caviar clambake?" Summer demanded as she and Ingrid hauled their reusable grocery bags out to the parking lot.

Ingrid glanced at the invitation. "Oh, it's a rich-person thing. They wear, like, old Levi's with Gucci and Louis Vuitton."

Summer tossed a sack full of fresh corn into Scarlett's backseat, then handed her car keys to Ingrid. "Jenna says it's because of Dutch."

"It probably is. Enjoy your caviar."

"But I'm not a caviar kind of girl. I'm more of a pizza and beer kind of girl. Which reminds me, I'm starving. Want to stop for lunch on the way home?" She buckled herself into the passenger seat as Ingrid cranked up Vivaldi on the sound system. "The social scene here is surprisingly exhausting. I feel like I'm pledging a sorority."

Ingrid backed up into a metal shopping cart, winced, and pulled forward again. "I'm surprised you're surprised. Haven't you always been popular?"

"With rock stars and rebels. Not with ladies who lunch."

Summer put on her sunglasses. "Is this how it is for you all the time? People trying to befriend you for the wrong reasons?"

"No, it's the opposite with teenagers." Ingrid missed sideswiping a yellow concrete post by mere millimeters. "No one invites me to anything because they think I'm a snitch."

"Killjoy by association?"

"Exactly."

"Dutch has been busy the last few days," Summer said, careful to keep her tone light. "Have you seen much of him?"

"Nope. I think he comes home for a few hours to sleep every night, but I have no proof." Ingrid shot a sidelong glance at Summer. "I thought he might be spending time with you."

"Uh-uh." Summer propped her feet up on the dashboard. "Haven't heard from him."

"Don't take it personally," Ingrid advised.

"Oh, I'm not. It's fine. He's not my . . . We're not officially . . . I'm not his parole officer," she finally finished. "He doesn't have to check in every minute of every day."

"Well. He could take two seconds out of his busy schedule to text." Ingrid braked for a yield sign. "But he gets like this when he's in crisis mode." She tsk-tsked and changed the music to Bach. "Boys."

"And we still don't know why he's in crisis mode?" Summer asked.

Ingrid shook her head as a stream of cars whizzed past them. "We can try to find out, though. Let's stop by his office and bring him lunch."

Summer put her feet back on the floor mat. "No."

"Why not?"

"Ingrid, *go*, already!" Summer cried. "Yield, not surrender, remember?"

Ingrid waited another few seconds before turning right. "Don't yell at me. I'm just trying to be cautious."

So was Summer. In her previous life, she would have called up a distracted boyfriend or sexted him or shown up at his office door in a belted trench coat with a wisp of black lace underneath. She would have seen it as a challenge to regain his interest.

But right now, she was too filled with doubt to view love as a challenge. She refused to beg for Dutch's attention. She was afraid that whatever she did, whatever he felt for her, it wouldn't be enough.

She felt weak, and she hated herself for it.

So she did nothing, and steeled herself for Dutch to do the same.

Late that night, Summer curled up in bed with the lights off and her smartphone on, vowing she'd go to sleep as soon as she beat this level of Candy Crush, when she heard a sharp smack against the balcony doors.

She thought it might be a wayward bird or a tree branch tapping against the glass panes, but before she could get out of bed to investigate, she heard more scraping, thumping, and finally a knock.

She froze, torn between lunging for the lamp switch and going into cardiac arrest, when she heard a familiar voice.

"Summer?"

"Dutch!" She scurried across the rug, fumbled with the latch, and opened the doors. "What are you doing? How did you get up here?"

He stepped into the moonlit room and took her in his arms. She couldn't see him clearly, but as soon as he touched her, her whole body craved more. More pressure, more pleasure, more of his taste and his scent.

He threaded his fingers into her hair and kissed her, first hard and demanding, then sweet and soft, then hard again. Together, they stumbled back onto the bed.

He was all over her, his body taut and solid and hot, but he went still for a moment as he brushed his lips over the sensitive skin of her throat and murmured into her ear:

"I missed you."

Before her mind could overrule her heart, she said it back: "I missed you, too."

chapter 27

"I just *consorted* with a Jansen man in Hattie's Huntington's house. And it was the best consortium of my life." Summer tried not to laugh too loudly as she rested her chin on Dutch's chest in the middle of all the fluffy white bedding. "We are going to get in sooo much trouble if we get caught."

Dutch draped one arm across her back. "Why do you work for her, again?"

"Extortion," Summer replied cheerfully. "It's a long story, but the short version is, I took one for Team Townie."

He wrapped his other arm around her and squeezed. "You're full of surprises."

"Look who's talking." She gloried in the feel of her bare skin against his. "The Boy Scout of Black Dog Bay, breaking and entering in the dead of night."

"You opened the door for me," he pointed out.

"Shh, you're ruining the mood."

"Speaking of the mood . . . In all the breaking and entering excitement—"

"So to speak."

"—I forgot to give you this." He leaned off the bed and sifted through the pile of discarded clothes on the floor until he found what he was searching for.

He handed her a flower so fresh that the scent of damp soil still clung to the velvety petals. She didn't have to turn on the light to know she was holding a rose.

"It feels good. It smells good." She inhaled deeply. "But is it bulletproof?"

"Like an armored tank."

It took her a few more seconds to realize what she *wasn't* feeling on the cool, slender stem. "You even took the thorns off? Damn, you think of everything."

"I've been told I'm thorough and responsible to a fault." She could hear the smile in his voice.

"Oh, you're definitely thorough." Her nerve endings were still humming. "So what have you been doing for the last few days? And don't say 'nothing.' Don't say everything's fine."

"All right." His voice sobered. "Everything is not fine."

"Thank you."

"Everything's going to hell."

Summer waited for him to elaborate, and when he didn't, she nudged his leg with hers. "I'm going to need specifics."

"Specifically, Hattie Huntington is sending everything to hell." He scrubbed his face with his hand. "That's all I can tell you for now."

"No, no, no. You can't leave me in suspense." She sat up. "What's that hissing old crone up to?"

He stroked her hair back from her temples. "Nothing's definite yet."

"If you tell me, I can help. Don't forget, I live with her."

"I can't say any more." Dutch's tone indicated that further wheedling would be useless.

"But it's really bad?" Summer asked.

His silence confirmed her suspicion.

"Why is she always so vindictive?" Summer remembered the grim lines in Hattie's face when the old woman talked about holding grudges and exacting revenge. "Why can't she use her powers for good, just once?"

"I wish she would." His voice grated with frustration. "I'm calling in every favor, reaching out to everyone I can, but you don't go up against Hattie Huntington and win."

"Just tell me what she's planning." Summer tightened her grip on the rose in her hand.

"I know she hates my family, but I always figured she had some sense of responsibility to the rest of the town." Dutch's whole body tensed. "She's owned half the town and ignored everyone for decades, and all of a sudden, she decides to twist the knife? Why now? I can't figure it out."

As Summer stared into the shadows, things clicked into place. She fell back against the soft down pillows. "I can."

The next morning, for the first time ever, Summer made it to the breakfast table before Hattie. She threw back two shots of espresso, skimmed the *Black Dog Bay Bulletin*, and was spoiling for a fight by the time Hattie arrived downstairs.

"I saw the dog," Summer announced before Hattie could even sit down. "Lavinia's dog. The Irish wolfhound."

Hattie adjusted the buttons of her navy and white cardigan and shot Summer a cool, assessing look. "Pshaw. You saw no such thing."

"Did you just say 'pshaw'?" Summer whipped out her phone. "Would you mind repeating that so I can record it for posterity?"

"Miss Benson, you just lost your phone for another day." Hattie held out her palm. "And if you're finished mocking my colloquialisms, I have a serious matter I'd like to discuss with you. It involves a gentleman caller in your room last night." She paused. "Although I suppose the term 'gentleman' may be an overstatement."

"Oh, sorry. Did we get a little too loud?" Summer used her linen napkin to dab imaginary sweat from her décolletage. "You know how those Jansen boys are. I just couldn't contain myself."

Hattie's knife rattled against her plate as she started shaking with rage. "Enough! I have warned you repeatedly, and now you have gone too far."

"Speaking of the Jansen boys," Summer interrupted, "I heard you're up to something extra diabolical."

The old lady froze, knife in hand. "Did you?"

"Yes, I did."

Judging by Hattie's smug expression, she expected Summer to beg and plead and promise anything in exchange for backing down.

Instead, Summer regarded her with a mixture of reproach and pity.

Hattie glanced out at the ocean, then back at Summer. "Well? If you have something to say, let's have it."

Summer nodded. "You know how everyone around here is always saying, 'Don't be bitter—be *better*'?"

Hattie didn't even dignify this with a response.

"Well, when I first got here, I thought that was bull. I wanted to be bitter. I *aspired* to it. Because I thought that would protect me. I'd never get my heart broken again, because I'd never be stupid enough to get close to anyone again."

Hattie let out an exasperated sigh. "Is there a point to this little pseudo-psychology lecture?"

"Yes. Being bitter is a choice. And your choices are making you miserable. They're also making me miserable. Apparently, they're about to make the whole damn town miserable."

"Including your Mayor Jansen," Hattie hastened to point out.

"Right. The guy that you hate for no good reason."

"Stop seeing him," Hattie commanded.

"Stop being such a stubborn, vengeful drama queen and *move on*," Summer shot back.

"You have overstepped your boundaries, Miss Benson. You sleep under my roof. I pay your salary."

"Fire me! I'm begging you! Actually, you know what? Fuck this—I quit. You and your lawyers can do whatever you want, but if you're going to go after Dutch, I'm done." Summer pushed back her chair and threw down her napkin. "I'm packing up my Hefty bags right now, and I'm never coming back."

Hattie looked panicked for a moment, but then her composure returned. "You know, all of this unpleasantness can be avoided if you'll simply—"

"No! No more bargaining and blackmail. I give up. This is an amazing town, Hattie. I've been all over the world, and I can tell you for a fact that this place is one-in-a-million. You're so lucky to live here, but you'll never understand that. You're willing— happy!—to ruin everything. As long as you can keep your fifty-year-old blood feud going strong."

"This isn't about my so-called blood feud."

Summer "accidentally" knocked a crystal serving bowl to the floor as she rounded the corner of the table.

"This is about my future," Hattie said.

"The future in which you make everyone else as miserable as you are?"

Hattie paused to sip her coffee, looking a little too confident. "You're advising me to stop harboring old grudges, Miss Benson? Do something productive with my life? Go abroad and see the world while I still can?"

"I think I made that pretty clear, yeah." Summer frowned as a dark sense of suspicion sank in. Somehow she'd just played right into her adversary's hands.

Hattie tilted her head, considering. "Perhaps you're right. Perhaps a change of scenery will change my perspective."

"Wow, I . . ." Summer nibbled her lower lip. "Really?"

"Yes. Your travel tales have piqued my interest. I *would* like to see Paris before I die."

Summer turned up her palm and addressed the heavens above. "Why is it always Paris? Why?"

"What's wrong with Paris?" Hattie asked.

"Nothing. By all means, go to Paris! *Bon voyage.* In fact, if you back off and stop threatening Dutch with whatever you're threatening him with, I'm happy to be your personal travel concierge. I'll plan your Paris trip myself."

Hattie's smile turned positively diabolical. "I'm delighted to hear you say that."

"Your wish is my command." Summer took this opportunity to snatch back her phone. "Do you have an airline preference? I can make some recommendations, if you'd like."

"Spare no expense." Hattie spread her snowy linen napkin across her lap. "We're not going to be backpacking through the Alps with a Eurorail pass. We only want the best of the best."

Summer's head snapped up. "'We'?"

"You'll come with me, naturally."

"Where? To France?"

"Yes. And then Italy, Switzerland, Germany, Ireland." Hattie spread jam across a piping hot scone. "Wherever we care to go."

"Um. Okay." Summer forced a laugh. "I can't really fly right now. My last flight scarred me for life. Literally."

Hattie dismissed this with an airy wave. "As you would say, it's time to move on."

Summer stood dumbstruck for a few moments, then asked, "And how long is this little European jaunt of yours going to last?"

"Not my jaunt—*ours,*" Hattie corrected. "I couldn't possibly manage all the luggage and logistics by myself. You will accompany me and continue to act as my companion. And it will last as long as I care to be abroad. Perhaps a few years, provided my health holds out."

"A few *years?*"

"I have a lot I want to see."

Summer chose her words carefully. "But I live here now."

"Temporarily, you said. Until Labor Day, you said."

"That was before I saw the ghost dog!"

"For the last time, Miss Benson, there is no ghost dog." Hattie looked as though it was taking every ounce of her self-control not to hurl her coffee cup at Summer's head. "I've lived here longer than anyone. If there were a ghost dog, I would have seen it."

"It's real," Summer swore. "Saw it with my own eyes."

"Perhaps you saw a hallucination brought on by an overabundance of hormones and alcohol."

"Oh, I'm not denying that hormones and alcohol were involved, but the dog was definitely real. Listen. I'm flattered that you want me to travel the world with you, but I'm staying put. I've already talked to Beryl about renting the apartment over her boutique, so—"

"You misunderstand. I'm not *asking* you to be my traveling companion. I'm *telling* you."

Summer struggled to remain calm. "And if I don't?"

"Then it will be very unfortunate for Mayor Jansen and all the other Black Dog Bay residents who have to suffer as a result of your obstinacy."

"You're the devil."

Hattie arched one elegant tan eyebrow. "I'm taking you on an all-expenses-paid trip around the world."

"Everyone was right about you," Summer said. "They all warned me! They said you were mean and spiteful, but I defended you!" She paused. "Well, I did at first."

"I'm touched by your loyalty." Hattie's smirk flattened into a grim line. "But the people who know me best told you who I was, and you should have listened."

"But I . . . But you . . . I want you to be better than this."

A hint of sadness crept into Hattie's smile. "For a woman who's so worldly, you're very naive. People show you who they are, and you refuse to believe them. You insist on trying to change them through wishful thinking and sheer force of will."

"Why would you even want a companion who has to be black-mailed into going with you? I like it here. I want to stay." Summer crossed to the window and stared out at the endless blue horizon. "I want to walk on the beach in the first snowfall. I want to board up the windows and ride out a hurricane with a bottle of booze and a deck of cards. I want to see my salt-resistant roses bloom in the fall."

"Roses." Hattie sniffed with disdain.

"Yes! Roses! I grafted the buds or whatever you call it, and I want to see them bloom." Summer turned back to her employer and begged, "Let me go. Let me stay."

"Just as you like. I'll let you stay. But remember, it's not I who will be inflicting suffering on the residents of this town. It's you."

chapter 28

"Finally!" Jenna paused in the middle of refilling the candy bowls as Summer walked into the Whinery. "It's about time."

Summer glanced out the plate glass window, where the blazing sun was beating down on Scarlett and the garbage bags piled in the convertible's passenger seat. "Settle down, ladies. It's the middle of the afternoon. Even I have to pace myself."

Hollis put down the paperback she was reading. "Wait until you hear."

Summer sat next to her. "Hear what?"

Hollis and Jenna exchanged a flurry of looks. "You'd better have a drink first."

Jenna tossed her a Hershey's Kiss. "And some chocolate."

"Let me see your manicure." Hollis grabbed Summer's hand and inspected her nail polish. "Might want to go see Cori for a touch-up."

"Did you two already start drinking without me?" Summer snatched her hand back. "You did, didn't you? And here I thought we were friends!"

Jenna and Hollis glanced at each other again, and Summer snapped.

"Stop! Stop with the meaningful looks and the cryptic comments and tell me what's going on before I beat it out of you."

"Okay." Jenna stepped out from behind the bar and sat down on the other side of Summer. "So. You know how everyone around here is always gossiping about everyone else?"

"Yes."

Hollis started bouncing around in her seat. "Well, right now, we're gossiping about you."

"About me and Hattie?" Summer crumpled up the Hershey's Kiss wrapper and ripped into a fun-size Milky Way. "Word travels fast, huh?"

"No." Jenna looked confused. "About you and Dutch."

Summer froze, a string of caramel dangling from her lip. "What about me and Dutch?"

Hollis crowded in closer, even though there were no other customers. "He's going to ask you to marry him."

Summer burst out laughing. "Warn me before you say these things so I don't spray caramel everywhere."

Hollis and Jenna stared at her, both of them wide-eyed and straight-faced. "We're serious."

"Very serious."

"Utterly and completely serious."

Summer stopped laughing and put down the candy bar. "No, you're not."

"Oh yes." Hollis nodded, her green eyes earnest. "I went over to Bethany Beach yesterday for an author event."

"She's a crazy stalker," Jenna explained.

Hollis's porcelain complexion glowed pink. "I am not! I know this guy from when I lived in L.A. He wasn't always a writer."

"So it's a guy?" Jenna asked.

"Yes."

"And is he attractive?"

"By whose standards?" Hollis demanded.

Jenna grinned. "Yours."

"Well." Hollis's cheeks got even pinker. "Yes."

"And did you happen to take this attractive male out for lunch after the event? You know, just to talk about books and writing and your glory days in Hollywood?"

"We did not have lunch!" Hollis looked triumphant, then muttered, "We had dinner."

"Uh-huh. I thought so. Stalker."

"Hello?" Summer raised her hand as if waiting to be called on in math class. "Can we get back to me and my problems, please?"

"You don't have any problems," Jenna informed her. "You're going to marry Dutch Jansen and live happily ever after."

"It's probably a great ring, too," Hollis added. "Knowing Dutch."

"There is no ring," Summer assured them. "You're high. You have been smoking a meth lab's worth of drugs."

"No, listen!" Hollis said. "This is what I was going to tell you before I was so rudely interrupted. So I was in Bethany Beach yesterday, and there was a jewelry store next to the bookstore. The door was open, and I thought I heard Dutch's voice when I walked by. Sure enough, there he was, looking into a display case with Ingrid."

"Oh." Relief flooded through Summer. "That's it? That doesn't mean he's going to propose. That doesn't mean *anything*. He was with his sister, for God's sake. They were probably getting his watch repaired."

Hollis shook her head, her eyes sparkling. "They were definitely looking at rings. The salesclerk handed one to Dutch, and he held it up in the sunlight, and then Ingrid said she liked it."

"Well, they were probably picking out a ring for her, then," Summer said. "For her birthday or something."

"Wrong again. Right after Ingrid said she liked it, Dutch said, 'But do you think *she'd* like it?' and Ingrid said, 'Maybe she'd rather have a diamond,' and then Dutch said no, it had to be a lavender stone."

"Lavender?" Summer's throat closed up. "That's . . ." *Perfect.*

"Well, what happened?" Jenna demanded. "Did he buy the ring or not?"

"I don't know," Hollis confessed. "I had to go be a crazy stalker."

"Priorities, Hollis. *Priorities.*"

"Maybe it's . . . um . . . a friendship ring," Summer stammered.

"Last time I checked, *friends* don't send each other silk panties in wineglasses." Jenna shot her a sly grin.

"They also don't end up in the police blotter for 'amorous activities' in the country club parking lot." Hollis grabbed Summer's hand and examined her naked fingers. "What's your ring size? Just in case anyone wants to know?"

Right on cue, the front door swung open and Dutch walked in.

Jenna jumped to her feet. Hollis grabbed her book and pretended to be reading. Summer shoved her hands under her thighs. You could practically hear waves of estrogen sloshing around.

"Is this a bad time?" Dutch stopped in his tracks when he saw their faces. "I can come back later."

"No, no, it's a great time." Jenna signaled to Hollis and sidled toward the back door. "We were just leaving."

"We'll be back in a few minutes." Hollis hopped off her stool. "If you have any, you know, news to share."

They nudged each other toward the back door, giggling all the way.

Dutch watched them go, his brow creased with bewilderment. After the back door slammed, he asked Summer, "What was that about?"

"Oh, nothing. You know how we do here at the Whinery." She tried to smile.

"Hey." He stepped closer and brushed a lock of hair back from her face. "You okay?"

"I'm fine." She kept her gaze trained on the floor. "There's just a lot going on right now."

"Everything's about to change, one way or another." He gave her a quick kiss on the cheek, then moved in for a more thorough kiss on the lips.

The sound system, which had been playing Kacey Musgraves's "Stupid," went silent. A few seconds later, the violin strains of Etta James's "At Last" poured out of the speakers.

Dutch pulled out of the kiss. "What's *that* about?"

"No idea." Summer had to laugh. "I'm pretty sure it's sacrilege to play that in here, though. I'm surprised lightning's not striking us down." She squared her shoulders and took a deep breath. "But I'm glad you're here, because I have some news."

"So do I."

Etta James kept crooning away about true love and Summer couldn't even maintain eye contact. "I kind of went nuclear with Hattie this morning."

"I don't want to talk about her right now." Dutch slid his index finger under her chin and tilted her face up. "There's something else I need to talk to you about first." His hand went to his pocket.

And just like that, she was back in the hospital bed, waking up to a splitting headache, a body covered in burns and bruises, a vase full of rotting red roses, and a man about to pull an engagement ring out of his pocket. She remembered how she'd felt when she found out Aaron was on the verge of proposing. Like she couldn't get enough air. Like she was about to pass out.

Right now, she didn't feel like she was going to pass out.

Right now, she felt like she was going to *die*.

Because she wanted to say yes.

She shoved off the bar top with both hands and sprinted out to the sidewalk, slamming the door against her shoulder as she went.

chapter 29

"Summer! Summer, come back!"

She ran, but he ran faster. His hand closed around her elbow before she reached the curb.

"What are you doing? Is your shoulder okay?"

"I'm fine!" She wrested away from his grasp. "Leave me alone."

"Let me look," he commanded.

She relented and let him roll up her short sleeve and examine the red splotch over her bicep.

"You're going to have a hell of a bruise tomorrow," he predicted. "You need to put some ice on that."

"I'm *fine*." She squinted in the midday sunlight. "I can walk it off."

"Stay here." He gave her a look of warning, then strode back into the bar and returned with a bundle of ice cubes wrapped in a pink dish towel. He handed the compress to Summer and led her across the town square to the weathered white gazebo by the bronze dog statue.

"I'm sorry." Summer sat down and pressed the cold pack against her skin. "I shouldn't have . . . I'm sorry."

He settled back against the wooden railing, waiting her out.

"You're probably wondering what the hell's wrong with me." Summer couldn't bring herself to meet his gaze.

"The thought has crossed my mind, yes. But I'm living day in and day out with a seventeen-year-old girl. I'm getting used to dramatic exits."

"That's not fair," Summer objected. "Ingrid is much more mature than I am." She took a moment to regain her self-control. To make sure she wouldn't say anything too rash or reckless. "I'm just upset."

"I can see that." He waited for her to elaborate, but she didn't want to tell him about Hattie. Not yet.

More silence. Families and small groups of heartbreak tourists trooped by, their flip-flops smacking against the planks of the boardwalk.

"Summer?" Dutch prompted.

She stared at the burnished bronze dog. "This is going to sound crazy."

"I'm listening."

"When I walked into the Whinery today, Hollis said . . . she said . . ." The more she thought about it, the more absurd it sounded in her own mind. She couldn't imagine how ridiculous it would sound coming out of her mouth.

But she couldn't ignore it, either. She couldn't do what she had always done—deflect, defer, deny the truth. This time was different. Dutch was different.

She was different.

"Hollis said you were looking at rings in Bethany Beach. Like, engagement rings." When he didn't respond right away, she set down the compress and covered her face with her hands. "I know. I sound like a delusional narcissist."

"I can't believe this." Dutch ducked his head, spearing his fingers into his thick brown hair. "There really is no such thing as a secret in this town." He straightened up. "I should have known that would get back to you."

"So it's true?"

He picked up the bundle of ice and held it to her shoulder. "You look like you're about to keel over."

"I need to sit down." She pitched forward, bracing her elbows on her knees. "I'm already sitting down."

"The reaction every man hopes for." He laughed drily. "Don't pass out just yet. It sounds worse than it is."

She rallied, putting her hand over his on the ice pack. "That came out wrong. What I meant was—"

"The rings were Ingrid's idea. She and I went to lunch, we passed a jewelry store, and she wanted to go in. We must've been in there for an hour, looking at settings and learning about stones. I think she's qualified to be a gemologist at this point."

Summer wrinkled her nose. "Ingrid doesn't seem like the type to fantasize about rings and weddings and big poufy gowns."

"She's not. She's already informed me that she'll be having a small ceremony on a cliff in Bali, *if* she ever decides to knuckle under to the patriarchy and shackle herself in the bonds of legal wedlock."

"Is that verbatim?"

He nodded. "Anyway, she's concerned that we're not moving things along fast enough."

Summer blinked. "You and I?"

"Yes."

"But we've only been dating for a few weeks. Engagement rings are definitely not part of our agreement!"

"I know. But no matter how mature she thinks she is, she's still seventeen. And she wants you to stay in town after tourist season's over. She wants us to knuckle under to the patriarchy and shackle ourselves in the bonds of legal wedlock."

"What do you want?" Summer asked.

He gave her a look. "I'm not sure answering that is in my best interests right now. You practically dislocated your shoulder fleeing me."

"Oh, come on." She leaned her shoulder against his. "Off the record."

"I think we've only been dating for a few weeks. I'm not ruling anything out, but we're still in the planning and development stages."

"Like floating a bill through subcommittee." Summer was surprised to hear the wistful note in her voice. "But it's only fair to tell you now: I'm not the kind of girlfriend you buy a ring for."

He rolled his eyes. "If you're worried about all the worn-out stereotypes of political wives, I can assure you—"

"No. It's not that I'm not political-wife material; it's that I'm not wife material. Period. Full stop."

"Says who?"

"Dutch, come on." She let her posture relax into a slouch. "I'm a temporary distraction from your real life."

"You're part of my real life," he insisted.

"I wish that were true." She dropped her hand, letting the ice pack rest next to her hip. "I'm so, so happy I met you and harassed you into going out with me."

"Me, too."

"But we're not going to last." She struggled to appear unaffected amid the swirl of guilt and fear and shame. "We're having fun. But 'fun' is kind of all I am."

"That's not true." He pressed his hand over hers, reassuring her while also preventing a second escape attempt.

"Isn't it?" She touched his hand. "What do you really know about me? We just met."

"I've made up my mind about you, Summer. I don't have to justify that decision." He smiled, those gunmetal gray eyes softening. "You're the girl who ran over my roses and helped me plant new ones. You're the reason I climbed onto Hattie Huntington's roof in the middle of the night. You are the exception to all my rules."

She remembered the first time she'd seen him working in his garden, focused and fulfilled. Gardening was something—the only thing—he did simply because he wanted to. Because it made him happy.

She had seen the world through his eyes that day. She had said the roses were magic, and she'd been right.

This tiny town by the sea was full of magic: the black dog, the resurrection of hope, the love they'd cultivated like a rose bloom unfurling in the sun.

She ached to tell him everything, to confide in him that he'd changed her forever, for the better. But all she could manage was, "You do have a lot of rules."

"A lot of rules and a lot of responsibilities, and I signed up for that. But when I'm with you"—he shrugged—"I don't feel so tied down."

"But that's what a relationship is. Being tied down."

"Not if you do it right." He gathered her into his arms, pressing his lips against her temple. "But I'd brace myself, if I were you. I think Ingrid might be getting ready to pop the question."

She laughed and got to her feet. "Can we stop talking and go make out in a parking lot or something?"

"I thought you'd never ask."

Summer sat with her back propped against Dutch's headboard, watching the waves sparkle under the golden sunset. The whole room seemed to glow, warm and quiet.

Very quiet. Dutch hadn't had a lot to say since he'd taken her home from the gazebo a few hours ago.

He'd gotten his point across, though. Several times.

She slipped out of bed, still naked, and walked over to the window. An amazing vista stretched out into the horizon—shingled roof hanging over a rainbow of roses edging into the white-capped waves. "It looks like it goes on forever."

He walked up behind her, still silent.

"But it doesn't." She tried to explain, to justify herself. "That was my life before this, Dutch. Shuttling planes full of people across the ocean. Around the world, full circle."

When he finally spoke, she could hear the smile in his voice. "Only to end up in Delaware."

She tried to smile, too. "Nothing goes on forever. Everything is finite, even if we can't see the end point from the starting point."

He was so close she could feel his body heat against her cool skin. "What about pi?" he asked. "What about a googol?"

"Google is an Internet search engine," she said. "Forever is a fairy tale." If she leaned back a fraction of an inch, she would be touching him. But she didn't.

"I'm not asking for forever," he said. "I'm asking for today."

"But what about tomorrow?"

"Don't focus on the end point. Focus on today."

She let herself lean into him. "I'm trying."

"I've got you, Summer. I will not let you fall."

She rested her head in the space between his chin and shoulder. *I love you,* she thought but did not say.

He loved her, too, she knew. More than she deserved.

"But what if you had to choose?" she asked. "Between me and Black Dog Bay?"

"Why would I have to make that choice?" He pulled back a bit. "That doesn't make sense."

"If you had to choose," she insisted.

He didn't hesitate. "I would find a way to have both."

"You can't always find a way," she said softly. "Love has limits."

chapter 30

"*Hey!*" Beryl called out from the doorway of Retail Therapy the next afternoon as Summer strolled by with an ice-cream cone. "Come in for a second. I need the latest gossip from the Purple Palace."

Summer ducked under the store's awning and took another bite of chocolate fudge ripple. "No gossip, as far as I know."

"Oh, there's always gossip around here. Scott says there's going to be some major construction projects starting up this fall."

Summer furrowed her brow. "Who's Scott?"

"My boyfriend. The one in concrete?" Beryl ushered her inside.

"Oh, right. The one who makes you watch baseball in bars that are not the Whinery?"

"That's him. He says something big is brewing, and everyone in the construction industry wants in on it." Beryl lowered her voice, glancing back over her shoulder at a pair of customers browsing the "grieving stage" racks. "So what've you heard?"

Summer nibbled her waffle cone, trying to quell the nervous flutters in her stomach. "Nothing."

"Are you sure? Hattie Huntington owns most of Main Street, and you live with her—"

"Not anymore. I moved out in a huff a few days ago."

"—and Dutch is the mayor and you're dating him. I figured you'd probably have the inside track."

Summer considered what Dutch had said about Hattie Huntington deciding to twist the knife after all these years. "Did Scott happen to mention what kind of development project it is?"

"He didn't know for sure. But something really big." Beryl wrapped her arms around her torso. "Which kind of worries me because, you know. Black Dog Bay is a small town, and we like it that way."

"I wouldn't stress about it too much," Summer said with a confidence she didn't feel. "How much can Hattie really do without getting approval from everyone else? I mean, she's rich and well connected, but she's not *invincible*. She's only one woman."

Major Developer Plans Luxury Hotel and "Brand Overhaul" of Town

"We're screwed."

The next morning, Jenna slapped the new edition of the *Black Dog Bay Bulletin* down on the bar and addressed the friends who had gathered for the emergency summit meeting she'd called at the Whinery. "Read it and weep."

The women crowded around as Hollis picked up the paper and began to read the article aloud:

> *Local land baron Harriet Huntington has approved a preliminary purchase and development deal with commercial real estate corporation KRKJ Holdings.*
>
> *Proposed plans include the construction of an oceanfront resort and several themed shops and restaurants in the town's main tourist areas.*

"The main tourist areas," Hollis repeated, looking up at her horrified audience. "Like where we're standing right now."

> *"We're very excited about the projected growth in this area," said KRKJ spokesperson Kami Mooth. "For years, Black Dog Bay has been known as a haven for heartbroken women, and with an increase in national press coverage, we believe that now is the ideal time to raise visibility. We aim to appeal to lovelorn singles all across the country with a new slogan: 'Lick Your Wounds in Black Dog Bay.'"*

"'Lick Your Wounds in Black Dog Bay'?" Summer leaned over Hollis's shoulder to examine the article for herself. "Does it really say that? Gross."

"Where on earth do they think they're going to fit a luxury resort?" Beryl fumed. "Every square inch of beachfront property is already developed."

Hollis kept scanning the article. "Miss Huntington's selling them her estate. All of it, including the beach rights. They're going to tear her mansion down to make room for the hotel."

"She wouldn't!"

"'The KRKJ team is unofficially known in development circles as "the Poconoids" for their proclivity for kitsch. Most of their successful ventures are reminiscent of resorts in the Poconos, which famously feature heart-shaped beds and martini-glass hot tubs.'"

"And by 'kitsch,' they mean 'tacky as hell,'" Beryl translated.

"How much of Main Street does Hattie actually own?" Summer asked.

"She holds most of the leases," Jenna replied. "Including mine."

"And mine," said Hollis.

"And mine," said Beryl. "Rents are going to skyrocket if they bring in franchises and a luxury resort. No way will I be able to renew my lease."

"Especially because they want to force us out," Hollis said. "Forget the Poconos. I Googled KRKJ this morning, and their 'vision' is like Liberace on Ecstasy. They're going to turn this place into the second coming of *Jersey Shore*." She pointed out the front window toward the bronze dog statue. "That's where MTV will start filming."

"There'll be Mardi Gras beads around that dog's neck." Beryl looked close to tears. "Lavinia Leighton is turning in her grave."

"This place'll probably turn into a daiquiri bar that plays 'I Will Survive' on repeat." Jenna scowled. "With a vomit bucket by the front door."

Summer held up her index finger and tried to clarify. "But wait. I thought Black Dog Bay isn't about hookups or revenge?"

"It's not. It's about healing. But why should reality stand in the way of progress?" Beryl shredded a pink cocktail napkin. "I wish we'd never gotten all that media attention."

"They're going to shut down my bookstore and start selling plastic ex-boyfriend voodoo dolls for twenty-five dollars a pop," Hollis predicted. "Just wait. They're going to do to this town what Madison Avenue did to Valentine's Day—turn it from something small and special into glittery, mass-produced, overpriced crap."

"Oh, and check this out." Jenna picked up the paper. "It says here, 'Our resort will offer a host of upscale amenities to cater to the newly dumped demographic, including a large gas fire pit on the patio where guests can burn their wedding gowns and mementos.'" Her eyes flashed in outrage. "They totally stole that from the Better Off Bed-and-Breakfast."

"Gas fire pit?" Beryl snorted. "That's just wrong. Everybody knows there's only one way to burn a wedding gown, and that's on a driftwood campfire."

"I told you," Hollis intoned. "Mass-produced, overpriced crap."

"'Although the town has a charming history, our goal is to

increase the market appeal and reinvent the brand. We've tentatively committed to naming the resort 'Cupid's Cove.'"

"Cupid's Cove?" Summer gagged.

"Where's the vomit bucket?" Beryl asked.

Jenna pulled a bottle of tequila out from under the bar, despite the early hour. "Shots for everyone. On the house."

Drops of tequila sloshed down on the newsprint as the businesswomen of Black Dog Bay clinked their glasses in commiseration.

"Here's to the end of our world."

Summer hung back at the edge of the group. "There has to be something we can do. I mean, aren't there, like, zoning laws, or council meetings, or . . . or . . ."

"Well, sure, there are all kind of laws." Jenna laughed bitterly. "But laws don't apply to people like Miss Huntington and her good buddy, the senator."

"She finally did it." Beryl slammed her shot glass onto the bar. "She hit the self-destruct button and she's taking us all with her."

"But why?" Hollis kept asking.

"Why does she do anything? Because she can."

"I called Dutch this morning," someone said. "He said he's working on it."

"He can work on it all he wants, but it's not going to change Miss Huntington's mind. You know how she is. There's nothing that can stop her."

"Well." Summer stood up and slung her handbag over her shoulder. "There might be one thing."

chapter 31

"*D*on't worry." Dutch squeezed Summer's hand when she finished recounting the emergency summit meeting. "We'll figure out a way around this."

"Why didn't you tell me about this before?" Ingrid sat at the Jansens' kitchen table, reading the newspaper article over and over, her jaw dropping lower with each perusal.

"Because I didn't want you to freak out." Dutch handed mugs of freshly brewed coffee to Summer and Ingrid.

"Too late." Ingrid spooned sugar into her cup.

Summer focused on the wisps of steam curling up from her coffee. "This is kind of my fault." When Dutch and Ingrid started to protest, she explained, "Hattie's doing this to make a point. And her point is, I better do what she says."

"No. This is not how it works. Everything's got to go through eighteen layers of bureaucracy." Dutch remained staunch. "They can't just start construction next week."

"Really? Then how do you explain the geological survey team Hollis saw down at the beach this morning?" Summer and Ingrid crossed the kitchen and peered out the recessed dormer window.

Sure enough, they could see trucks and workers assembled on the sand in front of the Purple Palace.

"This can't happen." Ingrid collapsed in a heap on the braided blue rug. "They can't tear down that hideous house and put up some hideous resort."

"And turn Main Street into the Snooki strip mall," Summer said. "Don't forget that."

"None of that's going to happen," Dutch said.

"Yeah—as long as I knuckle under to her demands and go abroad indefinitely with her."

Ingrid's eyes got even more panicky. "But you can't leave, either."

Summer stared out at the shoreline. Imagining how the view would change with the addition of a huge, hulking resort called "Cupid's Cove."

"Right?" Ingrid turned to Dutch. "She's not leaving, right?"

"She's not leaving," Dutch said. "Nobody's developing the shoreline and nobody's leaving."

They both looked at Summer.

"Say something," Ingrid demanded.

Summer lifted her mug halfway to her lips, then put it back down on the table. "If I stay here, that house is coming down, the new hotel is going up, and the local business owners are screwed. Hattie was crystal clear on her terms."

Dutch's composure finally cracked. "You're actually considering this."

Summer sighed. "I don't think I have a choice."

He strode over to the window. "It's not your job to fix this, Summer. It's mine."

"But you can't fix it!" Ingrid drew her knees up to her chest.

"I haven't figured out a way to fix this part of the problem in the three minutes since I found out about it," Dutch said. "Give me another three minutes."

Ingrid jumped up, pounded up the stairs, and slammed her bedroom door.

Dutch studied Summer, his expression unyielding. "How long have you known about this?"

Summer bowed her head and rested her hand on the back of her neck. "Since, um, since . . . Why do you ask?"

"I'm curious. Why didn't you come to me as soon as Hattie started in with all this?"

"Because I was too busy panicking about hypothetical engagement rings."

"You were over here for hours. You spent the night."

"I was trying to figure out what to do."

He didn't move, but she could feel a new distance opening up between them. "We're supposed to be a team."

She took a deep breath, tried to sound detached. "This isn't your problem."

"Of course it is! Black Dog Bay is my problem, Summer. *You* are my problem."

At this, her head snapped back up. "No, I am not."

"Yes, you are. And I'm tired of waiting for you to be ready to admit that."

Her words came out hurried and defensive as she tried to explain what Hattie had threatened and what it would mean. ". . . I can't be responsible for watching Jenna and Hollis and Beryl and Cori and Marla go out of business." She touched her chest, right over her heart. "I can't be responsible for ruining the town that your family built."

He remained remote, his expression stony. "You're not responsible for anything Hattie does."

"I'm responsible for my choices."

"Yes, you are." His eyes were flat and cold. "You choose to stay here or walk away."

Long, silent minutes passed.

"I have to go with Hattie." She focused on the churning gray waves and willed him to understand. "She gave me an ultimatum."

The chair legs scraped against the floorboards as he stood up. "Then I'll give you one, too. You either trust me or you don't."

She looked up at him, memorizing the features of his face. Remembering how she'd felt when he stopped talking to her for two days. The sharp, savage pangs of loss. The doubts, followed by the certainty that love was something she could have only for a limited time.

She imagined how she'd feel when he walked away from her for good. The sheer effort it would take to bring her back to a numb equilibrium.

"I don't want you to give up everything for me," she said softly. *Because in the end, you may decide I wasn't worth it.*

"You trust me or you don't," he repeated.

She knew what she should say, what she should do. She had to take that leap of faith and believe that he would catch her.

I can't.

She reached out to him with one hand. "I want to."

He turned and walked out of the kitchen, leaving her alone with the burning regret she knew she'd carry across the globe with her.

Summer splashed through the warm ocean shallows on her way to the Purple Palace. She could feel the gentle tug of the undertow with every step she took.

When she arrived at the luxurious mansion with the best view of the bay, she tried to envision what the Poconoid design team would replace it with. Neon? Gilt cupolas? Life-size cardboard cutouts of Channing Tatum and George Clooney?

By the time she reached the main entrance, she was in a rage.

For possibly the first time ever, Hattie opened the door herself. Her face looked strained, but her satisfaction was evident. "Back with an air of contrition, I see."

Summer met Hattie's triumphant smile with a cold, steely glare. "I hate you."

Hattie acknowledged that with a brisk nod. "I'll take that to mean you're going to accompany me to Europe?"

When Summer didn't reply, Hattie said, "The car to the airport will leave this house at nine a.m. on Thursday. Will you be here or not?"

Summer spun on her heel and walked away, wishing with all her heart that she could stay.

chapter 32

The next morning was mild and clear, and Summer spotted someone on the edge of Hattie's beach, where the surveyor's crew had been yesterday. When she walked out to investigate, she found Ingrid kneeling in the sand, using a garden trowel to scoop out a deep, narrow hole.

Summer lifted her hand in greeting as she approached. "What's up?"

Ingrid didn't look up from her work. "I'm building a sea turtle nest."

Summer crouched down next to her. "Do they have sea turtles this far north?"

"No. But sea turtles are endangered, so I figure that if I make the nests, they can't do any new construction near the shoreline." Ingrid wiped her forehead with the back of her arm and checked a photo she'd pulled up on her phone. "I think that looks pretty authentic, don't you? Now I have to figure out what to use for eggs."

"Oh, honey." Summer sat down, letting her knee graze against Ingrid's. "I don't think that's going to work."

"You don't?" Ingrid regarded the sand pit and nibbled her lip. "Well, then, I'll find another endangered species to exploit." She started typing on her phone. "What about an osprey nest?"

Summer took a deep breath. "Ingrid, I know this is hard, but Dutch and I—"

"You and Dutch?" Ingrid's fingers stilled. "Are you and Dutch even speaking to each other? I heard you guys fighting yesterday."

Summer tucked her hair behind her ear. "You, uh, you heard that?"

"I'm pretty sure they heard you in Baltimore." Ingrid hunkered down in the sand. She paused, then pleaded, "Don't leave. Dutch will forgive you. I'll talk to him."

Summer sucked in her breath as her heart squeezed. She knew too well what Ingrid was feeling right now. The helpless desperation of trying to fix someone else's relationship. The hope that if you could just find the right words, act the right way, you could erase sins and correct mistakes you couldn't even label.

For a moment, she was five years old again, feeling the cold soda seep into her dress and knowing, from the flicker of sorrow in her mother's eyes, that she had ruined everything.

"You don't need to talk to Dutch for me. Please hear me when I say this. What happened yesterday was between me and your brother." She placed her hand on Ingrid's arm. "We're adults."

Ingrid snatched her arm away. "Then act like it."

"I'm trying."

"Are you breaking up with him?"

"I . . . It's not that simple."

"I knew it." Ingrid nodded with grim certainty. "I knew he should have proposed when I told him to."

"It wouldn't have mattered." Summer waited until Ingrid looked up at her. "I'm not leaving because of Dutch."

"But you're leaving," Ingrid finished for her.

"Yes. But I don't want you to think—"

"Even if you break up, even if you don't like him anymore, you don't have to go." Ingrid looked up, her big eyes brimming with guilt. "I promise I'll stop bugging you about driving Scarlett and playing piano and buying makeup. I'll stop making you be my mentor."

"Being your mentor has been the highlight of my year." Summer smiled, willing Ingrid to smile back. "I wish I could stay here forever."

"Then do it. Stay."

"This isn't about just me. This is about everyone who lives in Black Dog Bay—including you."

Ingrid's expression cycled through a range of emotions as she chose her next tactic. The tactic that would change Summer's mind.

The bargaining stage. Summer was all too familiar with that, too. Except now she was her mother, making an impossible choice, walking away from someone she loved. Because staying here would cost the ones she loved too much.

"Just stay until I go to college," Ingrid said. "Who's going to help me apply to Tulane and Columbia?"

Summer, who had been carrying tissues around in her jeans pocket since the showdown in the kitchen, pulled out one for herself and one for Ingrid. "Believe me, I would stay if I could."

"That's just an excuse. You do whatever you want—you said so yourself."

A physical ache thrummed in Summer's chest. "We can Skype, FaceTime. . . ."

"You'll forget all about me," Ingrid predicted. "Once you're back in the real world."

"I will never forget about you," Summer vowed. "And I will see you again."

Ingrid's gaze turned hard. "No, you won't."

"Yes, I will. That's a promise, Ingrid. And I want you to understand something. Are you listening?" She faltered as she prepared to say the words that someone should have said to her when she was younger. "There is nothing you did to make me leave. And there is nothing you can do to make me stay."

Ingrid crumpled up her tissue and flung it into the sea turtle hole. She stopped crying and begging, and instead began to rage.

"If you go, I'm going to start doing drugs," she threatened. "I'll pierce my tongue, I'll chain-smoke, and I'll . . . I'll eat processed lunch meats."

She stole a glance at Summer to see if she was properly shocked.

Summer remained empathetic and impassive.

"I'll sleep with the mouth-breathing lacrosse jersey." Ingrid got to her feet and glared down. "I'll wear blue eye shadow with the wrong shade of lipstick."

Summer let out an involuntary gasp. "You better not."

"Why can't this be enough?" Ingrid opened her arms to encompass the sky, the sand, the sea. "Why can't you just be happy here with us?"

Summer stood up next to Ingrid. "Life isn't that simple. I wish it were, but it's not."

"Don't patronize me."

"Okay. I'm sorry."

"Everyone here loves you." The pleading note crept back into Ingrid's voice. "Including Dutch, even though he's being stubborn. Including me."

Summer took her hand. "I love you guys, too."

"Why aren't I enough?" Ingrid's voice broke. "Why does everyone end up leaving me?" She swiped at her eyes. "I know you're not my stepmother, or my sister, or whatever, but you're *something*, okay? You and I are something."

"We're definitely something, and we always will be." Summer cleared her throat. "I know what it's like to lose your mom."

"Did your mom die, too?"

"No, she . . ." Summer trailed off. "She left. She left my father and me for another man."

"Wow."

"Yeah. My father never got over it."

"Did you?"

Summer sighed and pulled a bag of M&M's out of her sweatshirt pocket. "I grew up. I moved on." *I walked it off.*

"Did you have to go to therapy?" Ingrid looked both horrified and hopeful.

Summer poured a few M&M's into her palm, then offered the bag to Ingrid. "Oh, I probably should have, but I preferred to work through it the old-fashioned way. Underage drinking and acting out with inappropriate men."

"And now you're doing the exact same thing your mom did," Ingrid accused. "You had your fun and now you're going to forget we ever existed. How can you do this to Dutch? He has spent his whole life taking care of this town, taking care of me. He deserves a girlfriend who loves him."

"Yes, he does," Summer said softly.

"He's too nice, right? That's the problem? He doesn't treat you like crap, so you're not interested?"

Summer flinched. "I get that you're mad, Ingrid, and I don't blame you. But please know that what I have with Dutch, what I have with you—hell, what I have with this whole crazy town—means more to me than I can ever explain."

"Who cares what it means to you? You're leaving to go travel the world with someone you allegedly hate."

"There's nothing alleged about it," Summer assured her. "I despise that bitch for real. And I swear to you, if there were any way I could stay . . ."

"Shut up." Ingrid stalked away.

"I love you," Summer called after her.

"Go to hell." Ingrid broke into a run.

And Summer felt more devastated than after any breakup she'd ever had.

That evening, Summer checked in for one last night at the Better Off Bed-and-Breakfast. She took the long way, doubling back through Main Street, trying to absorb all the vibrancy of this tiny town. The locals, the tourists, the summer homeowners and bored teenagers. How was it possible that she'd arrived here only a few weeks ago, aimless and utterly depleted? Somehow, while she was busy making friends and enemies and memories, she'd put down roots. Somehow, after years of surviving turbulence and changing time zones, she'd found a home.

But not for long.

Tomorrow, she'd be back to reality. Back to jet lag, the blur of ever-changing faces, hotel rooms with thick curtains and bland framed watercolors on the wall.

But no—Hattie Huntington would never settle for corporate chain hotels with laminate furniture and synthetic bedspreads. They would have the best of everything—lodging, food, clothes. Summer would want for nothing.

Yet she was giving up everything.

She reached the turnoff to the inn and paused, inhaling the ocean breeze laced with the faint scent of grease from the boardwalk fries and sugar from the saltwater taffy shop.

When she entered the hotel lobby, Marla greeted her with a welcoming hug and a freshly baked oatmeal raisin cookie.

"Did you hear?" Marla whispered, her blue eyes welling with tears. "Miss Huntington is going to let them come in and build a trashy, tacky resort. I'll never be able to compete."

Summer sat down on the sofa. "I heard."

"I can't believe it. I broke down and cried when Beryl told me, and I start crying again every time I think about it."

"Don't worry. She'll change her mind."

"No, she won't. You know how ornery she is." Marla dabbed at her eyes as she pointed at a trio of framed black-and-white photos on the wall. "For decades, this place has looked the same. Our guests have been able to sit on the porch and look out at the beautiful view and now . . . now . . ."

"She'll change her mind," Summer repeated, but didn't elaborate further. Any explanation she offered would only lead to questions and conversations and misguided attempts to help. She didn't want everyone to rally around her or condemn Hattie.

She couldn't bear an outpouring of support from the community she was about to leave behind.

After pausing to nibble her cookie, she said, "I was hoping you might be able to squeeze me into the attic room tonight."

"Of course, sweetie. I don't blame you one bit for getting out of that witch's house. How long would you like to stay?"

Summer inclined her head, feeling as aimless as she had the day she first checked in. "I don't know."

"Well, you're always welcome here. I'm kind of hoping you'll decide to stay past Labor Day. You and Dutch seem so happy. Just look at you—you're a new woman, and you've seen the black dog to prove it." Marla took a shuddery breath and regained her composure. "Want to go to one more bonfire, for old times' sake?"

Summer smiled wistfully. "Nothing left to burn."

"Well, then, it's official: You're healed." Marla dusted off her hands.

"Not quite. I need a favor. Can I borrow Theo's pickup truck and a flashlight?"

chapter 33

Early Thursday morning, while Hattie called the KRKJ real estate development team to inform them that the deal was off, Summer staked out the Jansens' front porch and prepared to say her good-byes.

She had to ring the bell three times before Ingrid answered the door.

Okay, *thirty*-three times.

Finally, Ingrid yanked the door open with the air of a het-up hillbilly about to discharge a shotgun. "Get off my porch before I call the cops."

"I came to say good-bye." Summer lifted her arms, offering a hug.

Ingrid shrank back. "Bye."

"Ingrid . . ."

"Bye." Ingrid tried to close the door.

Summer wedged the toe of her sneaker in front of the door-jamb. "I'll call you. E-mail you. Send you sheet music from around the world. Whatever you want."

"I don't want anything from you." Ingrid bristled. "And

while you're whoring around Paris, just know that I'm back here shaving my head and failing out of school and . . . and robbing banks."

"Well, then, you'll need a getaway car." Summer dangled her key ring and nodded toward the little red convertible parked in the driveway.

Ingrid eyed the keys with a glimmer of interest, then turned her face away.

"Take it," Summer urged. "I want you to have Scarlett."

"So you're getting rid of your car, too, now that it's not convenient for you to keep it? Wow, you're really cleaning house."

Summer knew that nothing she could do or say right now would help Ingrid heal. So she stayed right where she was and absorbed the full force of Ingrid's anger and pain.

Finally, Ingrid stopped seething long enough to ask, "Well? Why are you still here?"

"I'd like to see Dutch."

Ingrid's hands curled into fists. "He's not home, and even if he were, I wouldn't let you talk to him."

Summer nodded. "You're a good sister."

"Get out of here."

This time, Summer complied. But she left the car keys on the porch railing, the silver metal glistening against the white wood that had been preserved and cared for since the days Black Dog Bay first began.

Six hours later, Summer settled into a cushy leather seat, her mind flashing back to the last time she'd been in the first-class section of an airplane. The smell of wine and coffee. The stubbly-faced English guy handing her the magazine and offering to write a song about her. Kim's expression when she rushed back from the flight deck, bursting with news about Aaron and the diamond ring.

Now here she was, buckling her seat belt on another plane bound for Paris, this time as a passenger. She would drowse and flip through magazines while some other flight attendant presented her with hot towels, salads, entrée, dessert. She would sit, passive, and stare out the window at the sky.

As the pilot made his preflight announcements, Summer expected to be catatonic with terror. She'd assumed that she would need booze, pills, and a suitcase full of M&M's to get through taxi and takeoff. But she didn't feel terrified. Fear would have been preferable to the overwhelming ache of loneliness and loss.

Her old life was gone forever and her new life was about to begin, whether she liked it or not. This summer with Dutch and Ingrid and the women at the Whinery had just been an interlude. Simple and sweet and all too short.

She pulled her cell phone out of her bag.

"Stop texting," Hattie ordered from the seat next to Summer's.

"I'm not texting, I'm IM-ing," Summer informed her.

"Don't quibble with me—just stop. An obsession with one's mobile phone is both gauche and banal." Hattie wrapped her tiny white talons around Summer's wrist, then pushed up her sleeve to reveal pinpricks of blood and faded smudges of dirt. "What in heaven's name did you get up to last night?"

Summer snatched her wrist back. "Oh, this and that."

"You look like you wrestled a lynx."

"Just because I'm your prisoner doesn't mean you can interrogate me." Summer returned her attention to her phone.

"A prisoner flying first-class to Paris?" Hattie's laugh was thin and mocking. "Aren't you the one who told me to move on? Let him go, Miss Benson."

Summer tightened her grip on her phone. "Let *me* go."

"Fine." Hattie rearranged her cashmere shawl. "I'm merely trying to make life easier for you."

"So you keep saying. And yet my life keeps getting harder. Anyway, I'm not even texting him."

The lower half of Hattie's face disappeared in folds of featherweight cashmere. "Your heart is broken; I know. Be patient. You'll get over it."

Summer finally put down the phone and gave Hattie a glacial stare. "In fifty years? Just like you did?"

When the flight attendant took her place beneath the monitor while the safety video played, Summer had the surreal sensation of watching someone else live her life. If the engine hadn't burst into flames that night, she would still be flitting around the world, drinking and dancing and avoiding attachment. She would probably still be with Aaron, slowly sabotaging his attempt to get her to commit. She never would have met Dutch.

And she never would have had to leave him.

The flight attendant pointed out the nearest emergency exits. Summer watched the woman scanning the cabin, no doubt looking for able-bodied assistants among the frail and vulnerable.

Someone like Summer. Someone strong and scrappy, who could do what needed to be done.

"I am never going to get over this," Summer said, as much to herself as to Hattie.

Hattie didn't respond, and Summer assumed the older woman had drifted off to sleep.

But then, in the moment when the plane tilted, leaving the ground and taking flight, Hattie reached over and put her dry, cool hand on Summer's warm, sweaty one.

"Some things we're not meant to recover from. But in the end, you'll find the pain was worth it."

The next few weeks passed in a whirlwind of trips to museums, restaurants, ballet performances, and operas. Summer had seen Paris before, but never like this. Never through the scope of unlimited wealth and privilege. There was no waiting, no inconvenience, no sweating in the ripe urban humidity. Logistics clicked into place and life was easy—at least, from a practical standpoint.

One afternoon, as they left the Musée d'Orsay, Hattie turned to Summer and announced, "I've had enough of Paris. I'd like to go south and see the coastline before it gets too cold."

"Why don't we wait until the weekend?" Summer suggested. "I've a got surprise planned for you."

Hattie's gaze sharpened with suspicion. "What is it?"

"Well, if I told you, it wouldn't be a surprise, now, would it?"

Hattie was having none of this. "We're leaving for the coast tomorrow."

"Can't wait to go topless on the beach, huh? Fine, have it your way. I'll just make a few calls and rearrange a few things."

The next afternoon, Summer and Hattie arrived at a five-star hotel near the rocky shores of Cap d'Antibes. The white Renaissance Revival château was flanked on both sides by tropical gardens, beyond which Summer could see the ocean. The water was a startling shade of turquoise, darkening to cobalt along the horizon.

"Check it." She pointed out a massive white yacht silhouetted against a craggy cliff. "Do you think that's Paul Allen or P. Diddy?"

"Hmm." Hattie gazed up at the imposing, intricately carved stone facade. "I suppose this will suffice."

Another car pulled into the circular driveway.

A small, stout woman with curly blond hair, sparkling blue

eyes, and a jaunty red beret stepped out. "*Mon dieu*, Hattie. You look so *old*."

Hattie dropped her smart little satchel. "Pauline?" She clutched Summer's arm. "What is she doing here?"

"Same thing as you." Summer shrugged. "Reuniting with her long-lost sister."

chapter 34

"How dare you?" Hattie tightened her grip on Summer as her sister approached. "You know we're estranged. You know I don't speak to her. I told you—"

Summer interrupted. "You never once told me not to hunt down your estranged sister and fly her out to France."

"I shouldn't have to tell you things like that!" Hattie closed her eyes and shook her head, as if this would somehow erase Pauline from existence. "How did she find us? Did you conjure her with witchcraft?"

"I conjured her with Facebook." Summer rolled her eyes. "I keep telling you, there's this magical thing now called the Internet."

Hattie stiffened her spine. "I have no desire to see her ever again."

"I know."

"I have made my feelings very clear on this." Hattie trembled with rage, but Summer detected an undertone of fear. "You betrayed me."

"You've gone behind my back lots of times," Summer pointed out. "But then you tell me you're doing it for my own good. So now it's my turn."

When Pauline was twenty feet away, Hattie threw up her arms to ward her off.

Pauline stopped, still smiling determinedly. "Well, my goodness, Hattie, you got so thin. Don't you eat anymore?"

Hattie crossed her arms. "Not as much as you, clearly."

Pauline threw back her head and laughed, and Summer realized that she'd never once heard Hattie laugh. "Yes, I still love my chocolate and my cheese." She took another tiny step toward her sister. "I see you're still dressing like an uptight preppy."

"And you're dressing like a flower child slattern." To Summer's astonishment, Hattie took a step toward Pauline. "You got old, too, you know."

"Not as old as you. Your hair is so short."

"Yours is too bleached."

They each took another step.

"Still trying to hide your freckles under your makeup, I see," Pauline said.

"At least I'm aging gracefully," Hattie retorted. "It's plain as day you're using Botox."

Another step closer.

"And you're still mean and sharp-tongued as a snake."

"And you're still flighty and superficial."

"Some things never change."

Pauline pounced, throwing both arms around her sister.

Hattie made a halfhearted show of struggling, but only for a moment. "Get off of me! I can't breathe!"

"Ah, sisterly love." Summer clasped her hands over her heart. "Reunited and it feels so good."

"Let's go, you two. One foot in front of the other. Do I have to frisk you for weapons, or can you behave yourselves in public?" Summer dragged the Huntington sisters out of the hotel lobby to the sidewalk. Hattie had made another attempt to escape to the isolation of her hotel suite, but Summer had managed to head her off at the elevators. "We're off to do some bonding."

"What exactly do you mean by 'bonding'?" Hattie eyed her with suspicion.

"Yes." Pauline seemed apprehensive, too. "What does bonding entail?"

"Forced marches and alcohol. Hup, two, three, four." Summer led the way down a treelined path to the nearby town, which, despite being billed as a "quaint fishing village," featured gourmet restaurants, boutiques capable of obliterating an entire credit card limit in a single transaction, and an obscenely expensive *pâtisserie*.

Pauline flitted alongside her sister. "Hattie, I'd given up on ever talking to you again. I was so thrilled when you sent me that Facebook message."

"I didn't." Hattie stomped over a sewer grate in her spotless white loafers.

"I handle all her personal correspondence," Summer explained. "Just doing my job as her companion."

"I do not correspond with my sister," Hattie said. "Nor do I have a Facebook account."

"Yes, yes, you've made your point." Pauline confided to Summer, "I sent her Christmas cards for twenty years straight before I gave up."

Summer nodded. "She can be a little hardheaded."

"Runs in the family, I suppose." Pauline raised her voice as if her sister were deaf instead of ignoring her. "So, Hattie, what are you up to these days?"

Hattie kept her mouth closed and her gaze straight ahead, striding past charming cafés and breathtaking seaside vistas without out a second glance.

"She's still living in Black Dog Bay," Summer told Pauline. "Lording it over all the peasants."

"Really?" Pauline was practically shouting at Hattie. "I thought you hated that place." She told Summer, "When we were little, she used to say she was moving to New York as soon as she finished high school." To Hattie she said, "I'm living in California now, not that you asked. In a lovely little bungalow by Carmel. I make jewelry and grow my own vegetables."

Hattie said nothing.

"Married?" Summer asked.

"Twice," Pauline said. "The first husband divorced me, the second one died. But I've got lots of friends, always somewhere to go and something to do."

Summer shot a sidelong look at Hattie. "Do you golf?"

"Heavens, no." Pauline wrinkled her nose. "But I just started going to Zumba, and I think I might stick with it."

Summer linked her arm through Pauline's. "You're my favorite."

Hattie finally broke her silence. "Pauline's everyone's favorite." She jerked Summer away from her sister. "Don't forget who's paying you."

Summer drifted back toward Pauline. "Any kids?"

"Not officially, but I've got five godchildren, plus three cats, two dogs, and a goat named Millie."

Hattie came to a halt in the middle of an intersection. "Millie? As in Millie Palmer?"

Pauline blinked. "Who?"

Summer shepherded both sisters toward the curb as a car approached.

"Millie Palmer," Hattie said. "From Bayside Drive. The one who wore the bright pink hat to church and wouldn't stop pestering Mies Jansen. I'm sure you remember *him*."

Pauline gave Summer a mischievous wink. "Oh, really now, who can remember all that ancient history?"

"I remember it perfectly, so don't you dare try to rewrite it. You never cared how you hurt me, as long as everyone else liked you."

"Behave yourself," Summer hissed at Hattie. "Better, not bitter, remember?"

"Speak for yourself, Miss Benson."

Two hours and four authentic French macarons later, Summer had given up on brokering any kind of peace between the Huntington sisters, who seemed hell-bent on keeping their feud going for another fifty years. She savored a salted chocolate and caramel confection, lagging several yards behind Pauline and Hattie as they stormed back to the hotel.

"I can't believe I flew all the way to Europe and you still won't be civil to me." Pauline's patience finally snapped after a long afternoon in the sun.

"Then go home," Hattie snapped back. "I didn't ask you to come."

Pauline clicked her tongue. "You know, you turned out just like Aunt Nora."

"Take that back!"

"I'll take it back when you stop acting like Aunt Nora. Petty and prudish and—"

"And you wonder why I don't speak to you?"

"Girls!" Summer took another bite of salty caramel goodness. "Could you please dial down the negativity? I'm trying to have a moment with my macaron, here."

They both ignored her and kept sniping.

Summer grabbed Hattie's elbow with one hand, Pauline's with the other hand, and tried to bring them both back toward the center of the path. "Mies Jansen must have been a catch and a half, to be worth all this drama. Either explain to me what was so great about the guy, or shut up about him, already."

"Well, he . . ." Pauline paused for a long moment. "You know, after all these years, it's hard to remember."

Hattie let out a little squeak of indignation.

Pauline exchanged a glance with Summer. "I imagine Black Dog Bay is still a small town today, but back in the fifties, it was desolate. We didn't have many boys to choose from."

"There were enough that you could have found your own," Hattie sniffed.

"Not like Mies!" Pauline fluttered her eyelashes. "Mies Jansen was dashing and charming, and, oh, just a hoot and a holler."

"And he was mine." Hattie tugged up the neckline of her cardigan.

"Now who's stretching the truth?" Pauline swatted her sister on the arm. "He was Millie Palmer's before you stole him away."

"Hold up." Summer's jaw dropped as she turned to Hattie. "You *stole* him from Millie Palmer?"

"I didn't steal anyone; he went willingly." Hattie developed a great fascination with the foliage. "Millie Palmer wasn't right for him, anyway."

"But you were?" Summer asked.

"I loved him desperately." Hattie's voice had gone quiet and tremulous.

"Not as much as you love not speaking to people," Pauline muttered.

"Then how did he end up with Pauline?" Summer asked.

"He didn't end up with me," Pauline pointed out. "He ended up with that summer girl."

Hattie could contain herself no longer. "He *married* that summer girl, had a passel of bratty children with her, and rubbed it in my face every chance he got. And don't try to change the subject." Hattie shook her handbag at Pauline. "He only dallied with you because you lured him."

Pauline gasped in outrage. "Excuse me?"

Hattie addressed Summer as though her sister had never spoken. "She stole my dress and copied my hairstyle and tried to snare my boyfriend for herself without a shred of virtue or remorse."

"You *gave* me that dress!" Pauline cried. "You said it was ugly and you didn't want it anymore!"

"This is like the plot of a Sweet Valley High novel." Summer took another bite of macaron.

Pauline got up in Hattie's face, jabbing her index finger. "You're just mad because someone else stole the man you stole for yourself."

Hattie jabbed her index finger right back. "You know what you did! All these years and you still can't admit it!"

Summer tried to step in between them. "Time out, time out. Let's take a minute to cool down."

She had to duck out of the way before she lost an eye to all the index fingers.

"He told me he loved me," Hattie informed Pauline.

"He told me he *adored* me," Pauline shot back.

"Love is better than adored."

"It is not."

"Is, too."

"Is not."

"Ladies. If you're going to have a bar fight, let's at least have it in a bar." Summer plugged her ears and herded everybody back through the hotel gates and into the lobby.

The front of the property was steeped in tradition and classic architecture, but the back of the building opened up into a sleek, spare patio overlooking the coastline. Low wicker benches surrounded small glass tables, and hand-finished hardwood planks added to the nautical atmosphere.

"Is this the bar?" Summer asked a hotel employee in a white jacket and black tie.

"Champagne lounge, actually."

"The mother ship." Summer hustled the squabbling sisters over to the far end of the patio, where they continued to verbally assault each other on a bench directly above the beach. A server arrived to take their order, but Summer waved him off and headed over to the long, marble-topped bar herself.

"Bonjour." She gave the bartender her flirtiest smile and hoped it would compensate for her horrendous French. *"Serait-il possible de faire boisson spéciale?"*

"Of course, mademoiselle," the bartender replied in flawless English. "What would you like?"

"Well, we'll start with champagne. The good stuff."

He nodded and produced three delicate crystal flutes. "We have an elegant and harmonious 2004 Louis Roederer."

"That does sound pretty damn good." Summer pointed out Hattie. "Charge it to her room. Okay, so we'll start with that. And then, we'll need some fresh vermouth. . . ."

She returned to the Huntington sisters just in time to hear Pauline say, "Well, you were right when you said I was fast. He and I did all sorts of things in the backseat of his car, and you know what? I'd do it all over again."

Hattie sat up even straighter. "He respected me too much to even suggest such a thing."

Summer sat down and enjoyed the warm breeze ruffling her hair. "Drinks will be here shortly."

"Thank you, darling. You *are* a treasure." Pauline patted Summer's hand. Summer shot a satisfied glance at Hattie, who looked murderous.

"You should have gone parking with him, too," Pauline told Hattie. "Life is too short to be a slave to societal conventions."

"Am I hearing this right?" Summer asked Hattie. "You've been pining away over this fool for fifty years and you didn't even have sex with him?"

Hattie toyed with her slim gold wristwatch. "We were very much in love."

"Well, I would hope so," Summer marveled. "Dude better have been the hottest manslice in all of Christendom."

"He was very handsome in his youth," Hattie said. Then she turned to Pauline. "But he didn't age well." With an air of great conciliation, she admitted to Summer, "His grandson has much better bone structure."

"I went parking with the grandson," Summer explained to Pauline, who did a little chair dance in solidarity. "It was fantastic."

"Is the grandson a smooth talker, too?" Pauline asked.

"No, he's kind of blunt. Gets right to the point." Summer focused her gaze on the dark blue line where the ocean blurred into the sky and thought about the sea of roses blooming in Dutch's garden. "But he's really . . . He's so . . ."

"You're very much in love," Pauline finished for her.

"No, no." Summer shook herself out of her reverie. "I mean, I was. Maybe. Before we came to Paris."

Pauline shook her head at Hattie. "You ripped this poor girl away from her true love?"

Hattie's expression hardened. "It was for her own good."

Pauline's eyes were the same shade of blue as Hattie's, but the color seemed so much softer. "You must miss him terribly."

"I do." Summer turned her face away. "I haven't heard from him since I left Black Dog Bay. No call, no e-mail, no text . . ."

"Texts." Hattie snorted. "You young people today have no idea what you're missing. When I was your age, we sent proper love letters."

"Have you tried to contact him?" Pauline persisted.

"I left him a message." Summer gnawed on the inside of her cheek. "Haven't heard back."

"Just one message?"

"Trust me, I was loud and clear."

"Send him a love letter," Hattie advised, before she could stop herself. "Sorry. That was the south of France talking."

"Mies used to write me letters." Pauline took on a dreamy, faraway expression. "Long, romantic letters. And he'd always sign them, 'I love you more than you know.'"

Hattie nearly toppled off her bench. "Pardon?"

"'I love you more than you know,'" her sister repeated.

"But that's how he used to sign his letters to me!"

"What? No. Surely not!"

Summer shot to her feet. "Let me go check on those drinks." But the older women hunched closer together, blocking her way.

"I memorized every line he ever wrote to me," Hattie assured Pauline. "And that's how he signed his letters."

"Do you suppose . . ." Pauline's eyes widened. "You don't think that's how he signed his letters to Millie Palmer, too?"

"It's probably how he signed every letter to everyone." Summer sat back down.

"How cheap. How dull and disappointing." Hattie looked so stricken, Summer put an arm around her shoulders.

Pauline shrugged and wrinkled her nose. "Let's face it: Mies was nice to look at, but he wasn't a staggering genius."

"Yeah." Summer gave Hattie another little squeeze. "I'm sure plagiarizing himself was only one of his many faults."

Hattie mulled this over for a minute, then finally said, "Sometimes, after he came back from the dock, he did smell like fish."

Pauline brightened. "Remember his toenails? Ragged and unsightly."

"That's true," Hattie conceded. "And his mother was a terror."

"And his cousins were worse."

"And he was terribly vain."

"Always checking his part and combing his hair." Both sisters giggled. "Remember the boar bristle brush?"

"Who could forget?"

"We should look up Millie Palmer and see how she's doing." Pauline appealed to Summer. "Can you do that with the Facebook, dear?"

"Wow, it's like I'm back at the Whinery." Summer felt a stab of homesickness.

"What's the Whinery?" Pauline asked.

"Only the best bar ever," Summer said. "You two would fit right in if you ever get back to Black Dog Bay. Jenna, the owner, will make you a Cure for the Common Breakup."

"What's the cure for the common breakup?"

Summer motioned for them to clear a path to the glass table as the server arrived with three cocktails on a silver platter. "You're about to find out."

Hattie and Pauline opted to shoot death glares at each other in lieu of toasting.

"Cheers!" Summer said for all of them.

And then the sisters sipped, and their long-held bitterness simply couldn't withstand the bubbly sweetness.

"Delicious!" Hattie murmured.

"Divine!" Pauline cried.

Suddenly, Hattie put down her glass and pointed at the sand. "Oh my goodness! Look at that!" She wore an expression Summer had never seen before—amazed, excited, unguarded.

Young.

Hattie clutched her sister's shoulder. "Do you see it?"

Summer peered over the white metal railing, scanning the empty beach. "See what? What are we looking at?"

"Oh, he's darling!" Pauline clapped her hands in delight.

Summer still didn't see anything that warranted clapping and shoulder-clutching. The sand? The waves? A few fancy French seagulls?

Hattie and Pauline abandoned their champagne and clambered over the patio railing, narrowly escaping breaking a hip or two. Pauline grabbed a stick lying in the windswept patch of grass and hurled it across the sand. "Fetch! Go get it!"

And then Summer knew. Hattie and Pauline saw the black dog. He had somehow appeared, all the way across the ocean, to the woman who refused to believe in him.

After a moment, the sisters stopped pointing and calling and lapsed into silence, watching the antics of a dog unseen to everyone but themselves.

"Do you feel that?" Summer shivered as her arms broke out in goose bumps. "That's bonding."

Finally, Hattie startled out of her trance and looked back at Summer. "My goodness. Give me a hand, won't you?"

"Whoopsies!" Pauline flashed her panties at the bar staff as a gust of wind blew up her long, flowy skirt.

Summer laughed. "Are you sure you're not *my* long-lost sister?"

Hattie kept glancing over at the empty stretch of sand. "Was that some sort of sheepdog?"

Pauline straightened her clothes. "A Newfoundland, perhaps?"

"Irish wolfhound." Summer took Hattie's hand, and Hattie took Pauline's, and without another word, the three of them settled back into a circle, linked by heartache and hope.

chapter 35

"*Y*ou're doing an excellent job," Hattie announced the next morning when she joined Summer on a chaise lounge overlooking the azure waters.

Summer opened one eye just long enough to locate the straw in her sparkling water. "Thank you."

"By far, the best companion I've ever employed."

Summer adjusted her sunglasses and tilted her head back into the chair cushions. The warm sun and the damp breeze felt heavenly on her bare legs. "Except for the part where I told you to get laid, broke curfew, smuggled in a man you can't stand and had sheet-scorching sex with him, called you a vengeful drama queen . . ."

Hattie pursed her lips. "Yes. Except for that."

"And the part where I arranged a sisterly ambush at the swankiest hotel in Provence."

"Yes."

"And the part where—"

"My *point*, Miss Benson, is that I have high expectations of you."

"Yeah, yeah." Summer inhaled deeply, bracing herself. "So what are you making me do now?"

Hattie perched on the white cushions and said nothing further. Before Summer could ask any questions, Pauline strode onto the scene, looking as imposing as a septuagenarian in a floral sundress and a beribboned hat could look. "Hattie Huntington. Spit it out."

Summer put down her water glass, alarmed. "Oh, God. What?"

Hattie wrung her hands and gritted her teeth and clicked her tongue for several long moments before finally muttering, "You're fired."

"Excuse me?" Summer cupped her hand to her ear. "Did you really say I'm fired?"

Hattie's voice was practically a snarl. "Yes."

Summer clasped her hands over her heart. "Really? Truly?"

Hattie glowered up at her sister. "Yes. Effective immediately."

"Thank you!" Summer lunged out of her chair, threw both arms around Pauline in a bear hug, then moved on to Hattie. "Thank you, thank you, thank you."

"You're welcome." Hattie folded her bony arms over her bony chest and sulked.

Summer started to twirl with joy, then froze as a thought occurred. "And you won't call the Poconoids and the senator and give them the go-ahead to turn Black Dog Bay into Cupid's Cove?"

"Poconoids?" Pauline asked. "What on earth?"

Summer summarized the real estate development scandal, complete with a highly dramatic description of the Channing Tatum cutouts and a daiquiri bar with "I Will Survive" on repeat and a vomit bucket by the door.

"Hattie, *really*." Pauline shook her head. "You should be ashamed of yourself."

"Perhaps I should be." Hattie shrugged. "But I'm not."

"Well, don't worry, Summer," Pauline said. "I know the senator, too. In fact, he likes me better."

Hattie helped herself to Summer's water and took a long, angry sip. "Everyone likes you better."

"No one will be selling or developing the Huntington property as long as I'm alive," Pauline promised.

Summer shot a wary glance at Hattie. "You better outlive her."

"I fully intend to."

Hattie's sour expression didn't quite reach her eyes. "If I were you, I'd get out of my sight while the getting's good, Miss Benson."

"I thought you'd never ask." Summer threw her sunglasses, sunblock, and book in her bag.

"Would you like me to arrange for your flight back to the States?" Pauline asked.

"No, I'll be okay." When Pauline looked puzzled, she explained. "Up until a few months ago, I was a flight attendant. 'Standby' is my middle name. I can work the system like nobody's business. Besides"—she turned back to Hattie—"I'm not accepting any other offers from you. Ever. No more deals with the devil."

Hattie smiled and adjusted her wide-brimmed hat. "That's what you say now."

"You were a flight attendant? How exciting!" Pauline exclaimed. "So you could hie off to Mexico, or Switzerland, or Japan?"

Summer ticked these off on her fingers. "Been there, been there, been there."

"Fiji, Alaska, Johannesburg?"

"Check, check, and check."

"What a life you must lead. It must be like a travel brochure all mixed up with a soap opera."

Summer laughed. "You know, it kind of is."

"So where will you go?" Pauline asked. "Now that you can go anywhere you like?"

Summer stopped laughing. "I'm not sure."

The only place on earth she wanted to go might not welcome her back.

chapter 36

"Summer Benson." The ticket agent looked up when she read the name on Summer's airline employee badge. "Wait a minute. I've heard of you. You were on that flight that—"

"Yep, that's me." Summer deposited her overstuffed suitcase onto the luggage scale and tried to keep the conversation moving, but the ticket agent insisted on rehashing every detail of the emergency landing, then started calling her coworkers over to meet "the flight attendant who saved the six-year-old."

"So which airport shall I book you through to?" the agent finally asked.

A year ago, Summer would have been paralyzed with possibility. She could run off and start fresh in the tropics, the tundra, the teeming cities of Europe or Asia.

But today, her choice was simple. The possibilities, which once seemed infinite, had now narrowed down to three.

"Try Baltimore, Philadelphia, or D.C.," she said. "Sometimes, you just get as close as you can and hope for the best."

———————

Summer's plane landed after midnight and she went straight to the car rental counter.

"I'll take whatever you've got." She shoved her driver's license and credit card at the agent. "As long as it goes fast and the radio cranks up to eleven."

She drove through the night, and as she approached the shore, she opened the windows to let in the fresh air. The ocean smelled different now that autumn had arrived; the chill wind had a sharp tang to it.

By the time she arrived in Black Dog Bay, the sun had just started to rise over the Atlantic. She slowed the car to a near crawl. At this hour, the streets were deserted and fog rolled in from the ocean, imbuing the whole town with an air of magic and mysticism.

Scarlett was parked in front of the Jansen house, and Summer noticed that the little red car had acquired a few new scratches in the paint and dings in the bumper. She pulled the rental car alongside the convertible, turned off the engine, and adjusted the rearview mirror so she could brush her hair and apply lipstick and powder, though she knew that wouldn't disguise the dark undereye circles and fatigue etched on her face.

Then she stepped out of the car, scooped up a handful of white pebbles, and started pelting Dutch's window.

His curtains were drawn and her aim was terrible, so after she pinged the gutters a few times, she gave up and tried to hoist herself up to the porch roof.

Ten minutes, several lacerations, and one irreparably ripped pair of jeans later, Summer crawled across the cedar shingles and checked her reflection in the window. Her face glistened with sweat and her hair was windblown, but at least her lipstick hadn't smudged.

She rapped on the pane and did her best to look casual.

The heavy curtains parted and Dutch's face appeared on the other side of the window. She held her breath as his expression progressed from grumpy to confused to shocked.

She pressed her palm against the cool, smooth glass.

He opened the window, took her hand, and tugged her inside. The bedroom was warm and dark and smelled vaguely of Irish Spring. And she knew she was home. She had found the place and the people she would never walk away from again.

"Summer?" His voice was still thick with sleep. "What the hell?"

She gazed up at his face, ran her fingers along his unshaven cheeks. "I missed you."

He pulled her into his arms. She relaxed into him and let him hold her. She could feel the rhythm of his heart, and pressed her lips against the soft cotton T-shirt that covered his chest.

"I missed you," she whispered again.

He stepped back for a moment, holding her at arm's length. "I missed you, too."

"Uh-oh." She started to smile. "You're overenunciating again."

He held her face in his hands and gave her a very slow but very thorough kiss. "I'm pretty worked up."

She wrapped her hands around his wrists and kissed him back, then tilted her head toward the rose garden. "I see you got my message."

"Yeah." He tugged the hem of her blouse out of the waistband of her jeans.

She shivered, anticipating the feel of his callused hands on her. "I'd like to come back. I'd like to stay. I know it's not what we agreed on. . . ."

He backed her up toward the bed. "Works for me."

"Impressive." They stood at the bedroom window, gazing out at the message Summer had left for Dutch on the night before she flew to Paris. The small, simple symbol she'd formed out of lavender rose blossoms:

$$\infty$$

Summer assessed the lopsided loops with a critical eye. "Could you even tell what it was supposed to be? It came out kind of crooked."

"I could tell. Eventually." Dutch laughed. "It took a few weeks for everything to bloom, but I figured you were upset and GUI—gardening under the influence."

Summer gasped. "How dare you! I was up for hours, working in the dark! Give me some points for creativity."

"Must've taken you all night."

"It did. I scratched the hell out of my arms." She glanced down at her forearms, which were now smooth and unblemished. Her healing had been so gradual, she hadn't even noticed. "I thought about trying to plant them in the shape of lacy panties, but the logistics were tricky."

"I thought you didn't believe in forever," he said. "I thought googol was an Internet search engine."

"I believe in now," she said. "And I believe in you. Especially because you kept my roses alive, even though you would have been well within your rights to rip them out by the roots."

"Yeah, well, I figured that planting roses instead of running them over was a step in the right direction for you. And you did it the right way," he said. "See? I told you the broken part could grow back stronger."

She gave him a squeeze. "You think I don't listen, but I do."

There was a shuffling noise in the hallway.

"Dutch?" Ingrid called. "You okay?"

Dutch and Summer disentangled themselves, and Dutch cleared his throat. "Fine. Come on in."

Ingrid opened the door and poked her head in.

"Surprise." Summer lifted one hand in greeting.

"Oh my God. You're . . ." Ingrid's expression darkened as astonishment wore off and anger set in. "Well, look who came crawling back."

"Ingrid," Dutch warned.

"No, it's okay." Summer squared her shoulders. "Let her say what she has to say."

Ingrid folded her arms and looked at Summer, then at Dutch, then back at Summer.

"So you snuck back in the middle of the night."

Summer nodded.

"And you." Ingrid raised her eyebrow at Dutch. "You're just going to let her come home?"

Dutch nodded.

"Well." Ingrid loaded the word with her full seventeen years' worth of disdain. But Summer detected a little glint of hope in those gray eyes. "I guess this means I have to give the car back, too."

"Absolutely not," Summer said. "Scarlett's all yours."

Ingrid put her hands on her hips and tapped her index finger, considering this. "Fine." She pivoted and headed back down the hall. "You can stay."

"Good," Summer called after her. "'Cause I'm moving in."

"Whatever."

"Want to go get a mani-pedi at Rebound later?"

"Whatever." A door slammed, then creaked as Ingrid opened it back up. "Ten o'clock."

Summer leaned into the hallway and yelled, "I'm glad to see you, too!"

The door slammed again.

"Don't be fooled by all the 'whatever's,'" Dutch said. "She loves you."

"You think I don't know that? Please. I'm her mentor."

He pulled her back inside the bedroom and closed the door. "Are you really moving in?"

"It might be best." Summer nodded at the window she'd climbed through. "I'm pretty sure we're going to break the drain-pipes, the roof, and the gutter if I don't."

"Good point." He paused, then warned, "Once you move in, though, you're never moving out."

"That's kind of the point." Summer nodded down at the crooked infinity symbol in the garden. "If I move in, that means I can stop living out of a suitcase." Her eyes widened as the realiza-tion sank in. "I could . . . I could actually unpack."

Dutch smiled. "When's the last time you unpacked?"

"Never. And I have to warn you: I have a lot of stuff. I try to travel light, but as you know, I've accumulated a lot of baggage." She winked. "It's like a metaphor."

"I can handle it," he assured her. "I have big closets. Metaphor-ically."

When she closed her eyes to kiss him, Summer could smell the sea mixed with the faint perfume of fresh roses.

chapter 37

A few weeks later, as Summer and Ingrid sat at the piano in the living room, they saw lights come on in the Purple Palace across the bay.

"Did you see that?" Ingrid pointed out the window. "Miss Huntington must be back."

Summer seized on this opportunity to stop practicing her scales. She got to her feet and peered out at the twilit sky. "Must be."

"I heard she went all over Europe," Ingrid reported. "I heard she went to Ireland and Italy and Switzerland and Germany."

"You don't say."

"I heard she has a sister now, too."

Summer smiled. "Well, I think the sister has technically existed for about seventy-five years, but yes, the whole 'acknowledging her existence' thing is new. Her name's Pauline, by the way. She's nice."

"Anyone's nice compared to Miss Huntington." Ingrid stuck out her tongue. "I can't believe she came back. She has to know that everyone's going to hate her more than ever now that she almost sold us all to the Poconoids." Ingrid paused. "Not that she cares what anyone thinks of her."

"Oh, I think she cares a little," Summer said.

"I bet you're going to give her a taste of her own medicine." Ingrid rubbed her hands together. "I bet you're never going to speak to her again. I bet you're going to torture her just the way she tortured you. Right?"

They heard footsteps on the porch; then Dutch maneuvered his way through the front door holding a briefcase and a pizza box.

"Oh, good," Ingrid said. "You brought dinner."

"I did. I also brought the latest edition of the *Black Dog Bay Bulletin*. Hot off the presses." He watched Summer, waiting.

She tried to suppress her grin and played innocent. "Oh, really?"

"Yes, really."

Ingrid glanced between the two of them. "What?"

Summer turned up both palms. "Nothing."

Dutch put down the briefcase and handed his sister the newspaper. "Check out page three. There's a very interesting blind item in Hollis's 'New and Noteworthy' column."

"Isn't she a great writer?" Summer gushed. "So witty, so playful!"

Dutch just looked at her.

"What's a blind item?" Ingrid asked.

"It's a juicy bit of gossip that doesn't name names," Summer explained. "Kind of like a—"

"You want to know what a blind item is? This is a blind item." Dutch cleared his throat and started to read aloud. "'Which globe-trotting town savior is about to broaden her horizons by heading up the historical preservation society? After slaying at least two society dragons, the brassy blonde is a true testament to Lavinia Leighton's vision.'"

"That's not blind," Ingrid pointed out. "That's totally obvious." She turned to Summer, her eyes huge. "Wait."

Dutch dropped his head into his hands. "Tell me that doesn't mean what I think it means."

"Town savior?" Summer rolled her eyes. "That might be going a little far."

"You deserve it," Ingrid said. "If it weren't for you, that horrible old hag would've turned this place into Atlantic City. They should put a statue of you next to the bronze dog."

"That horrible old hag has a name," Summer said.

Dutch and Ingrid exchanged dismayed glances. "*Please* tell me that blind item doesn't mean what I think it means."

Summer took Dutch's hand and gave him a little kiss on the cheek. "It means what you think it means."

"But . . . but *why*?" Ingrid asked.

"Because I spent the whole summer telling Hattie to use her powers for good instead of evil, and she finally listened. She and Pauline are funding an official town preservation board to keep Black Dog Bay awesome." Summer stepped back. "Meet the new director and social media coordinator."

Both Jansens regarded her in silence for a moment. Then Dutch asked, "Is she blackmailing you into working for her again? Because if she is, I swear I will—"

"No. She's giving me an office, a salary, and a very generous charitable trust to make sure that Black Dog Bay never turns into Cupid's Cove. Oh, and also, I made her promise she'd vote for you in the next election." Summer winked. "You're welcome. The Huntington sisters and I have big plans. We're going to start by making sure the historical registry is—"

Her phone buzzed. "Ooh, incoming official e-mail. Hang on."

From: j.sorensen.mmat@gmail.com
To: prez@BDBHistoricalSociety.org

I'm sending you a summit flag for the K2.

J.

Summer laughed.

"What?" Ingrid demanded.

"Oh, I guess word's starting to get around. Jake Sorensen just checked in."

"Jake Sorensen's still in town?" Ingrid's gray eyes sparkled. "I thought he left after Labor Day to go . . . wherever it is that he goes."

"He did," Dutch confirmed.

"Are you going to e-mail him back?" Ingrid asked Summer.

"No," Dutch said firmly.

"Well, if you do, tell him I said—"

"No," Summer and Dutch chorused.

Summer put down her phone and focused her attention on Dutch. "So how did the rest of the zoning hearing go?"

Dutch took off his jacket. "Riveting."

"It was riveting for me, too," Summer assured him. "I thought it would be deadly dull—and don't get me wrong, it was—but something about watching you review all those variance applications in your tie and cuff links kind of gave me fever."

He gave her a thorough once-over. "I noticed. It was very distracting."

"So much fever that I went to Retail Therapy and bought a new lavender—"

"Hey!" Ingrid whacked Summer with a magazine. "Stop being inappropriate and start practicing."

"Don't be selfish; your brother needs help." Summer darted around the sofa and made a break for the kitchen. "I'll set the table."

"No, no, no." Ingrid snagged the hem of Summer's sweater. "Don't think you're going to weasel out of this. Sit down and finish your scales."

"She's just giving me hell because I made her rewrite a draft of her college application essay," Summer told Dutch. "Girlfriend needs to go to rehab for adverb addiction."

"I do not," Ingrid retorted. "And I don't know why you insist on editing it. You're the one who's always saying you're not a writer."

"Writer, no. Adverb police, yes."

"Well, then, I'm the piano police. Check your posture. Watch your wrists." Ingrid dragged Summer back to the bench.

Summer groaned. "No more scales."

"Yes, more scales. I told you—you're never going to be able to play actual songs if you don't get the basics down first."

Summer sat down and glanced over her shoulder at Dutch. "I have enough in my repertoire."

"You know *one* song," Ingrid pointed out. "'Heart and Soul.'"

"So what?" Summer patted the piano bench and Dutch sat down next to her. "You can do the accompaniment, right?"

"I can improvise."

"Good enough." She arranged her wrists in perfect position, then launched into the melody. "'Heart and Soul' is all you need in your repertoire. As long as you have the right partner."

Photo by Anna Peña

Beth Kendrick is the author of *The Week Before the Wedding*, *The Lucky Dog Matchmaking Service*, and *Nearlyweds*, which was turned into a Hallmark Channel original movie. Although she lives in Arizona, she loves to vacation at the Delaware shore, where she brakes for turtles, eats boardwalk fries, and wishes that the Whinery really existed.

Don't miss Beth Kendrick's next charming novel,

new uses for old boyfriends

Available from New American Library in 2015

chapter 1

"*If* I've learned one thing in this business, it's that everything goes out of style sooner or later." The jewelry store saleswoman lowered her loupe and gave Lila a condescending smile. "The whole 'timeless classic' line? It's a marketing myth."

Lila Alders nodded and tapped her fingernail on the glass display case. Rows of diamond rings sparkled in the light, each one representing a promise exchanged by two people coming together in trust and faith and hope.

And they had all ended up here: the relationship boneyard. An "estate jewelry" storefront sandwiched between a Starbucks and a pet groomer in a suburban strip mall.

The clerk clicked her tongue. "The setting's very dated and gaudy, but the stone itself is decent."

Lila kept her head down and waited. Waited to hear how much her broken promises would be deemed worth.

While she waited, she surveyed the rings: big stones and small, colored gems and flawless diamonds. She tried to imagine the men who had proposed with these rings: rich and poor, old and young, all of them in love with a woman they believed to be as unique and dazzling as these jewels.

And they had all ended up here.

The saleswoman tilted her head, her gaze shrewd. Lila knew she was being assessed for weakness. How desperate was she for cash? How much did she value this touchstone of her past?

What was the bare minimum she would accept?

She knew she should lift her chin and meet the other woman's gaze, but she couldn't. She'd been completely depleted—of confidence, of certainty, of the will to stand up for herself.

"We can sell the diamond, but the setting will have to be melted down and refashioned." The clerk picked up her pen and wrote a few numbers down on the pad in front of her. "Here's what we can offer you."

Lila glanced down at the figure and took a deep breath.

"I know it's probably not what you were hoping for, but the fact is, diamonds just don't hold their value." The woman's tone was both apologetic and insincere.

"But that's less than a third of what my husband paid for it eight years ago," Lila said, hating how tentative and soft she sounded. Then she corrected herself. "My *ex*-husband, I mean."

Carl had spent a ridiculous amount of money on this ring—a fact he managed to work into dinner conversations long after their wedding. He had lavished her with jewelry on holidays and anniversaries, and Lila had taken this as a symbol of his emotional investment. As long as the rings and necklaces and bracelets kept coming, she could rest assured of his devotion. She could feel secure in her marriage.

But now she was selling this showstopping engagement ring to help pay off the legal bills from the scorched-earth divorce that had dragged on for nearly eighteen months and left her burned out on every level. Because whatever she'd been to her husband—a trophy, a lover, a cheerleader—she hadn't been what he needed most. She knew this because he'd told her straight-out: "I just need someone new."

What he meant, of course, was that that'd he'd already *found* someone new. Someone young and fresh and sunny in ways that Lila would never be again.

She flattened her palm on the cool glass case and tried to rally as she looked at the number written on the pad.

You can do this.

She knew better than to accept an opening offer. She needed to negotiate, to demand every penny she could get.

You have to do this.

But she glanced up at the jeweler through lowered eyelashes, her eyes watering and her lip trembling. All the fight had drained out of her. The spark inside had flickered out.

"I . . ." She trailed off, cleared her throat, forced herself to start again. "I . . ."

"Come on now, ma'am," a deep, authoritative voice boomed out as a man in a navy merino sweater appeared at her side. "You can do better than *that*."

Lila's head snapped up. She recognized that voice. That voice had plagued her soul and harangued her attorney through eighteen months of mediation meetings and conference calls and court battles.

"Mr. Langley." Her entire body tensed. "What are you doing here?"

"Dropping off a necklace for my mother. She needs the clasp repaired." He sidled even closer, smiling as if they had just been introduced at a cocktail party. "Please, call me Brock. And don't look at me that way—now that the divorce is final, I'm no longer your ex's attorney."

"I'm not up for this right now." She looked back down at the numbers scrawled on the pad. "You won, okay? You and Carl got what you wanted. I don't want to talk about it anymore."

He held up both palms. "I don't want to talk about it, either. In fact, doing so would be a breach of client confidentiality." He was close enough now that she could smell the sharp, astringent undernotes of his hair gel. She had to swallow back a gag.

"I'd much rather talk about you, Lila." His voice was jovial, but his dark eyes gleamed with predatory intensity. "You're selling your ring?"

She sighed as the feelings of failure and shame settled in all over again. "Thanks to the billable hours you racked up with my attorney, yes, I am. Well played, Counselor."

Instead of taking offense, he seemed to soften. "Don't take that personally—I was just doing my job. And if you're selling your ring, I'll be more than happy to help you."

She glanced up, her eyes narrowing. "You want to help me?"

"Absolutely. I'm very good at what I do."

"Yes, I know. You made my life miserable for almost two years."

He chuckled again. "Like I said, nothing personal. But now that the case is settled, it would be my pleasure to negotiate on your behalf."

"I see."

"Pro bono," he assured her. "Do you happen to have the GIA certification?"

Lila knew the appropriate response here was to curse his name and spit in his face, but she found herself pulling an envelope out of her bag and handing it over. "Yes. We kept all the papers and insurance appraisals in our safety deposit box."

Brock pinned the store employee with the same look of aggressive disdain Lila remembered him giving her lawyer in court. "Excuse me, ma'am. What's your name?"

The employee shot Lila a glare that could melt a platinum ring setting into a puddle. "Norma."

"Norma." Brock squared his shoulders and scanned the certification papers. "Have you seen this?"

Norma made a phlegmy noise in the back of her throat. "I've seen it."

"And that's what you're offering for a stone this size, with this color and clarity?"

"The cut's more important than any of that." Norma folded her arms over her sensible cabled cardigan.

Brock held Lila's ring up to the light. "Well, I'm no gemologist, but this cut looks pretty damn good to me."

"That's the best we can do," Norma insisted. "That offer is more than fair."

Brock scoffed and handed the ring back to Lila. "Put this back in your purse. Norma, I'm taking a business trip next week to New York, where I happen to have a friend who works in the Diamond District. You're telling me that if I take this ring and show it to him, he's going to tell me that *that* is a fair price?"

Norma remained stone-faced.

Brock whipped out his cell phone and brought up some jewelry resale sites on his browser. "Because I'm thinking we could get a lot more." He double-checked his phone, then wrote a counteroffer on the pad. "Something closer to this."

Norma's lips thinned into a tight white line as she glanced at the figure.

"No? Okay, then. We gave it our best shot." Brock turned to Lila and placed a hand on her elbow. "Let's go. I'll take your ring to New York next week and get you a decent price."

"Oh, I couldn't—"

"No need to thank me." He steered her toward the door. "All I ask is that you have dinner with me tonight. There's a great new Japanese place near Central. Do you like sushi?" He raised one hand as he opened the door for Lila. "Thanks for your help, Norma. Have a great day."

Norma caved. "Wait." She uncapped her pen and wrote out a new offer.

The amount still wasn't enough to save Lila, but she needed

every bit of cash she could get right now. So she let go of all her old hopes and dreams and agreed to take the money.

But not before a tiny swirl of tarnished metal caught her eye. She leaned over the case, peering at a piece of jewelry in the very back corner. "What is that?"

Norma glanced up from the check she was writing. "It's a hair comb."

"May I see it?"

Norma obliged, muttering under her breath as she pulled out the velvet-lined display box.

The comb was obviously old, shaped like a flower atop two thin prongs. There was nothing flashy about it, but Lila couldn't look away. "What's it made of?"

"Steel, I believe. Dates back to the early eighteen hundreds."

"Not even silver?" Brock lost interest. "Can't be worth much."

"It's not. A hundred dollars, at most."

"I want it," Lila said. She ran her fingers along the faceted edges of the flower's petals. The steel had been cut like a gemstone, designed to look dainty despite its strength. "Tell you what—throw this in along with the check, and you've got yourself a deal."

Norma lowered her glasses and shook her head. "We already came to an agreement. You can't change the terms now."

"We did shake on it," Brock said.

Lila plucked her ring back off the counter and threatened, "Diamond District."

The saleswoman rolled her eyes. "Fine. But only because we've been trying to unload that thing for years."

"Thank you." A little thrill of victory surged through Lila as Norma placed the hair comb into a bag. "Thank you."

Then she remembered that this transaction wasn't finished yet. She still had to deal with Brock Langley, legal shark, master negotiator, and very determined dinner date.

"Now that we've settled that, let's move on to sushi." He reached for her again.

Lila's cell phone rang, and she turned away from him and reached into her bag. "Excuse me; I have to take this." She glanced at the screen. "It's my mother."

Brock headed for the door. "I'll wait right outside."

Before Lila could even say hello, she heard her mother's voice, strained and desperate.

"Lila? Lila, are you there?"

"Mom?" Lila pressed the phone closer to her ear. "What's wrong?"

"Where are you right now?" her mother demanded.

"I'm at the engagement ring boneyard."

"The where?"

"Never mind. I'm out running errands. What's going on, Mom? You sound—"

"Get in the car and come home right now. It's Daddy."

Lila froze beneath the warm, bright overhead lights.

"He's had a heart attack," her mother continued.

Lila opened her mouth and had to force the words out. "Is he okay?"

"No." Her mother's voice broke as she started to cry. "He's not okay. He's dead."

chapter 2

Steady, pounding rain drenched the windshield of Lila's SUV as she made the drive to Black Dog Bay, Delaware. The night sky was starless, the roads were treacherous, and Lila stayed in the right-hand lane of the highway, praying that she wouldn't skid on an oil slick or scrape a guardrail or misjudge her braking speed.

She had to stay focused. She had to stay in control. She had to keep driving and make good time so she could meet with the funeral director tomorrow morning.

Her father was dead. No matter how many times she repeated this to herself, she couldn't make herself believe it. Her father had more life in him than anyone she'd ever met, and it was impossible to imagine the scenario her mother described: her father seizing up and collapsing while cleaning out the gutters. Dead from a massive heart attack before the ambulance even arrived.

Her father didn't have heart attacks. And he certainly didn't clean out gutters.

The mental picture was so absurd that she started to laugh, startling herself with the sound. She must be in shock. Shock and denial. And that was fine with her, because she wasn't prepared to deal with what would come after the shock and denial wore off.

She wanted to turn on the radio and take a sip of coffee from the travel mug resting in the console, but she was too afraid to release her death grip on the steering wheel.

Buying this car had been a mistake; she could admit that. A huge mistake. Almost as huge as the vehicle itself.

Once upon a time, she had driven a sexy, silver, low-slung convertible. She'd breezed around town with oversized sunglasses and her hair streaming out behind her. She'd never given a second thought to issues like braking speed. But when Carl had announced he was abandoning her for something new, Lila had decided she deserved something new, too. And Carl deserved to pay for it. She'd strode out of the house, roiling with rage, and driven to the nearest auto dealership.

"I want the biggest car you have on the lot," she told the first salesman she saw. "Fully loaded: leather seats, sunroof, power everything."

The salesman didn't miss a beat. "Backseat DVD player?"

"Sure, why not?" she'd replied, though she had no children. She didn't even have a dog. There'd be nothing in her backseat but baggage after Carl sold the house with the spacious walk-in closets.

"Do you have a color preference?" the salesman asked as he led her toward a line of shiny new vehicles.

"No." She pulled out her checkbook. "Let's just get this done before my husband closes the joint accounts."

And that was how she'd ended up with this all-wheel-drive behemoth with an interior large enough to set up a pair of sofas and a coffee table. This sumptuous, supersafe SUV—or, as she privately referred to it, the "*FUV*."

She'd driven back home in a spurt of renewed optimism, feeling invincible.

Then she'd turned in to the circular driveway in front of their stately brick home and realized that she had blind spots the size of a small planet and insufficient clearance to maneuver the vehicle into the garage. She'd had to park outside and slink in to face the derision of her soon-to-be ex.

Except Carl hadn't been waiting for her in the house. He'd vanished, taking his laptop and golf clubs with him, leaving a certified letter from his accountant explaining that because his businesses had been "gifted" to him by his father, she wouldn't be entitled to any portion of his company's equity or revenue going forward.

All her rage and optimism sputtered out after that. Hopelessness set in as the divorce dragged on and she lost everything she valued.

But she still had this FUV cocooning her within steel crossbars and countless airbags as she cruised along Route 26. She had a world of comforts at her disposal—heated leather seats, climate control, enough cupholders to accommodate a case of cola, and, of course, the backseat DVD player. She had signed the purchase agreement thinking that she was buying a sense of safety and protection.

Ding.

Lila instinctively tapped the brake as she glanced at the dashboard. An orange alert light in the shape of an exclamation point was blinking. She had no idea what that meant, but she knew it was bad.

Reminding herself to stay calm, she watched the road ahead and maintained her speed.

One hazard light wasn't the end of the world. She could call Triple A. How did the Bluetooth system work again?

Ding.

Another light illuminated—this time, the engine temperature alert.

Ding.

The oil level alert.

Ding.

The battery life alert.

BEEP-BEEP-BEEP.

The antitheft alert blared to life at eardrum-shattering decibels.

Lila didn't realize she was screaming until she heard the sound of her own voice in her ears in the split-second pauses between *beep*s and *ding*s.

Her fingers clenched the steering wheel so tightly her wrists trembled. She tried to focus on the road, but all she could see in front of her was a cluster of red and orange lights announcing crises she hadn't even imagined.

She glimpsed a gas station on her right and swerved into its parking lot, skidding on the wet pavement and jumping the curb in her haste. For a moment, she worried the enormous hulk of machinery would simply topple and roll over, but it righted itself with a shudder.

The cacophony of *beep*s and *ding*s continued. She threw the vehicle into park and started jabbing at buttons on the dashboard and key fob. Nothing changed—the lights kept blinking; the alarms kept blaring.

And just like that, her inner rage resurfaced. All rational thought deserted her and she was *furious*—at Carl, at this overpriced car, at herself for being stupid enough to think buying it would change anything. Even at her father for dying and necessitating this drive on this road in this weather.

She heaved the door open and jumped out, stumbling on the retractable assist steps that automatically unfolded.

"Shit!" She fell into a gasoline-scented puddle. Though she managed to catch herself with her hands, the water splashed onto her cheeks and collar.

The car alarms kept sounding.

She grabbed the edge of the massive metal hood and pulled. Nothing budged. She could barely see; her hair was plastered to her face in the icy downpour.

Cursing at the top of her lungs, she ran back to the driver's-side door, flung it open, and felt around the floor mats until her hand connected with the glossy copy of *Vogue* she'd bought a few days ago. She opened the magazine and perched it on her head like a makeshift hat, then resumed wrestling with the hood.

She startled as a hand pressed down on her shoulder.

"Stop." A calm, authoritative male voice filtered through all the honking and dinging.

She shook him off, then redoubled her efforts.

"You can't pop the hood that way." The man, wearing a base-ball cap and a dark wool jacket, held out his palm. "Give me your keys."

Lila hesitated for a moment, worst-case scenarios flashing through her mind. If she handed over her keys, this stranger could steal her car. She'd be stranded here, shivering and alone.

Without the hulking, heavy vehicle that she could barely drive. *Good.*

She repositioned the magazine on her head and pointed toward the driver's-side door. "They're in the ignition."

The man stepped onto the metal ledge, reached into the SUV's cabin, and cut the engine.

Everything stopped at once—the dinging, the honking, the fury and despair.

Lila listened to the raindrops spattering against the magazine cover during the long, lovely pause.

Then the engine rumbled to life again as the man turned the keys in the other direction.

She started to protest, but the words died on her lips when she realized that she could *hear* the engine now. She could also hear the steady squeak of the windshield wipers. All the alarms had been silenced.

The man stepped back out of the SUV and nodded at her. "This model has a lot of electrical problems. Probably a short somewhere."

She swiped the back of her hand over her eyes, trying to get a better view of her rescuer. "How do you know? How did you do that?"

He ignored her question. "You'll be fine for the next few days, but get it checked. Should be covered by the warranty."

She started to thank him but he was already gone, walking toward a pickup truck on the other side of the parking lot.

As she watched him leave, a chord of recognition struck somewhere deep down in her memory.

Something about his voice and his stride. Something both foreign and familiar.

"Hey!" she called after him. "Have we met? Do I know you?"

His reply got lost in the noise of passing traffic.

Lila climbed back into the driver's seat, buckled her seat belt, and just sat for a few minutes. Relishing the heated seats and warm air gusting out of the vents. Watching the dashboard for any more emergency lights.

Finally, she put the FUV into gear and started back down the highway to her hometown.

And five minutes later, when she passed the quaint clapboard sign adorned with the silhouette of a Labrador retriever—WELCOME TO BLACK DOG BAY—she realized why she'd found that stranger so familiar.

They *had* met. She *did* know him.

But, of course, there was no way she would recognize him in a situation like this—stressed and grief-stricken and drenched in a midnight storm . . .

And fully clothed.

If she didn't know for a fact that the turn radius of the FUV was equivalent to an aircraft carrier's, she would have pulled a U-turn across the narrow lanes of traffic and sped away from the tiny shoreside town where everyone remembered everything.

And nothing stayed secret forever.